LUST

THE FIGHT CLUB, BOOK SIX

BECCA JAMESON

ACKNOWLEDGMENTS

To my fans! Thanks to all of you for loving my fighters and sticking with me through six books! Love you all.

CHAPTER 1

Zane swung into the passenger side of the ambulance and somehow managed to shut the door and buckle himself in before jerking his phone out and pressing speed dial for Rider.

Vance drove. He turned on the siren before they pulled away from the fire station and headed west. "Rider called this in?" Vance glanced at Zane, who nodded as he listened to the phone ring on the other end.

"Come on. Come on. Pick up."

"Zane."

Zane exhaled briefly before speaking. "Rider. You hurt? Emily?"

"No. No. We're both fine. Called this in from my neighbor's house. Two doors to the left. You on the call?"

"Yep. Be there in a few minutes. What's the situation?"

"Emily went outside to sit on the patio and heard screaming. She yelled for me, and I ran in the direction of the noise. Her name's Abby. She just moved in about a month ago. We've only met a few times. I think Emily has talked to her more than that."

"Dude."

"Yes?"

"What's Abby's problem?"

"Shit. Right." There was a pause, and then Rider lowered his voice. "She's trapped under her back patio."

"Come again?"

Rider's voice grew more muffled. "Apparently there were kittens under the patio whining. Abby crawled halfway under to rescue them." He was practically whispering.

"Rider? What the hell are you not saying? I can barely hear you. Is it a secret that your neighbor is stuck?"

"Fuck. Man. I'm trying not to chuckle," he mumbled. "It's not funny. A piece of the porch slipped and pinned her underneath."

"And this is funny how?" Zane held on to the handle above the door as Vance rounded a corner.

Rider cleared his throat. He sounded more serious when he spoke again. "Uh. Well…"

"Never fucking mind, dude. We're pulling in. Be back there in a second." Zane ended the call and dropped the cell next to him in the console.

"What was that about?" Vance asked as they jumped from the ambulance and made their usual fast-paced walk to the back of the truck to grab their packs.

The Vegas heat was already stifling this morning. Zane felt the hot sun burning the back of his neck. "Not a fucking clue. Some woman is trapped under her porch. Not sure what Rider was mumbling about, but somehow he finds this humorous."

Vance tipped his head and grinned. "You never know. I've only been with the department six months myself, but Lord have I already seen my share of weirdness." Vance heaved his pack higher up on his shoulder as they both rounded the side of the house.

The first person Zane saw was Emily, Rider's fiancée. She was kneeling next to the steps of the back porch, leaning forward.

Rider grabbed Zane's attention next. He jogged into Zane's line of sight. "You're gonna need some tools to extract her. I think there's a nail jabbing her."

Zane nodded, furrowing his brow as he rounded the steps and came around Emily. And then he hesitated. *Jesus.*

Whoever Abby was, she had the best fucking set of legs he'd ever seen, and the finest ass too, made all the more obvious by the fact that she wore cut-off jeans that were short enough he could see the rounded globes of her amazing ass peeking out from underneath.

And that was all he could see because the rest of her was hidden under the porch.

Vance didn't seem nearly as affected. He immediately kneeled at Abby's other side and set a hand on her thigh.

Zane gritted his teeth. For some fucked-up reason that made not one lick of sense, he didn't like Vance fondling the sexy legs. He felt the irrational urge to swat Vance away and take his spot next to the sweetest ass he'd ever seen.

A slightly repressed chuckle to his right made Zane whip his gaze to find Rider staring at him, his lips pursed and his eyes dancing with mirth.

The man was right. This was not a laughing matter, but holy mother of God, Rider knew Zane well. He'd clearly been trying to find a tactful way of warning Zane about Miss Sexy Legs and hadn't managed to get the words out before Zane arrived.

Vance's voice jerked Zane back to face the situation. "I think we need some tools, Zane. Call for backup."

Zane didn't like the sound of that. He rushed forward, ignoring the request and kneeling on the ground behind Miss Legs, intent on figuring out what on earth had her so stuck they needed more equipment.

Emily leaned out of his way as Zane placed one hand on the ground beside Abby's hip and lowered his face to peer under the porch.

Fuck.

The first thing he noticed was the board that had slipped and fallen on her ass just below her waist. The second thing he noticed was the nail sticking out the top of the board, rusted and crooked. If that nail was as long as he suspected, a good portion of it was currently puncturing her ass.

And then he heard her voice for the first time. She sniffled and then spoke softly. "Can you lift it off?"

Zane twisted his gaze to Vance, who raised his eyebrows and stood. "Okay, then. I'll call it in. *You* talk to the woman."

"Abby," a tiny voice informed them.

As Vance moved to step back a few paces, Zane took the spot he vacated. "Abby. Ma'am. My name's Zane. I'm a medic with the fire department. We're working on it. Hang tight, okay?"

"Zane…" It sounded as though she was trying his name out on her lips.

He leaned closer, trying to get a better look at her. But it was too dark under the steps and all he could see was a mass of black hair. "I'm right here, Abby. Hold on, hon."

"I'm scared. And dirty. And embarrassed."

Zane chuckled low. "I'm sure you are. Don't worry. Nothing to be embarrassed about. Shit happens." He touched the board lying across her back and started to lift it. It barely budged.

Abby squealed. "God. Stop. Oh my God." Her legs tensed; her toes, tucked in an old pair of sneakers, curled under to brace herself.

Zane released the board slowly. *Shit.* "Okay. Okay. I won't touch it again." He shifted his gaze to follow the length of the board. It had dislodged from the bottom of the porch but remained wedged tight on one end. The only lucky aspect of this situation was that it had stopped short of putting all of its weight on Abby. It was long and heavy.

"It hurts so bad." She began to cry.

Her sobbing tore a hole in Zane, and he tried to shake the irrationality of the way he felt about this woman he'd never seen. Fine legs and a fantastic ass, albeit an impaled one, were not usually the only criteria he used to select a woman. A serious case of pure lust.

Sirens wailed again. He knew they were getting close. "There's a fire truck almost here, baby. They have more tools than the ambulance." He leaned in, squeezing himself a few inches under the porch alongside her, telling himself she needed the moral support. And why the hell was he assigning her endearing nicknames? *Baby? Jesus.*

A small hand, covered in dirt, wormed its way toward him and grabbed his as he reached closer to brush her hair back. He still couldn't see her face, but he felt the wetness of her tears running down her cheeks. "It hurts, Zane."

"I know, baby. We're gonna get you out of this. I promise." *The nail must be deep.*

He thought she nodded as she gripped his hand tighter. Her fingers dug into his palm. He didn't give a fuck.

She rested her cheek on her other arm bent under her head. "I've never been so humiliated in my life."

Zane stroked the back of her hand with his thumb. It was all he could do to soothe her. "You're going to be fine. Think about something else." He glanced around in the dark and spotted a flashlight next to her. It wasn't on. He needed to talk to her to keep her calm. "Emily said you were looking for kittens. Where are they?"

She sniffled. "Damn things ran out as soon as I wiggled under here and got stuck."

He chuckled at her cussing. She was feisty. He liked feisty. *What are you thinking, man? Who cares if she's feisty?* "Figures. Squirrelly little things. Can't trust them to stay still for one minute," he teased.

"Are you making fun of me?" She winced. "Never mind. I'd make fun of me too."

Zane reached for the flashlight with his free hand.

"Batteries are dead," she muttered.

"Figures."

"Yeah. I'm not having a good day. Better watch out. The house might fall on you." She didn't laugh. In fact she winced again. At least he'd managed to keep her mind off her problem for a few minutes.

Voices behind Zane told him the cavalry had arrived. He twisted his head an inch to see better, but Abby gripped him harder. "Don't leave. I'm scared."

"Not going anywhere, baby," he whispered, holding her firmly. "I've got you."

Two men from the station moved closer. He watched their feet as they shuffled forward to assess the situation.

Zane spoke to them from his semi-hidden location. "There must be a nail sticking out the other side of that board. She's pinned pretty good."

"Got it." That voice belonged to Gavin. That meant the other legs were undoubtedly Troy's. Good men. They would get her out of this mess, but Zane's chest actually hurt for the pain she would endure as though she were his own wife. He stopped breathing for a second at the absurdity of that thought.

The men discussed their options for several moments and then leaned in closer. Troy spoke. "Gonna have to hoist this board off her. We'll use a jack. Zane, can you hold her steady when we're ready?"

"Yep." He hated every bit of this. Usually he could remain completely disassociated when on a call. Always. Not usually. He was trained to separate his emotions while at work.

Not this time. Not this woman. Not Abby.

She whimpered again. "What's he talking about?" she mumbled.

Zane inched farther under the porch. He was almost in the same predicament as she was now, his back grazing against the underside of the wood. His face was nearly level with hers, though he couldn't see her features clearly. Her hair was a tangled mess all around her, long thick locks blocking his view, concealing her further in the darkness. He could barely make out her lips, and only because she licked them. "They're going to use a jack, kind of like a car jack, to lift the porch off you."

She sucked in a breath. "That's gonna hurt like a mother fucker."

Zane chuckled. "Yes it is, but the alternative is spending the rest of your life under this porch in the dark waiting for the rusty nail to kill you slowly."

She almost giggled, her body shaking as she took in his words. "Don't make me laugh. That hurts even more."

"Sorry, baby." He stroked her hand again. "I'm going to let go of your hand and brace your legs now."

She gripped harder. "Not sure I like that idea."

"It's not my first choice for this morning either, baby."

She released his grip, curling her hand into a fist and tucking it under her chest. She took a deep breath. "Zane."

"Yeah."

"I'm really, really stuck. It feels like a ten-inch nail is running into my ass."

"I know. And we're going to get you out from under here. And it's going to hurt. And then I'm going to take you to the hospital and they will fix you up."

"Ready?" Gavin asked from above.

Zane wiggled his hand out from under the porch and gripped Abby's thigh right below her ass cheek. He held her tight.

She tensed, every muscle under his hand firming. "Shit."

"You okay, Abby? They're going to start lifting now."

"Mmm hmm. Too bad the most action I've had with a man in months is beneath my back porch with a nail impaling my ass, but sure. Go for it."

Zane chuckled. He held her tighter, gripping her thigh and biting his cheek to stave off his ridiculous reaction to her sexy ass. Her fucking perfect sexy ass. Firm. Smooth. An excellent handful. *And impaled with a rusty nail, you asshole.*

Abby screamed as the jack lifted the porch. Her body jerked, but Zane held her firmly in his grip, his fingers digging in to her thigh, oh so precariously close to her pussy.

"Son of a bitch," she yelled. "Just fucking do it already."

"Can you move any faster?" Zane twisted his face to shout.

Troy leaned over. "Trying."

And then the jack stopped a few inches above her ass, and Gavin spoke again. "That's all we can do. We're going to have to cut the nail. It's embedded deep."

Abby squealed. "What did he say?"

Zane held her hand tighter and wiggled his other arm back under the porch to brush her hair off her face again.

"They have special tools to cut through the nail, Abby. It's gonna be okay."

She shook her head. "No. God. No no no."

He held her face in his hand. "It's the only way. Normal procedure. Without knowing how deep that nail is, we need to transport you to the hospital without removing it. Let them handle it."

"Oh God." Her voice squeaked with renewed panic. "Can't they just fucking pull it out?"

"I wish they could, baby." He brushed tears from her cheek. He couldn't see her face, but he could feel her fear with his fingers. Her lips were pursed as she set her other cheek on the ground in defeat.

A loud noise filled the momentary silence.

Abby stiffened.

"Can you hold her steady again, Zane?" Gavin asked.

Zane reluctantly released her face to maneuver his hand back down to her thigh and hold her steady.

She tensed every muscle in her body, her thigh and ass stiff beneath his grip as the noise grew closer.

"Quicker, Gavin," Zane yelled.

"On it," Gavin responded.

Zane gritted his teeth and held his breath alongside Abby as the saw did its work, carefully cutting through the nail between the board and Abby's butt.

Suddenly the noisy saw disappeared, the board lifted off several inches, and the light of day filtered under the porch.

Abby yelped and then she squirmed. "Oh God. Get me the fuck out of here."

Zane scooted back, keeping his face low to make sure she was truly cleared, and then he grabbed her by the hips and dragged her out from under the house slowly, careful not to let the nail become embedded any worse.

9

"Shit. Shit shit shit," she screamed.

As soon as she was clear, still lying on her stomach, Zane shouted instructions. "Clean gauze. Saline. Hurry." He leaned down to speak directly to Abby's ear, covered in her hair. "Hold still, baby. Let me secure the site and get a gurney."

"'K." Her voice was soft, but her breathing was heavy.

Zane took several items from his partners as they were handed to him. Vance kneeled on Abby's other side. He already wore a pair of sterile gloves, but he only held Abby steady as Zane put his own on. Bless Vance for whatever possessed him to realize this was Zane's gig. Zane didn't even look up to make eye contact with his partner.

Abby's shorts were torn. He carefully lifted the denim over the nail and tugged her low-riding shorts down a few inches, revealing the thick rusty nail and angry puncture at the top of her right cheek, oozing blood. He grabbed the bottle of saline that landed in his hand and poured it over the wound.

Abby flinched, but she didn't scream again.

Thank God. If he heard her make that sound one more time, he would surely melt. He would gladly go the rest of his life never hearing that fear and pain coming from Abby's lips again.

Next, he grabbed the offered gauze and draped it gently around the wound.

"Shit," she muttered, but not as forcefully this time.

"Hang on, baby." He taped the gauze into place across her lower back and butt cheek and then moved a few inches away from Abby for the first time since this entire fiasco began. "Gonna lift you onto a board now, Abby."

"'K."

Vance stuck the stiff board up against Abby's side. Zane

tucked his fingers under her hip and shoulder while Vance did the same on the other side.

"One, two, three," Vance said. Together they eased her from the ground to the board, leaving her on her belly.

Abby whimpered again, but she didn't cry out.

Zane mirrored Vance as they lifted the board onto the gurney and then hoisted it from ground level to his waist. He brushed her hair from her face. Her hands were balled up under her chest as he tucked a lock of thick black hair behind her ear. Tears smeared her cheek. Mascara ran down her face.

And he'd never seen anyone more beautiful. She took his breath away. Huge blue eyes blinked up at him. She licked her full pink lips and gave him a smile. "Thanks," she whispered. She wiggled out a hand and grabbed his where it hovered at her ear.

"Any time." He smiled down at her but forced himself to stand straighter.

Vance started pushing the gurney. Zane took the other end. As they wheeled her up the slight incline toward the side of the house, Zane caught Rider's gaze for the first time since he'd arrived on the scene.

Rider's brow was furrowed in natural concern, but his lips were tipped up at the corners. The bastard was smirking. He wrapped his arm around Emily and held her to his side. Zane watched as he kissed his fiancée's forehead and pulled her tight. It was a natural reaction anyone had after something intense made them grateful for their unblemished lives.

As Rider set his cheek against Emily's head, he smiled at Zane and lifted his brows.

How did the damn man know him so well?

Zane turned his gaze back to the woman he was hauling around the house. He wanted to stroke his fingers through her thick hair and kiss her temple the way Rider had done to Emily. That wasn't even close to reasonable or possible, however.

And he needed to get his head out of his ass. He didn't know this woman. Just because her butt was fucking fantastic and she had the nicest legs he'd ever set eyes on didn't mean he should race out and buy her a ring.

Hell, he'd probably never see her again after he dropped her at the hospital. Whatever tone he'd heard in her voice and whatever look he'd thought he'd seen in her eyes, both were a result of her stress and fear. To think this woman had even one tiny thought toward him romantically was ridiculous.

CHAPTER 2

Zane leaned back in the kitchen chair and took another sip of Emily's delicious coffee while she sat across from him fighting a giggle. Kayla, Gage's girlfriend, bustled around Emily's kitchen making lunch. It was a well-known fact that Kayla didn't cook.

Zane had come home with Rider after sparring at the gym. Normally he considered himself lucky when one of the other Fight Club members brought him home to be fed by their woman, but he had his doubts about Kayla. He'd been conned into thinking Emily would be cooking. He'd eaten Kayla's cooking before. The woman could easily fuck up a sandwich. He fought to keep from grinning as he watched her fumble around with lunch meat, cheese, and bread.

Rider sat across from Zane, his back to the kitchen. His eyes danced with laughter as he twisted his neck around. "Kayla, you don't have to go to all this trouble. We could have ordered pizza or gotten burgers."

"Nope. I've got this." She shuffled around as though it were an emergency, nearly stumbling several times as she fought against the growing puppy at her feet that continuously wove a path in circles around her ankles. "I'm practicing." She pointed a sharp knife at the men and narrowed her gaze. "I need you guys to be good little guinea pigs so I can impress Gage later with my new culinary skills."

Zane hardly considered sandwich making a culinary skill, but for Kayla it was a leap.

Zane looked down at the cute furry little guy at her feet. "Don't you have that beast trained yet?" he teased.

Kayla gasped. "We've only had him a few months. He's still a baby. Give me a break." She giggled and rolled her eyes. "Though I must admit, I am kinda shocked Gage doesn't have him sitting like a soldier yet. I think he's got a soft spot for little Jove."

Zane chuckled. "I'm certain in the end he will be the best-behaved canine in the state. After all, his master is the best-behaved K-9 trainer in the state." Zane took another sip of his coffee as a knock sounded at the front door.

Rider pushed from the table. "I've got it. You expecting anyone, Em?" he asked over his shoulder.

"Not that I remember." Emily lifted her head from where she was perched at the island watching her friend "cook."

Kayla was focused on making the sandwiches as though she were being graded.

"Hey, Abby," Rider said from across the greatroom. "We've been meaning to check on you. Come in."

Zane turned his head toward the door and fumbled his mug as he attempted to set it on the table. It almost fell over. Hot coffee sloshed over the side as he righted the cup, but he barely noticed the slight burn. He yanked his hands away and wiped them on his jeans as he swallowed his shock, not over the spilled coffee, but the woman currently entering the house.

He pushed his chair back and angled himself to face the sexy guest who had starred in more than a few of his wet dreams over the last week since he'd pulled her from under the porch.

"Oh, I'm sorry," Abby muttered as she came into view. "I won't bother you. You have company." She held out a Tupperware container. "I just wanted to…uh…" Her gaze landed on Zane more directly, and she stopped, both walking and talking.

Two seconds passed that seemed more like two hours. Zane finally managed to get his brain to send messages to his legs and stood, not without almost toppling the kitchen chair behind him, however.

"Hey," Abby said. "Zane, right?"

"Yes." He nodded. "How are you?"

She ducked her head, but not before he noticed the flush crawling up her cheeks. And holy fuck she was gorgeous. He'd been nearly speechless over her long sexy legs and even sexier ass the other day. He'd barely had a chance to see much of her face under her thick black hair, dirt, and tears. He was surprised she recognized *him* at all.

Today she wore a cute, pale-pink sundress that hugged her tits to perfection and flowed out over her hips to extend halfway down her thighs. Thighs he remembered well. Toned. Smooth. Silky. *God, I'm in so much trouble.* Zane plopped back down on his chair when his knees threatened to buckle. Since when did a woman get under his skin like this?

Rider broke the silence. "Come on in. Have you eaten? We were about to have lunch." He stepped toward the kitchen, nodding for Abby to follow.

"Oh, no. I don't want to intrude," she said, lifting her

face toward Zane as she spoke to Rider's back. "I, uh, I brought you some cookies. As a thank you, for, you know, rescuing me." Her gaze remained on Zane as though she were speaking to him, but she held the container out to Rider, who took it and set it on the table.

"You didn't need to do that. And besides, all I did was call for help," Rider said.

Zane stared at Abby, catching Rider's glance back and forth between them out of his peripheral vision.

"Really, I should have brought some to the fire station, but I felt weird about that," she stated as though apologizing to Zane.

Rider pulled out a chair and pointed at it. "Sit. Lucky for you, the real rescuer is currently visiting for lunch, so he can eat the cookies himself, and you'll have killed two birds with one stone."

Zane jerked his gaze to Rider, who now stood behind Abby, his brows raised in mirth. *Two birds with one stone? What decade are we in?*

"I should be going, actually." Abby took a step back.

"Don't be silly. Stay. Sit."

Emily came up behind Rider and wrapped one arm around him. "Really, Abby. I insist also. Kayla's making sandwiches. There's plenty." She leaned back. "Have you met Kayla?"

Abby shook her head and stepped toward the kitchen. "I don't think so."

Kayla met her gaze and smiled. "I'd shake your hand, but I'm knee deep in cheese and lunch meat."

Zane fought against laughter. Only Kayla could look so flustered over something so simple. He knew Gage was totally head over heels in love with this woman, but it clearly had nothing to do with her cooking.

Rider tugged Emily to his side and kissed her forehead.

"No offense, babe, but it's impolite to poison the neighbors. If you expect us to make friends with anyone, it would be better if you ordered pizza now." He wrapped both arms around Emily as he finished, pinning her hands to her sides, and Zane understood why when Emily squirmed in his grasp. She was about to slap him for teasing Kayla so mercilessly.

"Seriously? Rider, that's rude." She struggled to free herself, giggling. When she gave up the fight, she looked at Abby with a grin. "Don't listen to these imbeciles. Kayla is perfectly capable of making sandwiches."

Rider held her tighter, her back against his front. He shook his head. "We don't actually know that yet."

Emily broke free and elbowed Rider in the ribs. "Stop it. They're just sandwiches. Let the woman practice on us." She stepped away and gave Abby a quick girly hug greeting. "How's your, uh, butt?"

Abby smiled, having not moved or spoken a word during that exchange.

The puppy chose that moment to change his victim and angled for Abby's ankles.

Rider swooped down and grabbed the little fellow before he could scratch up Abby's legs. Zane was glad. He hated to see anything marring those perfect shins or the cute feet currently strapped into silver sandals. Her toenails were painted pink. When he let his gaze roam up her body until he met her gaze, he found her eyes on him again. *Shit. She must think I'm an ass, staring at her like this.*

Her face flushed again, and she licked her full lips several times.

Zane thought he would moan out loud if she didn't stop. The thick black hair that had concealed her face the first time he met her was pulled back into a heavy ponytail that hung down her back in long waves. Her blue eyes managed to hold him captive, and she scrunched up her tiny button nose as she answered Emily's question. "Better. Sore. I'll live." She grabbed the back of the chair in front of her and held on, but didn't sit. It had only been a week. Her ass would still hurt.

Rider stepped back several paces as Emily returned to the island.

Abby still held Zane's gaze, and as far as he was concerned, she could do so for eternity. She was that cute. *Cute? Dude, you don't do cute.*

Finally, she spoke to him again. "Thanks for, um, pulling me free."

"Any time." He smiled and leaned forward, his elbows landing on the spilled coffee he'd completely forgotten.

Emily dashed forward with a towel. "Let me get that." She lifted the mug, set it out of Zane's reach, thank God, and proceeded to wipe up the spill and Zane's elbows. "I guess I got it too full. Sorry about that."

Bless her. She'd done no such thing, but it was sweet of her to cover his stupid, star-struck ass.

Abby turned her gaze to Emily. "I really should go. I have to, uh…things. Thanks for the offer. Let's do lunch one day. Yeah?" She turned to look at Kayla. "Nice to meet you, Kayla."

"You too." Kayla waved her knife-yielding hand.

Abby backed up as she spoke, and Zane feared she would trip and fall any second as she paid no attention to anything but making a hasty escape.

The way he stared at her, unable to drag his attention from her unbelievable body, he couldn't blame her. And he couldn't stop himself. He'd been mesmerized by her legs and ass the first time he'd seen her. Adding her face and chest had done nothing but cause him to drool.

Emily stepped away from the counter and walked Abby

to the door. "Yes. Let's make plans. I'll call you when it's less hectic around here."

They were at the door and then out on the porch before Zane could formulate a sentence. Abby didn't glance back. And apparently Zane's jeans were glued to the chair because he couldn't seem to lift himself.

He finally jerked his face toward Rider when he heard him chuckling. "Dude, that was the singularly most impressive loss of speech I've ever seen. I knew you found her ass attractive the other day, and I can't say I blame you, but you're totally smitten."

Zane winced. "Smitten? What kind of word is that?" He wrapped his hands around his coffee mug and pulled it closer. Emily had set it almost out of reach when she cleaned up his mess. It was still hot. He didn't bother to attempt to lift it and take a sip, knowing his hands would be shaking.

The front door shut with a snick, making Zane flinch and turn his gaze toward Emily.

The woman was outright laughing as she approached, holding her belly. She wiped tears from the corners of her eyes as she managed to speak finally. "Sorry." She held up one hand. "I was holding that in for the last five minutes."

Rider stood at the island now, helping Kayla bring plates to the table. He shook his head, his mouth still turned up in a smirk. "I was struggling myself. What did Abby say to you?"

"She was so embarrassed, her face was bright red." Emily stopped at the chair where Abby had stood.

"Do you think she was interested?" Rider asked.

Zane rolled his eyes. "Come on, guys. Don't be ridiculous."

"Oh, hell yes. She even face-palmed and paced the front porch."

"What?" Zane straightened his spine.

Emily grinned so wide her face had to hurt. She nodded. "She said she thought her mental image of you had been an apparition, but now that she's seen you up close and personal, she realizes you're hotter than you were under the porch covered with dirt."

"You're shitting me?" Zane squeezed his coffee mug tighter, surprised it didn't explode.

Emily shook her head and tucked her lower lip in between her teeth to keep from giggling more.

Kayla eased a plate in front of Zane. "I thought she was smitten also, and I've never even met her." She grinned.

"Huh," Rider began. He headed toward the table carrying several more plates. "Double date?"

Zane shook that idea off quick. "Hell no. No way."

"Why the hell not?" Rider asked.

"For one thing, you two wouldn't be able to keep from chuckling all evening. And for another thing, that woman is way too sweet for the likes of me."

"I don't think you should judge her that quickly," Emily said. "She's a tough gal. She deals blackjack for a living at the Crystal Palace."

"Seriously?" Zane was surprised by that. Dealers were hard-nosed and smart as hell. *Maybe she isn't as demure as she appears on the outside.*

"Yep."

Zane gritted his teeth and then threw in the towel. He slumped forward, hating to admit he was head over heels for this chick he knew so little about. "Give her my number."

"Don't have to." Emily pulled a slip of paper from her jeans pocket and held it out, her smile spreading farther.

Zane released his coffee and reached for the scrap. "I feel like I'm passing notes in third grade." And his day suddenly looked much brighter than it had so far. At the very least, he now had the ability to ask Abby out, confident she wouldn't turn him down. It had been a while since he'd dated a vanilla woman, but it wasn't unheard of. He could do this.

How could he not?

CHAPTER 3

Abby finished chopping vegetables, wiped her hands on her towel, and headed for the front door. She'd jumped when she heard the knocking, feeling rather shaky from her visit to the neighbors' house. It had only been a half an hour and she was still running through the ridiculous conversation she'd had with all four people and feeling a bit idiotic.

Giving Emily her number had been presumptuous. First of all, Zane was way out of her league. And second of all, she hadn't demonstrated she even had a handle on the English language.

She found herself shocked into further disbelief when she opened the door to find the man dominating her thoughts standing on her porch. He was leaning casually against her doorframe, and the grin on his face almost made her moan. He was sexy in general, but even more so when he smiled.

"Hey," he said, righting himself in front of her. "Emily gave me your number." Nothing about his stance said he agreed with her thought that he was out of her league.

Abby licked her lips and straightened to her tallest. "And yet this is not my phone," she teased.

Zane chuckled. "Can I come in?" The sound of his laughter sent a chill down her spine. How could he manage to be so buff and sexy with a laugh that awakened every fiber of her being?

Abby stepped back, her fingers releasing their tight grip on the door as she pushed it farther open. "Of course. I was just making a salad. Did you eat Kayla's sandwich, or did she botch it up too badly?"

He chuckled again. "Nope. It was fine. I ate every bite. Of course I would have no matter what to avoid hurting her feelings."

God. He's sweet too…

"I didn't mean to interrupt your lunch."

She shrugged. It would be hours before she could swallow a bite now that Zane was in her living room. "No worries. It'll wait. Sit." She pointed toward her couch, wincing at what he must be thinking about the strange floral pattern. In fact the entire room was decorated in the same mauve and maroon and pink gaudy spray of roses.

Zane didn't comment, though his brows did knit together as he scanned the mauve chair across from the couch and then the group of pictures on the wall opposite that featured garden prints. "You like roses," he finally stated. "A lot."

"Nope." She took a seat in the pink chair and tucked her feet under her. "Not particularly. And I'll never want to see one again after living in this house." She met his gaze. "I'm renting the place. The owners are on sabbatical for six months. It worked out perfectly since I just moved here and arrived with very little of my own belongings."

"Ah." He leaned back against the couch, looking far more comfortable than he had at Emily's kitchen table. He crossed one leg over the other, setting his ankle on his knee. Giving him her number had apparently fortified him to consider her a sure thing. He wasn't cocky precisely, but more confident than the man who'd spilled his coffee on his own hands when she'd entered Emily and Rider's house. "That would explain the dozens of pots of roses on the front porch."

"Yeah. I hope to hell I don't kill them. Mrs. Lamphry wouldn't be too pleased. She left specific instructions and seemed genuinely relieved to find a female renter. She told me several times how very glad she was that a woman's touch would care for her plants. Obviously she doesn't know me well. I didn't have the heart to tell her I knew nothing about roses or any other living flower and the poor unsuspecting plants would surely recognize this and wither in my presence alone."

Zane laughed again, his deep baritone making her squeeze her legs together at the onslaught of wetness gathering between her legs.

Yep. She was doomed. Every cell in her body came to life and took notice. Even the dormant nerve receptors in her pussy were on full alert.

Zane finally spoke again. "It can't be that bad, right? A little water every once in a while should keep them alive. They looked good to me."

"We'll see. I'm not convinced." She smiled. It was impossible not to.

The way his tight T-shirt stretched across his rock-hard chest made her mouth water. His deep blue eyes penetrated her as he stared at her. His biceps were so large they stretched his shirt. And the tattoos she could make out peeking from under his sleeves made her curiosity reach new heights.

"You must work out a lot." Those words fell from her lips unbidden, and once again she felt a bit stupid.

He didn't seem to mind, though. "I fight. Mixed martial arts. So yes. I work out most days pretty hard and the other days I spar with the other guys."

"Oh. Well, that explains it. Does Rider fight also?"

"Yep."

"Figured. You both have the same build. But you have a day job." Apparently he didn't fight fulltime.

"Yes. I'm not professional. It's just for fun and to keep fit. I'm an amateur fighter. All the guys at my gym are." He set his foot back on the floor and leaned his elbows on his knees, staring directly at her, assessing her it seemed.

She found herself leaning back, even though there were several feet between them. The intensity of his gaze made her feel self-conscious.

Finally he spoke again. "Listen, Abby. I need to be honest with you."

She nodded. Honesty was a good policy, but she didn't get the feeling she was going to like this particular version.

"You are smokin' hot. I nearly bit my tongue the moment I saw your sweet ass sticking out from under your porch. I didn't even need to see your face to know you would blow me away. And you did, dirt and messy hair and all. Did you ever find them?"

She blinked at his abrupt change of subject. "Find who?"

"The kitties. I never saw them."

"Oh, well, they ran out from under the porch as soon as I wiggled toward them. Never saw them again." She didn't know how she managed to answer his question with her chest pounding so hard at his previous statement. *He thinks I'm hot?*

He smiled. "Anyway, the thing is I could ask you out on

25

a proper date, and we could go see a movie and do dinner and I could bring you back home and kiss you sweetly on the lips with promises of more, but I'd be lying to you by omission if I did so."

She could hardly keep up with his rambling. What was he talking about? She stiffened at the possibilities. Maybe he was married. Or had a girlfriend.

Zane narrowed his gaze, and his face grew serious. "I'm a Dom."

Now she froze. Perfect. Just her luck. *I finally meet a sexy man who makes my panties wet, and he turns out to be some sort of deviant.*

"Do you know what that means?" he asked when she didn't move an inch or comment.

She closed her eyes and exhaled slowly. "Yes." Visions of her one and only friend in Vegas so far filled her mind. Lauren was the first person she'd met. She was a cocktail waitress at the casino where they both worked. And she was in a very fucked-up relationship with a Dom.

Before Lauren, Abby hadn't known much about BDSM. She'd gotten an earful in the last few weeks. The woman was sweet, but Abby feared she was in a horrible situation. Lauren denied it, but Abby thought the man she was seeing was beating her.

"Abby, look at me." His voice was soft, but firm at the same time.

She found herself lifting her face and opening her eyes to meet his gaze.

"You're petrified."

She swallowed.

"I think you either have the wrong idea, or you've had a really bad experience in the past." He leaned farther forward, not close, but infringing on her space nonetheless.

She remained still.

"I didn't tell you that to scare the shit out of you. I only told you so you'd have all the cards in front of you face up. It wouldn't have been fair for me to ask you out and later fill you in on my preferences." He paused. "I've hit a nerve."

She cleared her throat. "Yeah." She should have suspected. Right? Huge buff guy. Sexy as shit. Tattoos sticking out from under his T-shirt. Short spiked hair in messy disarray on his head. He screamed bad boy.

He furrowed his brow again. "I'll leave if you want." His voice was calm. Nothing about him spoke of danger.

And she needed to shake him out of her system now before anything started between them. There was no way she was going down a perverted path into the dark world Lauren spoke of. No fucking way. She worked too hard to get where she was today. She had a steady job that paid well, a rental home that met her needs, and she was finally making progress on her first novel when she wasn't working at the casino.

She didn't need a man. And she certainly didn't need a Dom. Any ideas she'd entertained over the last few days since getting stuck under the porch needed to purge themselves from her system and go away. Thank God Zane had been man enough to lay all his cards face up, as he'd said. At least she wouldn't spend countless nights investing herself in him only to find herself in a miserable situation that made her fear for her safety. She was a strong, independent woman, not someone who would allow herself to be pushed around by anyone, especially not a man. "I'm sorry, Zane. I just can't. That's not who I am."

Suddenly, the ache in her ass where she'd been impaled three inches by a rusty nail throbbed. Probably from adrenaline. She leaned to one side, wincing, to alleviate the pressure.

"Does it still hurt?"

She jerked her gaze back to Zane. "Sometimes."

"That nail was long. I'm not surprised. I was more surprised by how well you managed to compose yourself while my men freed you. When I saw it, I was shocked you hadn't been either screaming or passed out."

"I guess my endorphins kicked in, but I do believe I cried on your arm."

He smiled. "Expected. No worries." He glanced down at her lap. "You sure it's not infected?"

She glared at him. If he thought she was going to show him her ass right here in her living room, he was sadly mistaken.

Zane leaned back and lifted both hands. "I didn't mean anything by that. I was just wondering if you'd been back to the doctor."

"It's all good," she managed. "They numbed the area as soon as I got to the hospital, and I hardly knew what was happening while they removed the nail, cleaned the wound, and stitched me up. The worst part was the tetanus shot. I got the stitches out yesterday."

"Right. Okay. Well, I'm gonna go." He stood, rubbed his palms on his jeans, and rounded the couch to put several more feet between them.

Why did a stabbing feeling fill her chest at the thought of him leaving? It was exactly what she wanted, or needed him to do. Damn the part of her that wanted him to remain right where he was, providing her with the most amazing eye candy and the deep sexy voice to accompany it.

Instead, she uncurled herself from the chair and stood, folding her hands across her chest and tucking them under as though she were cold. He was going to slip away, and she was going to let him.

Zane walked to the door, opened it, and then hesitated. He turned around to face her where she stood rooted to the floor. "I'm sorry, Abby. Sorry for bothering you and sorry for whatever happened to put that look on your face. I am a Dom. I can't apologize for that, but I'm not an ass. If you've had an unpleasant experience with domination in your past, I'm truly sorry. I won't bother you again." With that, he left, shutting the door gently behind him.

The small snick of the door shutting finalized the brief interlude of excitement. Damn. Too bad she had to let that one go. But there was no way she would head down the path he suggested.

CHAPTER 4

Abby had just finished her salad when another knock sounded at the front door. Was he back? The idea made her nervous. She hoped he wasn't the kind of guy who wouldn't accept *no* as an answer.

She peeked out the window first, relieved to find Emily standing there, and then she opened the door.

Emily held up a bottle of wine. "Figure I owe you one."

Abby smiled. "You don't, but I never turn down wine." She opened the door farther and let Emily in. "Come on in. I'll grab glasses. It's five o'clock somewhere, right?" It was midafternoon in actuality, but who cared. Abby didn't have to work again until Monday. Sure, she should have been writing, but there was no way she could capture the muse after facing Zane.

"Zane told me what happened. I'm sorry about that. I didn't mean to push you into anything." Emily spoke as she followed Abby to the kitchen.

"No worries. And I doubt Zane really knows what happened, so he couldn't have accurately told you anything." Abby reached for the wine glasses on the second shelf and then fumbled around in several drawers until she found a cork screw. "I'm still getting used to where things are around here."

"I don't know how you can even do it. Isn't it strange moving into someone else's house?" Emily asked as she propped up on one of the stools at the island.

"It's a little weird, but it's also cool, if you can stand the floral-patterned everything." Abby turned up her nose as she popped the cork.

"Yeah, that is a little overkill. Mrs. Lamphry loves her roses."

"I thought Zane's eyes were gonna bug out when he first came in. He probably thought I was somewhat whacked."

"And in the end the tables were turned." Emily giggled.

"True. And you can set Zane straight about that. I'm sure he left here thinking I had personally been burned in a past relationship with a Dom. That isn't the case."

"Ah good. I was worried." Emily's shoulders lowered as she relaxed and took a sip of the Merlot.

"I'll admit, I'm not an expert. In fact, if you had asked me a month ago what I thought about the lifestyle, I would have said I was intrigued. I'm familiar with Google." Abby chuckled. "But then I started working at the casino, and I met Lauren. She's in a seriously fucked-up relationship with some Russian guy, and I don't want anything to do with that. I quickly realized there was no way I wanted anyone to boss me around, and I certainly wouldn't want them to hit me."

Emily gasped. "The guy hits her?" Her eyes were wide.

"Yeah. She hasn't told me as much, but I can see the bruises, and her personality is changing. She was such a sweet girl when we met. I was excited to have found a friend, someone I could take lunch break with and go for drinks with. And then this guy comes along and sweeps her off her feet, and now she's a different person."

"Jesus. That's awful. And not at all the way I would describe the D/s lifestyle. Does she belong to a particular club?"

Abby shrugged. "Not that I'm aware of. But this guy has taken over her life. He calls her incessantly to make sure she's where she's supposed to be. He comes into the casino just to check on her and then leaves. I've seen him. He's a bear, always scowling and glancing around as though someone's waiting to snatch his woman when he's not looking. And the craziest part—he's so much older than her. Like fifty. Gray hair even." Abby shivered.

"That's plain weird, Abby. Rider and Zane aren't like that. Neither are any of their friends."

"I was going to ask you if Rider was a Dom also. I just didn't want to pry."

"Yeah. And believe me, he doesn't have some strange control over me like that. Real Doms would never hit a woman without her permission, and they certainly don't hold the power. The submissive is the one who rules."

"How do you figure that?"

"I have to give Rider permission to dominate me. Without it, he has no control. It's a daily give and take." Emily set her elbows on the island and leaned forward. She smiled huge. "Believe me, that man makes it worth my while. Every time I submit to him, he takes me to new heights."

Abby crinkled up her nose and held up a hand, laughter spilling from her lips. "TMI."

Emily giggled too. "Hey, I wouldn't trade it for the world. I never would have pegged myself as submissive, but the first time I walked into Extreme, the club we belong to, I was titillated."

"Huh."

"The club has rules. If anyone breaks them, they have to leave."

"What kind of rules?"

"The premise of D/s is for play to be safe, sane, and consensual. No skin can be broken. No marks that last more than a few hours, and by that I mean raised welts from floggers or spanking. Everyone has a safe word. If they use it, play stops. The object is to let yourself feel free from the release, not to get hurt."

"It sounds like Lauren's in a totally different sort of relationship. There are some Russian mafia in this area. They can be intense. They don't always play by the rules. The local cartel is not a nice group of guys. The Russians tend to stick together, and they're known for behaving outside of the law."

"Geez. I figured she was in trouble. It could be worse than I thought."

"Possible. Rider and Zane know a few Russian fighters. They might be able to give you some insight. Or perhaps Gage."

"Who's Gage?"

"Another member of The Fight Club. He's Kayla's boyfriend. He works for the K-9 unit at the police academy. Zane told you he's an MMA fighter, right?"

"Yes. But what's The Fight Club?" Abby took another long drink of the wine and then grabbed the bottle to refill both glasses as she sat in the stool next to Emily. They were going to need more wine.

"There are six guys who happen to belong to the same gym where they work out and fight together. They also belong to the same BDSM club. The one I mentioned. Extreme."

"Wow."

"Yeah, it's confusing, but they're great guys. I've gotten to know most of them pretty well by now. All upstanding citizens. None of them would ever lay a hand on a woman in anger. Trust me."

"Huh. Maybe I judged too quickly." She thought about Zane sitting on her couch, his frame sucking the oxygen out of the room. His smile lit up his face. His deep blue eyes held a world of mirth until she'd turned him down.

"It's understandable. And I didn't mean to pry. I just wanted to check on you. Zane asked me to, actually."

"He asked you to check on me?"

"Sure. He was worried about you. Thought you'd had an abusive relationship in the past."

"Yeah, I didn't really mean to give him that impression, but it all happened so fast, and then he was gone. I'm way too strong to allow myself to be abused."

"Apparently, if you had the balls to send a sexy man like Zane packing before he barely got through the door." Emily giggled again.

"He *is* sexy, isn't he?"

Emily rolled her eyes. "All six of them are. I get tongue-tied in their presence. Naturally, I'm partial to Rider, but hey, I'm in a relationship, not dead." She shrugged.

"I feel kinda stupid now."

"Don't. Hell, until you've been inside the club a few times and watched the scene, there's no way for you to truly realize what the lifestyle encompasses. I was so stunned when I first started going that I spent three Friday nights sitting in one spot people watching, until Rider came to me and wormed his way into the booth across from me."

"Oh God. I would have died."

"I thought I would, believe me. Rider fills a room. And his intensity when he's in a dominant mode is enough to send sparks through the air. I'll warn you, if you're interested, Zane is the same. It's intense, but smolderingly hot."

A shiver shook Abby's frame, and she took another fortifying gulp of wine. "Hotter than when he's rescuing women from under porches?"

"Oh yeah." Emily's smile broadened. "He's got a variety of sides. In regular society he's a perfect gentleman. Quiet. Tidy beyond belief. Anal. When he's in the ring, he's all business. He turns into a wild man. It's impressive to watch. They dubbed him 'The Animal.' He takes on an entirely different demeanor."

"Yikes. And at the club?" Abby shivered picturing Zane standing above her. Her hands shook as she set her glass on the counter.

"Sex on wheels, girl. Don't tell Rider I said that. I've seen him do a few scenes with women. Believe me, they always come back for more. Jenna and Katy have been around longer than me. I'm sure they could tell you a few stories."

Why on earth did that make her panties wet? Abby pinched her legs together and tried to shake the arousal she felt just thinking about letting Zane dominate her. "Who are Jenna and Katy?"

"Jenna is Mason's fiancée. Katy is Rafe's wife, two other guys from The Fight Club. They're the sweetest women. The best part about meeting Rider and joining his gaggle has been the friendships I've developed with the other women."

"I might have judged a bit too harshly."

"No biggy." Emily grinned. "If you're interested, you can go to the club with me any time. I'd be happy to show you around."

"Yeah, I think I'll pass for now. The whole thing scares me."

"I understand. If you change your mind, just let me know."

Abby lifted her glass and downed the rest of the wine in one gulp. She felt hot, as though she had a fever. Was it the wine, or was it all this talk of hot MMA fighters who dabbled in BDSM and sported tattoos?

CHAPTER 5

First thing Monday morning when Abby got to work, she ran into Lauren in the locker room. "Hey. How was your weekend?"

"It was okay." Lauren didn't turn to face her. She was bent over strapping her shoes on. She wore the usual uniform—tight skirt, too short, bustier, also skimpy, and high heels. Lauren definitely had the body for the outfit, so she was the perfect person for the job. Her breasts spilled over the top of her bustier and her ass filled her skirt perfectly, giving her a true hour-glass appearance. Her long brown hair was thick and naturally wavy, and it looked fantastic when she wore it loose. It did not come from a bottle.

That would be why men hit on her. And that would be why Lauren kept this job. It paid well. Abby knew she was also taking classes at the local community college. She was pursuing a degree in restaurant management. In the meantime, waitressing at the casino paid the bills and allowed her to pay for school also.

Something was off with the woman this morning. She

wasn't her usual chipper self, nor had she made eye contact with Abby. "Lauren?"

Finally, she stood and faced Abby. There was a bruise on her face below one eye.

"Lauren..." Abby reached out a hand, but Lauren backed up a step.

"I ran into the wall on my way to the bathroom. It's no big deal."

"Lauren," Abby repeated. She was no more buying that than a local beachfront property.

"Gotta get out there. I'm almost late." Lauren breezed by Abby and pushed through the door to the noisy casino.

Abby took a deep inhale and headed to her station also. She was a good dealer, and she knew it. That was why she'd come to Vegas in the first place. She'd moved here from Tunica, Mississippi, where she'd learned everything there was to know about blackjack and had worked at the casino from the moment she was old enough.

Vegas was the place to be. The money was better, the housing was cheap, and the adventures were far more exciting than anything in Mississippi. Dealing cards wasn't a life ambition. Writing was. But in the meantime, making money to support herself was paramount. She was good at it. Her dad had taught her from a very young age. She had an excellent memory and fast hands. And she knew she wasn't hard on the eyes. She wasn't Lauren, but she looked fabulous in her black hose, short black skirt, and tuxedo shirt. Her own hair was almost black, thick, and hung in layers down her back when she wasn't working. At the casino, she wore it in a ponytail, one of the many rules.

After checking in with the supervisor, Abby took her spot and immediately had three older gentleman at her table. Pushing thoughts of Lauren out of her mind, she smiled at her first victims and proceeded to take their money.

She had a steady round of customers all morning, and never found Lauren anywhere during her hourly ten-minute break. So, it was a relief to run into her when it was time for lunch. "Lauren. Hey. Lunch?"

"Sure." Lauren smiled, but her face was swollen and looked painful.

They grabbed their lunch bags from their lockers and found a corner table in the break room to eat. "Are you going to tell me what really happened?" Abby asked. She wasn't about to let this go.

Lauren didn't say anything for several seconds.

"Look, I'm not stupid. I know you're seeing that Russian guy, and I know he's rough with you. Can't you just break up with him?"

"I wish," Lauren muttered.

"What do you mean? End it. You're not happy, and he's been hitting you for at least two of the four weeks since I met you."

Lauren lifted her face; her eyes were watery but she held back tears. "It's not that simple, Abby. He's…"

"He's what?"

"Not the kind of guy you say *no* to."

"Pardon?" Abby didn't know any kind of guy she wouldn't hesitate to say *no* to. In fact she'd just two days ago turned down the hottest man on earth. Granted, she hadn't gotten him out of her mind since then, but still.

"Look, I'm handling it. Can we talk about something else?"

Abby stared at the top of Lauren's head where it hung toward the table. Lauren never let her head hang, or her shoulders slouch for that matter—both of which were her current stance. "I think you need help."

Lauren's face shot up. "Of course not. Don't be silly. Anton just likes things a certain way. I'm clumsy sometimes."

"Lauren, you should hear yourself. You're brainwashed. Men don't hit women because their food isn't hot enough."

Lauren's shoulders slumped again. "I know. I know. I've got it. Don't worry, okay?" She grinned, but it didn't reach her eyes.

Abby didn't bug her anymore, but she kept a sharp eye on her demeanor. It wasn't good.

Two hours later, a man sidled up to her table while she was between patrons.

Abby lifted her face to smile at him and froze. It wasn't Anton but one of his lackeys. She'd seen his boys around the casino with him a few times. This man was just as scary.

"Anton sent me over to tell you to mind your own fucking business, bitch." He said all this under his breath without moving a muscle to match the strength of his words.

"What?" Abby stared in disbelief. "Are you talking about Lauren?"

"Who else would I be speaking of? Stay away from her, and stop filling her head with shit, or you'll find yourself with a shitload of problems of your own. Are we clear?"

Abby licked her lips and nodded.

"If I have to speak to you again, I won't be so polite."

Abby nodded again, and before she could blink, the man disappeared.

She glanced around. No one was looking at her. Not even the shift manager who was busy talking to another dealer.

Shit. Fuck. And shit. She glanced up at one of the many cameras trained toward her table. What she should do if she had any sense would be to turn around and report the asshole immediately.

Instead, four other men, partially inebriated, sidled up to her table, and two seconds later, Lauren showed up to take their orders. As she finished, and before Abby had completely regained her composure, Lauren turned toward Abby and gave a shaky smile. "Whatever he said, he means it. Stay out of this. Please. For my sake."

Abby nodded. She realized if she turned that guy in, Lauren's life was liable to get a whole lot worse really fast. She decided to wait until they were both off and then confront Lauren again.

The rest of the day passed slowly. Abby's hands shook more than usual, and that sucked because her hands were the key to her job. When she finally clocked out and headed to the locker room, she ran into Lauren at her locker again. "What the fuck, Lauren? Why would you tell your boyfriend about our conversation?"

Lauren jerked her gaze upward. "I didn't tell him anything. Anton's like omniscient or something. I just saw his guy talking to you and figured it had to do with me."

Abby shivered. "That was one scary asshole. You have to get yourself out of that mess. And fast."

"I'm fine." Lauren's movements were jerky as she hastily grabbed her purse from her locker and turned around. "Please, Abby. Stay out of this. I've got it." She glanced up at the corner of the room.

"You don't have anything, Lauren. It's not safe. Hell, it's not even safe for you to go to your car right now." Abby followed Lauren's gaze and spotted the camera in the corner. Had Anton watched their earlier exchange? Is that how he knew Lauren had spoken to Abby? The idea made her cringe. Holy fuck. If that Russian guy had the clout to monitor the camera in the break room, what else was he capable of?

"Don't be silly. Let it go." With that Lauren practically ran from the room.

Abby took her time. She plopped onto the bench next to the lockers and reached for her stuff, wishing she'd done something different. Anything. Lauren was going to get hurt, and Abby had no idea what to do about it. She wasn't stupid. She knew she'd been threatened. She also knew Lauren would suffer even more if she called the cops or reported the incident.

Disturbed and exhausted, Abby grabbed her purse and headed for the parking garage. Minutes later she was in her Hyundai Santa Fe and pulling out of the lot.

She drove with both hands on the wheel, heading home on rote memory, paying almost no attention to her surroundings. She couldn't shake Lauren's face from her mind. And she had no idea what to do about her friend's problems. Nothing she could think of seemed wise. Suddenly, just outside of town, a car veered into her lane, headed straight toward her.

Abby screamed. She had just seconds to yank the steering wheel to the right to avoid a head-on collision. And that was the last thing she remembered.

~

As Vance pulled up behind the mangled car off the side of the road, Zane winced. The front end had hit the embankment so hard it had completely buckled. He would be surprised if the unconscious victim in the front seat lived, judging from the extent of the damage to the vehicle.

Two police cruisers were already on the scene. An officer shouted toward Zane as he jumped down from the ambulance, grabbed his bag, and jogged faster than normal to the driver's side.

"What'cha got?" Zane asked.

"Female. Mid-twenties. Unconscious. Lacerations to the head," the officer said. He had managed to get the door open and was kneeling with both hands inside the car holding the woman's head upright.

"Fuck," Vance said as he entered from the passenger side.

"What?" Zane asked.

"Dude, this is the same woman we pulled out from under the porch last week."

Zane lurched forward until he could peer into the car around the officer and took a deep breath. *Fuck indeed.* "I've got her," he told the cop as he replaced the officer's hand with his own and let the man wiggle out of the tight space.

Vance called off her vitals. At least she was alive.

"Abby. Can you hear me?" Zane asked.

Nothing.

Vance didn't speak as he left Zane, crawling back out of the passenger seat. Zane knew he would be going to get the stretcher and the neck brace.

"Abby. Baby," he whispered, pulling her eyes open one at a time. No response. Her respirations were steady, her pulse also, but she didn't wake up.

It took less than five minutes to get her out of the car and into the ambulance, and then Vance sped away from the scene toward the hospital. Zane rode in the back, checking Abby's pulse every few seconds. "Did anyone mention what happened?"

"Yeah. Several people stopped. Apparently a car swerved into her lane, forced her off the road, and then righted itself and kept going."

"Seriously?" Zane almost screamed that one word. Who

the fuck ran someone off the road and then kept going? That was insane. Unless it was premeditated. But no one in their right mind would want to hurt Abby. She was new to the area and too sweet for her own good.

When they pulled up to the emergency room, Zane took the head of the stretcher and led the way. He shouted out her vitals to the doctor on call and followed them until they reached the exam room. It would be futile to attempt to enter with Abby. No way would the hospital staff allow it. But he sure as shit wasn't going to leave the hospital. Instead he paced outside the door for a moment, running his hand through his hair.

Vance stood next to him. "You okay, man?"

"Nope."

"Didn't think so. I'll call the station and let them know you won't be returning with me."

"Good." Zane didn't look up. He kept pacing.

A nurse ran by, and Zane grabbed her arm. "Sorry. The woman I just brought in?"

"Yeah?"

"I know her. Could you please let me know what's happening?"

"Sure, Zane. I'll be right back." She smiled. He didn't even know her name. Christy or Chrissy maybe? She knew his.

He paced some more. He barely knew Abby, and she'd totally turned him down last week, but he couldn't stand the thought she might be seriously injured or worse.

It took fifteen long minutes for the nurse to return, and this time he made a note of her nametag. Chrissy. "Hey, Zane. She's awake."

Zane exhaled a long breath. Thank God. "Is she okay?"

"She needs stitches in a few places and a staple or two.

And she has a concussion, but she should be fine. She said it would be okay if you came back."

Zane wiped his hands on his pants. Why did the woman make him nervous?

"She doesn't have family nearby, and she didn't want us to call anyone."

"Great. Thanks, Chrissy." Zane followed her through the doors leading to the triage unit and into the curtained section where Abby lay on a narrow hospital bed.

The first glance made him wince, thankfully before she noticed him. He schooled his reaction quickly before stepping up to her free side. A nurse stood at her other side, preparing a tray of sutures. "Abby." He took her hand.

She turned her head his direction and opened her eyes just enough to see him. She even lifted the corners of her perfect mouth in a slight smile. "Hey. You keep rescuing me."

"Yeah. If you keep this up, I'll have years of job security."

She gave a short giggle. "God, don't make me laugh. It hurts." She reached with her free hand and touched her forehead. "How bad is it? Be honest."

"The car? Totaled. You're gonna need a new one." He grinned wide, knowing she hadn't meant that at all.

"My face, Zane."

He smiled again. "Not bad, baby." He wasn't lying. He knew from experience there was never any correlation between the amount of blood present and the size of a facial wound. It always looked so much worse than it was until they cleaned it up.

The nurse to her other side explained. "The plastic surgeon is on his way, sweetie. He'll fix you up. In a few weeks no one will know anything happened."

"See?" Zane squeezed her hand, threading his fingers through hers when she hung on to him.

"Zane."

He knew she wanted more information. "Small cut above your eye won't take more than a few stitches. Small cut on your chin about the same. They look clean. Nothing jagged."

"There's two on top of your head too, sweetie," the nurse added. "We'll staple those. No one will see them."

"Staple?" Abby dug her nails into his hand. He didn't give a shit.

"It's normal, baby. You'll be fine. They'll numb the area first."

The doctor came around the corner then. He smiled at Zane. "Randolf," he greeted Zane. "You know Miss Burns?"

"Yep. She's a regular customer," he joked.

"That can't be good."

"Two times. *Two*," Abby said. "That hardly makes me regular."

"Yeah, but in as many weeks. And always I'm needed to extricate you from somewhere."

The doctor washed his hands and turned around, pulling his gloves on. "There's a good story in there, I'm sure."

"Yep. You should see what she did to her ass last week."

"Zane," Abby squealed before she could stop herself. She winced.

"Sorry, baby."

The doctor shined a pen light in each eye and then sat on the swivel chair the nurse pulled up behind him. "Yep, you have a concussion. Did you hit the steering wheel?"

"I don't remember."

"Were you wearing a seatbelt?"

"Yes."

"She was," Zane agreed.

"Did the airbags deploy?" the doctor asked.

"They did," Zane responded.

"Okay. Well, could have been worse. You must've bumped your head. Either the airbag or the steering wheel could have given you a concussion. And I'm guessing the windshield shattered. I'm going to fix you up, and then you can go home. You'll need supervision for twenty-four hours. Do you have someone who can do that for you?"

Abby furrowed her brow, breaking the skin open again on her forehead until a trickle of blood oozed out.

"I'll do it." Zane lifted her hand to his face and brushed it against his cheek. He had no idea why. Nor did he understand his deep-seated attraction for this woman. A woman who made it perfectly clear two days ago she wasn't interested in his brand of sex. He had no business butting into her life. But he also knew she didn't have someone else, so the choices were to remain in the hospital overnight or go home with him.

"All right then, let's get started." The doctor ignored Abby's reaction and proceeded to sew her up.

Zane didn't release her hand and continued to hold it for all the stitches and the staples. He did manage to pull his cell from his pocket and send a one-handed text to Gage to come pick them up.

When the doctor finished and sat back, tugging off his gloves, he spoke again. "I'll have the nurse discharge you into Zane's care. You can make an appointment with your regular doctor to have the stitches and staples removed in about a week." He patted her free arm and stood. "Nice to see you Randolf." With that he left.

"God, my whole head hurts." Abby lifted her hand to her eyes and pressed.

"It's gonna feel even worse when the local wears off. You can take acetaminophen, but that's about it with a concussion. I've got some at the house." He stroked his

47

hand up her arm and cupped her cheek gently. "Think you can sit up?"

"Not sure I want to."

He smiled.

"Zane, you can't take me home with you. That's insane. You barely know me."

"I can. It's already settled. Or we can go to your house if you prefer. But it'll be easier at mine. I know my way around, and all you're going to do is sleep."

"I need to call my boss."

"I'll do that when we get you settled."

"I need to call my insurance company."

He stroked his thumb across her flushed cheek. Even injured and bloody she was gorgeous. Her hair had come free of her ponytail and lay fanned across the pillow. Someone had removed her bow tie and tucked it in her shirt pocket so it wouldn't get lost. Although he feared the white tuxedo blouse might be a loss. It was covered with blood stains. "Baby, one thing at a time. Relax." He stood and leaned in to kiss her forehead, knowing it was risky and irrational and not giving a fuck. She was so damn cute, and flustered even more so.

She frowned at him.

"Stop squishing your face. You're tugging the stitches."

A nurse came in and held up a clipboard for Abby to sign, and right behind her an orderly pulled up a wheelchair.

Zane helped Abby sit with one hand pulling on hers and the other going to her back.

She moaned, which made him want to get her home and settled quickly so she'd be more comfortable. "Where're my shoes?" She glanced down at her feet.

Amazingly her hose were not snagged. How she'd managed that was beyond him.

The nurse held up a bag. "Right here. The police officer grabbed them from your car and drove them over. You must be a movie star," she teased.

Zane took the bag, hung it on the wheel chair, and helped Abby stand next to it and then sit. "I've got it," he told the orderly, who shrugged and followed them out the front door.

"You don't even have a car here," Abby said, twisting her head backward to face Zane.

"I have friends." He grinned at her. "And there he is now."

A black Jeep Wrangler pulled to the curb, and Gage jumped out to round the hood. "Hey, Zane." He patted Zane on the shoulder and looked toward Abby. "You must be Abby. I'm Gage. I think you met my girlfriend, Kayla, the other day. Don't worry. I'll have you home in no time, and then you can rest."

Abby nodded.

Zane helped her stand and nearly lifted her bodily into the back of Zane's Jeep. He scooted her over and climbed in beside her.

Abby stared at him awkwardly. "I can manage. You don't have to sit in the back with me."

He didn't respond. But he wished she wasn't so argumentative about him helping her. He reached for her seatbelt, buckled her in, and then did his own. As Gage slipped back into the driver's seat, Zane wrapped his arm around Abby and eased her head onto his shoulder.

She sighed and relaxed into him, seemingly giving up the fight to be cared for. "Gage is one of your Fight Club, right?"

Gage glanced in the rearview mirror. "I am. Work for the K-9 unit at the police academy."

49

"Emily tell you about The Fight Club?" Zane asked. There wasn't really any other explanation.

"Yeah. Among other things," she admitted.

Hmm. Other things. Like what?

He didn't ask. For one thing, she was barely lucid. For another, he didn't want to discuss her possible discussion with Emily in front of Gage. "Thanks for picking us up, man."

"No problem. Vance said he would get someone to bring your car home in a while."

"Right. Thanks for handling that too."

"And he said he already talked to the station about you having tomorrow off."

"Perfect. I appreciate it, Gage."

"No problem. Let any of us know if you need anything," Gage added.

Zane was a lucky bastard. The Fight Club was a fantastic group of guys, both in and out of the ring. Most of them had women by now, well, everyone except him. Conner had been the last one to bite the dust recently. That left Zane. The lone bachelor. But Zane held Abby tighter and prayed he might win her over. Or perhaps he would have to throw in his Dom card for her. She was that fucking awesome. If she hated the lifestyle, maybe he would be willing to give it the kibbutz. Maybe.

CHAPTER 6

Abby didn't know how long the drive to Zane's house was. She fell asleep against his shoulder, his rock-hard shoulder that she nestled her cheek against even though it was made of stone.

The next thing she knew, the car wasn't moving and Zane was lifting her into his arms. "Mmm."

He held her close to his body and strode to the front door.

She didn't open her eyes. She couldn't actually. "So tired…" she mumbled.

"I know, baby." He pushed through the front door that Gage must have opened for them. She didn't hear the other man say a word. And then Zane was settling her on a very soft bed. Marginally, in the back of her mind, she also realized she was still wearing her short black skirt, the one that barely covered her ass standing and certainly couldn't have covered anything by the time he carried her to what she presumed was his bedroom. His scent filled the space.

Her eyes opened a slit as he pulled the comforter up to her chin. "I'll get you some Tylenol and then you can rest, but I have to wake you up every few hours to make sure you're okay."

"'K." She winced as she turned to one side and snuggled into Zane's bed. His pillow. She inhaled Zane everywhere. It was dark out. She didn't know what time it was.

Zane sat on the edge moments later, holding two pills and a glass of water. "You want something to eat?" he asked as she lifted her head just enough to take the pills.

She shook her head. "No. My stomach is queasy."

"That's normal." He brushed her hair from her face and continued to stroke her skin.

It felt fantastic to have someone take care of her. It had been a long time since she'd been pampered. "I'm putting you out," she muttered. *Hell, I'm in your bed.*

"Not at all. I feel privileged." He leaned in and kissed her forehead. "Sleep, baby. I'll be back soon." With that, he released her and padded from the room, leaving the door open a crack and flipping off the light.

Holy shit. She was in Zane's bed in Zane's house. Her head hurt like a truck hit it—which it sort of did.

It seemed like only moments passed before she felt the bed dip and a warm hand land on her cheek. "Baby. Can you wake up?"

She moaned and burrowed farther into the pillow, aware she was curled up in the same position she'd been in when she'd first lain there. But she pulled one eye open a sliver.

Zane smiled. "What year is it?"

"Huh?"

"Just answer, baby."

"Two thousand fifteen."

"What's your last name?"

"Burns." Why was he asking her this stuff?

He grinned again. "I think you're good. You passed."

"Passed what?" she whispered.

"The concussion test. You do remember you were in an accident, right?" He stroked a hand down her arm. She could feel his warmth through the blanket.

"Of course." She turned onto her back, slightly more awake. Her skirt bunched up around her waist uncomfortably. "Could I borrow a T-shirt or something to change into?"

"Of course." Zane stood and stepped to the dresser. He returned with an enormous black tee that probably would look tight on him but would swallow her whole. Perfect.

She pushed to sitting, cringing at the pain in her head and at every location where she'd been sewn shut. She reached for the top button on her shirt, but her fingers wouldn't cooperate.

"May I help?" Zane sat back down on the edge of the bed. He lifted her chin and met her gaze. "Let me get the buttons, and then I'll leave you to the rest, okay?"

She nodded, feeling a flush race from her face to her chest. She wasn't ordinarily very modest by most standards, but the idea of the sexy hunk helping her get out of her clothes was almost more than she could stand. The end result would be much more comfortable though, so she let her hands fall to her sides and tugged the comforter out of the way enough for Zane to unbutton her work shirt.

He made quick progress getting her unbuttoned while she held her breath. Even though she was concussed and her head hurt like fuck, she wasn't dead. She was aware of his fingers grazing her nipples through her bra as he worked. She was also aware that he held his own breath.

When he finished, he set his hands on her shoulders and eased the shirt away from her body. "Here. Hold it up to your chest, baby." He handed her the T-shirt and she

53

clasped it to her front, shocked when he reached behind her to undo her bra. It fell forward, releasing her tight chest that seemed about two sizes too big for that particular bra all the sudden.

He lifted her chin to his gaze again. "Slip the shirt on, baby." He stood and turned around and she realized he meant *now*. As in, while he wasn't looking.

She quickly pulled it over her head and lay back against the mattress, exhausted as though she'd gone for a run, not pulled on a shirt. "'K," she said.

Zane turned back around. He didn't say a word. He simply pulled back the covers and quickly unzipped her skirt. He tugged it down with a little help from her when she lifted her hips, somewhat mortified, but also freakishly aroused even with a concussion. Or perhaps because of the concussion.

The man even peeled her black tights off next, leaving her in just panties that were visible because the T-shirt was bunched up around her waist. She tugged the shirt down, lifting her ass off the bed again slightly and wondering what pair of panties she'd left the house in that morning.

The next thing she knew, Zane was tucking her back in and kissing her forehead again. "Sleep. I'll be back." He left.

She was too tired to think and closed her eyes again, knowing it would be short lived.

~

Zane paced a hole in the living room floor as he downed his second beer. He tried watching TV, but nothing caught his eye and the noise was irritating. All he could think about was the gorgeous woman in his bed. And his brain was burned with the images of her fucking hot creamy skin, which he'd seen way more of than he should. Her bare shoulders had nearly undone him. He'd totally stepped over the line when he tugged off her skirt and hose. Her black lace panties had stopped his heart.

And then he'd left the room, filled with the scent of Abby, and begun this incessant pacing once again. What else was there to do? He'd spoken to her boss, explaining the situation. The man was beyond nice and had told him to have Abby call him when she was feeling up to it. Then Zane called the station and got a ribbing from his own boss, who chuckled when he told him he had him covered for the next few days.

Next, Zane had called Abby's insurance company, easily finding her insurance card in her purse. He reported what he knew and filed a claim on her behalf. She would have to call and follow up with that again later, but it was a start. At least the ball was rolling and the company could assess the car. Though Zane knew it wouldn't take a rocket scientist to come to the conclusion it was totaled. He still couldn't believe Abby had come out of it as unscathed as she had.

He glanced at his watch. Midnight. He would wake her again now and then try to sleep for a few hours. On the couch. The cold hard leather couch.

He entered the room again as quietly as possible, though there was no need since his main goal was to wake Abby. He sat on the edge of his bed as he had already several times and stared down at her for a moment. The light from the hall was enough to illuminate her features. Her mouth was parted, and she breathed easily. Her brow wasn't scrunched up in sleep, and he hated that when he woke her, she would be reminded of the pain and furrow her eyebrows again.

Zane lifted her hand that wasn't tucked under the covers and drew it to his cheek. Her skin was as soft as it looked. Yep, he would totally give up BDSM for this woman. Anything to keep her in his bed. She looked perfect there.

He inhaled deeply and then cupped her face with his other hand. "Abby. Baby, wake up."

A soft moan escaped her lips, and she turned toward his hand, burrowing her cheek against it. He thought she smiled too.

"Baby, wake up," he repeated. He stroked his thumb across her lower lip, enjoying her smooth skin.

She opened her eyes a slit, and then they fluttered while her tongue darted out to lick her lips and thus his thumb. So fucking sexy. And he felt like an ass thinking such a thing when she was not alert enough to be aware of his hard cock and his roving mind.

"Mmm. Has it been two hours again already?"

"Yeah."

"What do you want to ask me this time?" she muttered without meeting his gaze. In fact she pulled his hand, the one holding hers, up under her chin, rolled to her side, and tucked his fingers between her and the pillow. "I'll tell you the president is Mickey Mouse and his wife is that sexy woman who takes a lot of flak for not wearing sleeves."

"Ha ha." He leaned closer. "Funny girl. What's my name, smarty pants?" He held his breath, regretting the question immediately. If she didn't quickly respond, he would be hurt, sort of.

"Mmm. Let's see. The doctor called you Randolf. But in my mind, I've been stuck on Hot, Sexy, Tattooed Guy From Under My Porch." She took a few breaths while his eyes went wide, and then her eyes shot just as wide, and she lifted her head to stare at him. "Did I say that out loud?"

"Yes." A grin spread across his face until it hurt. "And I liked it. Hot, Sexy, Tattooed Guy, huh?"

She shrugged. "Ugh. I've given you a complex. Now you'll be all smug." She flopped back onto the pillow and winced, her free hand tugging out from under the covers to examine gently the various wounds. "Can I have more Tylenol?"

"Yeah. It's right here. If you give me my hand back, I'll open it."

She met his gaze and gasped, clearly unaware she was resting on his palm under her chin again. She released him immediately and moaned. "Gah, you scramble my brain."

He snickered as he dumped two more pills from the bottle and then held them up to set in her hand. He tucked his hand behind her head and lifted just enough for her to pop the pills in and take a drink of water. "Do you feel any better?"

"I think so, though I'm rambling at the mouth as though I were on stronger pain killers. What time is it?"

"Midnight."

"Have you slept? You can't get up every two hours and come in here to check on me."

"Of course I can. That's the general idea."

She shook her head. "You need to sleep too."

"I will. In two hour shifts. I've made a bed out of my couch." He stroked her face again, unable to resist. "I'm hoping if I manage to keep you locked in my room in my bed long enough, I'll start to grow on you, and you might consent to a date."

She inhaled sharply.

"A vanilla date." He shrugged when she narrowed her gaze at him. "Thought I might try your way, if you'll have me."

"My way?"

57

"Yeah, vanilla. I used to be able to do vanilla before I entered the lifestyle. Surely I could do it again."

"Hmm," she muttered, pulling her bottom lip between her teeth as though she had a secret she wasn't sure she should share. "Maybe I should hold my tongue then and not tell you I was thinking of giving your way a shot."

He lifted both brows. "You must have a concussion." He eased his hand into her hair and threaded his fingers through the thick locks. He stared at her hair, knowing he needed to escape this room fast before he went too far. Their combined innuendo was more than he could tolerate. "Sleep, baby. I'll take a nap and set an alarm to check you again in a few hours."

She grabbed his free hand and tugged. "That's crazy. I'm in your bed in your house. It's king-sized. It would be horribly rude of you to leave me here all alone. What if I wake up and I'm confused about my surroundings?" The imp batted her eyes at him.

What the hell was she proposing?

She pulled his arm farther. "I'd rest much better if you were next to me."

He gulped. "Next to you? In the bed?" He wasn't an imbecile. Of course that's what she meant, but he needed to wrap his mind around her proposal.

"Yes." She paused while he remained frozen, unable to meet her gaze. "Jesus, Zane. I didn't mean to be so presumptuous. If I'm way out of line, forget I said anything." She released his hand and scooted a few inches away.

Finally, he managed to jerk his gaze to hers. Her face was whiter than usual, and she looked a little embarrassed, her eyes darting past him to stare at some undisclosed location beyond him. And then he made a decision. He stood, walked into the master bath, shed his clothes, and tugged on a pair of flannel sleep pants.

Seconds later he was back at her side, climbing over her, and slipping under the blankets until he was situated alongside her. He pulled her back into his chest and kissed the spot behind her ear before he spoke again. "Not presumptuous, baby. I was just trying to avoid making you uncomfortable. I'll warn you, though. I can't control my body's physical reaction to this arrangement, but I'll do my best to be a gentleman."

"Never asked for that."

He froze again, his lips hovering at her ear. "Abby…" he warned.

"Yes?" she asked demurely.

"Go to sleep. I'm not in the habit of having sex with concussed women."

She snuggled closer to him, holding the hand he had draped over her body in both of hers between her breasts. "Who said anything about having sex?" she asked, the picture-perfect example of coy.

Zane licked a line down her neck from her ear to her shoulder until she shivered. "I did. And I intend to make good on it as soon as you aren't wincing every time you move, sexy." He gripped her hands with his between them. "Now stop wiggling before my cock gets a mind of its own and takes over my body, rendering me unable to be responsible for my actions."

"Mmm…" her voice was fading. "How did I land such an altruist?"

"How did I land such an imp?" He kissed her shoulder and then laid his head next to hers, catching the scent of her hair—floral shampoo.

"Mmm," she repeated, rubbing her ass against his cock.

He wanted to spank her sexy ass for being such a tease,

but he was afraid at this point she would enjoy such a thing. Besides, her ass was probably still sore from last week's impaling nail.

She might not think she was submissive, but he suddenly wasn't so sure about that. Given the opportunity, she might find she enjoyed some aspects of BDSM. Perhaps not all, but they might be able to come to a compromise.

Zane closed his eyes as he realized Abby's breathing had evened out and her grip on his hands loosened. It took him a while to fall asleep with her perfect body against him, but he eventually managed.

CHAPTER 7

Abby awoke slowly, gradually becoming aware of her surroundings. The first thing she knew was it was day, the sun filtering in though the partially open blinds. The second thing she knew on the heels of the first was she wasn't in her own bed. And the rest crashed into her mind quickly. The car accident. Zane. The concussion. Zane. The hard body pressed behind her. Zane.

And then the pain. Holy shit her head hurt. She moaned as she twisted around to face the hard body behind her. She squeezed her eyes shut against the ache of tight stitches and the throb inside her head.

"Hey, baby." Zane's strong arm settled on her belly as she landed on her back. "Let me grab the Tylenol."

She didn't move as he reached across her and nabbed the bottle of pills and the bottle of water. He sat up, popped two pills into his hand, and then lifted her head to help her swallow them. When he eased her back down, she opened her eyes a slit.

He was frowning. "One to ten, how bad?"

She thought about that for a moment. "Um, maybe a seven."

Zane settled back alongside her and set his palm back on her belly. Her naked belly. Her T-shirt, or rather *his* T-shirt, had worked its way up her body during the night. "Go back to sleep. You'll feel better in a little bit. Let the drugs get into your system."

"Mmm." She didn't have the energy for more than that yet. Her eyes fluttered shut. The last thing she wanted to do was move. So his plan was best. As she drifted back into dreamland, she was acutely aware of his firm palm rubbing her stomach. It felt so good...

The next time she opened her eyes, she was alone in the bed. She could smell coffee and her stomach growled. She hadn't eaten since lunch yesterday.

Testing her ability to move, she slowly sat upright and twisted her body so her legs dangled off the edge of the bed. The world didn't spin, so she assumed she might be up for more movement. She took a deep breath and eased her body off the bed until her feet hit the floor.

That was when the door opened. "Abby. Baby, hang on." Zane rushed across the room and took her arm. "Why didn't you yell?"

"I think that would have been the worst thing I could have done. Besides, I'm fine. Just getting my feet under me." She glanced down, realized the T-shirt hadn't fallen into place, and quickly tugged the cotton edges so it fell over her hips and covered her panties. *Geez.*

"I'll help you get to the bathroom, and then you can do your thing."

"K." She couldn't decide if she was more mortified or intrigued by this turn of events. "I'm pretty sure you're the first person I've ever been to third base with before the first date."

Zane chuckled. "Baby, that wasn't even close to third base. Your sports analogies are a mess. If that's what you call third base, you're in for an unbelievable inning when I do finally get a hit."

She had to fight to keep from giggling. She wasn't entirely sure she followed his line of thinking, but the important part was he made the mood light, his voice sent a shiver down her body, and his hand wrapped around her arm made her feel cherished.

When they reached the bathroom, Zane flipped on the light. "I set a towel for you on the side of the tub. Figured you might like a bath over a shower."

She felt stronger already. "Sounds like heaven."

"I even have bubbles." He winked at her as he turned the tap on and waited with his hand under the running water while it warmed up.

"Why on earth do you have bubbles?" She regretted the question as soon as it left her mouth. She didn't want to know the answer.

Zane lifted up a pink bottle with a mermaid on the side. "My niece. She likes her baths."

"Ah." Well, then. Why did that make her entire body warm?

Zane stood, satisfied with the temperature, and wiped his hands on his jeans. "You get settled. I'll bring you a tray. Coffee. OJ. Toast. I think you can handle those three so far."

"Perfect. Thanks. Can you grab a hair band from my purse?"

"Of course. I'll see what I can find."

She stared at his chest as he passed her where she leaned against the doorframe. He was too wide to pass through, and his hard chest brushed against her front. Her nipples jumped to attention, which didn't abate when he paused and cupped her face with one hand. He kissed her forehead and then left her to pad from the room.

Abby blinked at his retreating back. Everything about him was defined. He was chiseled from stone. And she wanted to see what was under the tight black T-shirt, not just the muscles, but the tattoos.

Instead, she licked her lips and made her way farther into the bathroom, pushing the door shut behind her. She thought about locking it, but that seemed absurd. And besides, he was going to bring her a tray. So she needed to get her ass in the tub quick and make sure there were ample bubbles.

After using the adjoining toilet room and brushing her teeth with the brand new brush she found on the counter, she slipped the T-shirt over her head and stepped out of the panties.

The water had risen high enough to cover her body by the time she lowered herself into the tub, letting her hair fall over the edge to keep it somewhat dry. She couldn't get the top of her hair wet yet with the staples. The water felt heavenly. The heat was just what she needed to soothe her muscles. Now that she wasn't lying in bed, her entire body ached. She popped the top on the bubbles, smiling at the scent of cotton candy, and poured a good amount into the flow coming from the tap. When the bubbles had risen enough to relax her, she flipped off the spout and leaned back in the water.

Bliss. Perfection.

She glanced around the room. Emily wasn't kidding. Zane was very organized. Everything in the room was precisely placed. Even the towel he'd left her was folded perfectly on the counter.

She closed her eyes for several minutes, not opening them until she heard the door squeak.

"You good? Can I come in?" Zane asked, his back to her, his ass pushing the door.

"Yep." *If you don't mind the fact that I'm naked and wet in your tub and your sexy frame is filling the room, making me squeeze my legs together.* It was downright ridiculous how her body reacted to him, her physical reaction completely obliterating the pain in her head.

Zane set the tray on the edge of the tub and handed her a hair band. "What sounds good first? Coffee or juice?"

"Juice. I probably need the sugar to jump start." She tucked her hair up in a messy bun.

He lifted the glass, and she took it from him. It tasted delicious, and she drank the entire thing before handing him back the glass. "God, that was good. I needed that."

He chuckled. "I can get more."

"Nope. Coffee." She grabbed the mug off the tray next.

"Sugar? Cream?"

"Please."

Zane spooned a heap of sugar into the mug and then poured some cream from the refrigerator carton.

"Perfect. Thanks again."

"Any time. How's your head?"

"Better. A dull throb. Could be more from the staples than the concussion."

"True." Zane set the plate of toast next to her and stood. "I'll let you relax. Don't slip under and drown on my watch, though." He narrowed his gaze while he teased.

"Got it. No problem."

Zane left, shutting the door with a quiet snick and leaving Abby to fend for herself. She ate the toast first, used the variety of products on the edge of the tub to wash, and then lay in the water until it cooled. Getting out and facing the man in the other room was going to be a challenge. He did things to her just looking at him. He sucked the oxygen from the room with his frame. And his smile made her mouth go dry every time.

She managed though, drying off with the enormous towel he left her and then shrugging into the clean T-shirt he'd set on the counter. No way was she going to put her panties back on. But on second thought, as she made her way into the main section of the house in search of Zane, maybe she should have.

"Hey," he said as she padded into the living room. "I got you all set up on the couch. Throw blankets. Pillows. More coffee."

She headed straight for the spot he pointed to from where he stood in the kitchen. The floor plan was open, the kitchen, family room, and dining area all one big space. Nothing was out of place. Even the chairs at the table were pushed in perfectly. A plant sat in the middle of the table.

Indeed, he had a little nest for her on the sofa. It looked out of place in the room. She glanced across at his television and the many DVDs and CDs lining the shelves on both sides, every single one precisely lined up. She was almost afraid to sit down for fear her butt would indent the couch cushion. Finally, she slipped into her spot, tugging the T-shirt over her bare ass, and covered herself with the blankets. "I'm gonna be spoiled."

Zane came around to her side and sat in the center of the couch, lifting her feet onto his lap. "How do you feel now?"

"Better. Almost human. I think I'll live."

"The concussion was mild. I'm sure you'll be fine in a few days."

"I might not be dealing blackjack this week." She leaned her head on the arm of the couch and stared at the ceiling. "I've only been there a month. I obviously don't have vacation time or sick leave coming to me. That part sucks.

Thank God I took COBRA from my last job, or I'd be screwed."

"Will you be okay financially?"

"Yeah. I just don't like it."

Zane set a hand on her knee and idly stroked her leg under the covers. His gaze pinned her to the couch. "How do you manage to look that sexy covered in dirt under the porch or covered in cuts and bruises?"

She flushed, heat rising up her face. "Whatever." She rolled her eyes to deflect his compliment.

He chuckled. "Yeah. Whatever. I can't wait to see you fixed up. I'll probably faint."

"We wouldn't want that. I'll keep the grunge look going for now to avoid injury to you."

He grinned wider. "You could, but you might feel awkward when we go out to dinner."

She lifted her brows. "Dinner?"

"Yeah. A date."

"A vanilla date. Thought maybe you were kidding last night." She giggled. "Can you do that?"

He leaned toward her and tucked a lock of hair behind her ear. "Of course. I was vanilla once. I'm sure I can do it again. I told you so."

"And I might have mentioned deciding to give your world a try."

His eyes danced with laughter. "Let's not get carried away. You're concussed. I thought *you* were kidding last night. Or at least confused."

"Nope. I figure I owe you after rescuing me twice." She had trouble breathing with his face so close to hers. "And maybe Emily talked me down from my initial fear of all things BDSM."

"I'm glad, but the reality is I like you, and I want to take you out on a real date, and it doesn't have to be anything beyond the normal. I thought I could walk away Saturday. I *did* walk away. It seemed like the right thing to do. But I can't get you out of my head, nor can I seem to keep you from climbing in my ambulance." He cupped her face and stroked her cheek with his thumb as he spoke.

She liked that. She liked everything about him.

"Speaking of Emily, she said she would go by your house and grab some things for you. If you want anything specific, you can call her. She knows where the spare key is."

"*I* don't even know where the spare key is."

"Well, the rose lady had Emily water her plants on occasion." Zane lowered his hand to her shoulder and down her arm until he held her hand in his. His thumb kept moving, now stroking the back of her hand instead of her cheek. It was safer, but the damage was already done. She was totally head over heels for this guy.

"Of course. Mrs. Lamphry and her roses."

"Also, the police need a statement from you. I told Rider he could do it when he and Emily stop by. I hope that's okay."

"What sort of statement?"

"Just your take on the accident. No big deal. You weren't conscious at the scene, so now they need to fill in the blanks."

"I doubt I can fill in any blanks. I can't remember much before I woke up in the hospital."

"Did you at least get a good look at the other car?"

"What other car?"

Zane's brow furrowed. "You never saw the car that ran you off the road?"

"No." Abby shook her head. Her heart beat faster. "Were they okay?"

Zane hesitated. "They left the scene, baby."

"What do you mean? How do you know there was another car, then?"

"Witnesses. Several people stopped. Nobody got the plate. The guy swerved into your lane, you veered to the right to avoid the head-on collision, and he corrected himself and continued driving."

"Holy shit. People saw that?"

Zane nodded. "Several people."

"Why? Did he maybe not know what happened?"

Now Zane shook his head. "Not a chance in hell. The accident was fast and loud. You hit the embankment, baby. Hard."

"Who would do that?"

Zane shrugged. "That's what the police are trying to figure out. Apparently you won't be much help."

"None." She closed her eyes and leaned her head back once again. Nothing. She didn't remember a single detail for those last few minutes.

$\sim$

On Thursday evening, Zane stepped up to the cage at the gym ready to spar. Conner was his partner. Of all the members of The Fight Club, Conner was by far the most intimidating as far as Zane was concerned.

The man was a beast. Nobody beat him in the ring, and on top of that, he was the oldest of the group. At thirty-eight he was fourteen years Zane's senior.

Nicest guy, though. Friendly, calm, laid back...until he hit the cage. And his fiancée, Sabrina, was the sweetest. Conner doted on her as if she were made of glass, especially since she'd gotten pregnant.

"Hey, Zane. You ready?" Conner asked as Zane entered through the fence.

"Yep. How's Sabrina?"

"Feeling better. Still has morning sickness. Though I have no idea why they call it that since it lasts all day. Other than that, she's officially moved in. Her house is sold. Now, if I could just get her to chill and let me take care of her so she could concentrate on writing her novel, everything would be perfect."

Zane smiled. Sabrina was an editor. Conner had been nagging her to give it up and work on her masterpiece for months.

Joe, the owner of the gym, came in behind Zane and shut the gate. "I don't have a lot of time, but I'll help you out for a few minutes."

"Sounds good." Conner bounced on his feet, popping his neck left and right. It made a cracking noise both times. "I'm getting too old for this."

"Hardly," Zane added as he squared up with Conner. "I pray to God I'm as fit as you when I'm your age."

"Hell, I wish I had been," Joe said. "I was never as strong as you guys are back in the day. Nobody was. Y'all are made of steel these days."

Conner threw a few jabs at the air. "Saw Rider yesterday. He said you were holed up with a woman." The man grinned.

Zane rolled his eyes as he stretched the tight muscle in his thigh. "Holed up? It's not like I had her tied to the bed or turned over my knee. The woman had a concussion. I was a total gentleman."

Conner chuckled. "Uh huh. I heard she was all legs, and I know how you feel about legs."

"True. They are smokin' hot. Not gonna deny it. She's agreed to go on a date with me Friday."

"A date?" Conner stopped jumping to clutch his chest.

"That's rich. When was the last time you went on a vanilla date?"

"Can't remember. High school maybe. But she's worth it. Trust me." Zane jumped forward. "Now, give me what you've got before I catch you unaware and knock you on your ass, old guy."

Conner laughed harder, but he got into position, and the two of them started the workout.

∾

On Friday night, Zane stood at Abby's front door, smoothing his hands down his shirt and taking a deep breath. He felt like he was fifteen the way he'd stressed about this date all week.

Abby had insisted on going home after two nights in his care. Her head no longer hurt, and her cuts were healing well. Zane took her to pick up a rental car, and that was the last time he'd seen her. He'd texted her every day, but he hadn't gone by her house. He didn't think he could control himself around her another minute, and she needed to heal before he saw her again. Because the next time he was in her presence, his lips were going to devour her.

He lifted his hand and knocked on her front door.

When it opened, he froze. Abby stood there wearing a tight black skirt that left plenty of long legs extended for his perusal. Her blouse was a deep purple, thin enough to hint at the black lace bra underneath. It had a collar, but Abby had left the top few buttons undone, leaving enough cleavage to make him drool.

He swallowed. "Abby… You… Uh…" He met her gaze. Except for the tiny stitches on her forehead and chin, no one would know she'd been in a serious car accident a few days ago. Her hair was down and hung in full waves down her back. Her blue eyes looked almost purple against the tones of her shirt. He let his gaze roam back down her body until he reached her feet. Strappy black heels finished the outfit. She wasn't wearing hose.

The thought of running his hand up her bare leg made him swallow again.

"You want to come in?" She held the door open wider and stepped back. "I just need to grab my purse." She turned and walked farther into the house, giving him a view of her perfect ass encased in the black skirt. It swayed fantastically when she walked.

Swallowing was no longer his primary concern. He was more worried about choking.

When she returned, purse in hand, he hadn't moved. "Ready."

There was no way he could do anything before he tasted her. She may not like him messing up the glossy lipstick she'd carefully applied before he arrived, but tough. Zane grabbed both her hands, pulled her closer until they were chest to chest on her front porch, and lowered his face to claim her mouth.

He'd only meant to taste, but immediately got swept into another dimension when their lips touched. Before he could stop himself, he angled his head to one side and deepened the kiss, his tongue slipping into her mouth to claim every inch.

She moaned against him, her hands moving from his hands to his biceps as he lifted his fingers to wrap them around her waist. The sounds she made stiffened his cock instantly. If he shuffled forward another inch, he would have her belly pressed against his length.

Instead he concentrated on her lips, the way her palms wrapped around his arms, her nails digging into his skin.

She tasted like her lip gloss, berry or something. He could stand there kissing her for the rest of his life and be content. Sort of.

When his knees threatened to buckle, he finally broke free, setting his forehead against hers and gasping for air. He let his hands trail up her sides until they rested under her breasts. "Jesus, Abby."

She nodded subtly. Her lips were swollen, and when she reached out her tongue to lick them, he groaned.

Gripping her tighter, he eased away from her until several inches separated them. "Have I mentioned you look amazing?"

"No." She smiled. "You look pretty fantastic yourself."

"We should go to dinner. Like now. Before I change my mind and push you into the house instead."

"Mmm." She didn't move, and Zane's libido shot even higher. Lord, she was going to kill him.

With a deep breath, he yanked the door closed, took her by the hand, and led her to his truck.

"I don't know if I can climb into that thing, Zane." She laughed as he held the door open.

Zane grabbed her by the waist and easily lifted her into the seat. "Problem solved."

She gasped. "Okay then." Zane watched as she situated herself and pulled her seatbelt on. Her damn legs were so sexy, and he could see most of them now that she was sitting and her skirt had risen. Of course he'd seen them in their entirety several times, including the day he met her—the moment he knew he wanted her, even before he saw her face.

Such a leg man… He shut her door and rounded the hood, taking deep breaths and hoping he didn't act like an idiot all evening. Usually he was calm, organized, prompt. People said he was anal. But small details seemed to disappear in her presence when his focus narrowed in on her and he lost track of everything else around him.

He turned toward her as he started the truck. "Italian?"

"Sounds good." She crossed her legs, tugging again on the hem of her skirt.

What Zane wanted to do was command her to spread her legs instead. He wanted to reach between her legs and see if she was wet. Or better yet, have her touch her pussy and show him how wet she was. But this was a vanilla date. And he kept his mouth closed and pulled away from the curb, wondering how he was going to make it through the evening in vanilla fashion, especially if Abby continued to fidget next to him, her bottom lip caught between her teeth, clearly nervous.

She hadn't been nervous while his tongue had been in her mouth…

It took ten minutes to get to the restaurant he'd chosen. Zane tried to make small talk. "How's your head?"

"Fine. Not noticing anything inside, but the two staples itch like hell, as do these stitches. I'll be glad when I get them out tomorrow. Thank God my doctor has office hours on Saturdays."

"And then you're going back to work?"

"Yes. Monday. My boss is being very understanding. I know it's been hard on everyone else having to cover my shifts."

"You didn't have much of a choice."

"Not at all. Dealing takes a lot of concentration. My head was swimming for the first few days. I hope I'm completely capable on Monday, or I'm gonna get fired."

"I'm sure you'll do great." He glanced at her, finding her hands fisted in her lap, pressing on the hem of her skirt. "I'd like to see you deal sometime."

She rolled her eyes when he looked at her again. "God

no. It makes me very nervous when someone I know comes to my table. Always has."

"How long have you been dealing? I thought you just moved here."

"Yeah, but I've been dealing blackjack my entire life it seems. My dad taught me as soon as I could hold the cards, and then when I was twenty-one, I started working at a casino in my home town."

"Where's that?"

"Tunica, Mississippi."

"Ah, so that's why you know how to gamble."

"Yep. Interestingly enough, my father doesn't gamble. He's never been inside a casino. But he loves blackjack. Has always played it for fun with poker chips."

"Funny. And your mom? Do your parents still live there?"

"Yes. They're older. They had me late in life. I never went to college because by the time I was eighteen, they needed me more at home. My dad retired from working an assembly line before I graduated high school. My mom doesn't get around well anymore. So, I did what I knew best and worked at a casino. I lived at home. Three months ago my parents told me it was time for me to spread my wings. I was terrified at first, but they sold the house and moved to a retirement community, giving me no choice."

"What made you decide to come to Vegas?"

"Who wouldn't?" She giggled. "It's so beautiful here. The weather is awesome. The cost of living is low. And I make way more money dealing here than I did in Mississippi."

"Did you ever think about going back to school?"

"Uh huh. I started taking classes online a few years ago. It's a slow process that way, though. I thought I wanted to be an English major, but after several classes, I realized what I really wanted to do."

"And what's that?" he asked as he pulled into a spot at the restaurant. He turned to face her.

She had her head tipped to one side. "Hm. I've never told anyone. I think I'll keep it to myself for a little longer."

He raised both eyebrows and grinned. "Seriously? A secret life ambition you aren't willing to share?"

"Yep."

"Intriguing."

"I'll just leave you guessing for a while." She unbuckled her seatbelt as Zane did the same and pushed his door open.

"Hang on, I'll be around to help you down."

Abby opened her door, but Zane got there in time to watch her swing her legs around and set her hands on his shoulders to hop down. *God, those legs are divine.*

Zane took her hand and led her into the restaurant. Luckily it wasn't too crowded yet for a Friday night. They managed to get a table quickly. "Do you drink wine?"

"Love it."

"Red? Cab or Merlot?"

"Either one would be great."

The waitress came over, and Zane pointed out a bottle of Merlot. After she left, he leaned on his elbows and soaked in more of his lovely date. "You're absolutely stunning in purple."

"Thanks." She touched a finger to her forehead. "These stitches really pull the outfit together."

He smiled. "They're hardly noticeable. You look perfect."

"I talked your ear off. Tell me more about you."

Zane shrugged. "I'm not nearly as interesting, to be honest."

"That's impossible. What little I know about you makes you more interesting than anyone I've ever met." She tucked her hair behind her ear. "I don't know a single MMA fighter, for example. Nor have I met an EMT. And definitely no one who practices BDSM. So, every aspect of you is new and fascinating."

"Well, when you put it like that, I sound kind of cool." He pumped out his chest in mock exaggeration. "But really. I'm from here, born and raised. I have a sister. She's two years older. Mari. She's married and has one daughter."

"Ah, your niece. The one who likes bubble baths."

"Yes. She's a gem. Love that little stinker."

"How old is she?"

"Four."

"When did you start fighting?"

"I've been fighting for about six years."

"You're so...buff." She wove a hand through the air, encompassing all of him. "How can anyone compete against you?"

He smiled. "Well, all the fighters are about like me. If not, they'd get crushed. I work out a lot."

"I'm sure."

The waitress returned with their wine and then read off the specials for the night. Zane easily chose one, and Abby surprised him by also selecting from the verbal list. Neither of them had opened a menu. The waitress took their menus back and promised to return shortly with salad and bread sticks.

Zane lifted his glass and took a sip. "Mmm. It's good."

Abby did the same. He watched her tip the glass back and set it on her lips, wishing he was that glass. The way she drank the wine was like an art form. Her tongue reached out to lick her lips before she took a drink, making him squirm in his seat. "Can I watch you fight sometime?" she asked as she set her glass down.

"Sure. Have you ever watched it on TV?"

She shook her head. "No, but I'm intrigued. Emily told me about your Fight Club. Do your friends' girlfriends and wives go to watch?"

He nodded. "They do, some of them reluctantly and others with enthusiasm." He wasn't kidding. "Jenna and Katy aren't fond of the sport at all, but they occasionally go to support Mason and Rafe. Emily and Kayla, on the other hand, Rider's and Gage's significant others, love it. Sabrina is Conner's fiancée. She also loves watching, but she's newly pregnant, so she doesn't come as often right now. She suffers from morning sickness most of the time. I'm sure Emily is coming to the exhibition we're having tomorrow night. If you want to go with her, she'd probably love the company."

"Cool. I'll call her tomorrow. What's an exhibition?"

"It's a night when we spar at the home gym just for practice. Nothing serious. A good place to check it out. Some of the larger arenas are crowded and overwhelming. Fans of MMA can be very intense."

"Maybe I'll do a little research in the morning so I'm not ignorant."

"You can. Emily's pretty astute by now. She'll fill you in with a play-by-play I'm sure."

"So, do you make money when you win these things?"

He shook his head. "Nope. Not as an amateur."

"And you don't have aspirations of going pro?"

"No. Though not for lack of interest. I've been approached by both legal and illegal venues."

"Really?" Her eyes widened. "Illegal?"

"Underground."

"That's a real thing?"

"Of course. And around here, there's a large Russian contingency of underground fighters. I have a few acquaintances who are involved."

"Huh. That's interesting. Russians you say?" She visibly shuddered.

"Yes. Why?"

"I have a friend from work, Lauren, who's dating some Russian guy. Made me think of it. Well, dating is perhaps a loose term."

"What do you mean?"

"I think he's bad news. In fact, he's the reason I reacted so harshly to your initial BDSM declaration. Lauren told me he was a Dom. She was all excited at first, but then she changed, quickly. I think the guy's abusing her."

"Shit." He reached across the table and took her hand. "I'm sorry. That sucks. No wonder you were so skittish. BDSM is not like that. Not even close. Not the kind I practice, anyway."

"Yeah. Emily set me straight after you left my house last week."

"I'm glad. And listen, yes, it's a part of who I am. Yes, I would love to introduce you to that side of me, but for now it's good enough I told you about that part of myself. I'm not going to pressure you in any way. I mean it. Nine days ago, I would have said there was no way I could date a vanilla woman."

"And then?"

"And then I got this call from Rider and found the sexiest legs I've ever seen sticking out from under her porch, and everything I've ever resolved to hold true evaporated."

"You can't be serious." She held his gaze, tugging on her hand, but he didn't release it.

Instead he gripped her hand tighter and reached for the

other one to hold them both. "As a heart attack. And then I crawled under that porch, and knew I wanted to get to know that woman better. Immediately. I had no idea how I was going to go about it, but you made it easy when you walked into Rider's house a few days later, all cute and sexy, carrying a tray of cookies, which were delicious by the way."

The salads arrived, and Zane was forced to release Abby's hands to make room on the table. He took another sip of wine, thinking this evening was going splendidly.

She narrowed her gaze at him. "You don't seem like a Dom."

"Well, I'm controlling that side of me. I'll be honest. And besides, I don't think you really have the right idea. Until you see D/s in action, you might have a skewed concept of what's entailed. Certainly not abuse, like your friend Lauren. Is she still seeing that guy? There are some Russian mafia around here that are bad news."

"I don't know if she's still with him. I haven't talked to her this entire week. I texted her after the accident, to let her know I wouldn't be in, but the only response I got was terse. I'm worried about her to be honest. Seems like she's in over her head.

"The guy sent a man to my table once. Last Monday in fact. The day I had my accident. He told me to stay out of his business." She shivered and then took a long sip of wine. "It was weird."

"The guy threatened you?" Zane held his fork midair.

"No." She shook her head and then stopped. "Well, maybe. I guess so. I have no idea how he even knew I was involved. That's the weird part. I talked to Lauren about him earlier that day at lunch and told her I thought he was bad news, but how the hell would he have known that a few hours later while we were both still working? Lauren said she didn't tell him a thing. I got the feeling he was watching us in the break room somehow." She shuddered.

Zane set his fork down. "Do you know his name?"

She thought for a second. "Something strange. Anton. That's it."

Fuck. He pulled out his phone and sent a quick text to Rider.

Dude. Abby knows Anton Yenin. He was bothering her at the casino before the accident.

"What are you doing?"

"Alerting Rider." He set the phone down. "Sorry. Go on. My mind is running ahead. Why didn't you say anything about this guy?"

She looked perplexed. Her brow furrowed again. "To whom?"

"The cops? Me? Anyone really."

"Honestly, I never thought about it again until just now. Completely left my mind after the accident."

"The accident. The one where someone ran you off the road and tried to kill you? That accident?" His heart was pounding.

Abby opened her mouth, but nothing came out. She set her fork down with a clank and stared at him.

"Baby, I'm thinking there could be a connection." He reached across the table for her hand and gripped it with his again.

"Surely not," she muttered. "I mean what did I do?"

"Well, if you tried to talk your friend Lauren into dumping Anton Yenin, there's no telling what happened between then and when he threatened you. That guy is very bad news. Don't you find it a bit too coincidental that a few hours later someone ran you off the road?"

She shook her head subtly. "I really thought it was an accident, and someone either didn't realize what happened or they were too scared to stop after mistakenly crossing into my lane."

"I might have agreed with you until you told me about the rest of that day. Now I'm not so sure." His phone beeped on the table. Zane released Abby reluctantly to grab the cell.

Rider: Shit. That's not good.

Zane: Exactly. I'll get back to you later. Thanks.

"What'd he say?" Abby asked.

"He's concerned."

She shook her head. Worry etched her face. She wasn't smiling any longer, and her skin was pale. "Why do you know this guy?"

"Everyone in MMA knows Yenin. He runs his own underground fighting ring. He has approached several of us to fight for him over the years. He even tried to blackmail Conner into fighting for him a few months ago."

"Jesus."

Zane smiled. "Forget all this. Let's enjoy our evening. We can look into it more later."

She nodded briefly and glanced at her plate. "Surely it's all just a coincidence."

"Probably," he lied. He didn't like one bit of the scenario, but until he could talk to Rider or someone else at the station, there wasn't much he could do.

Tomorrow.

They ate their meals, chatting about more mundane things for the rest of dinner. He tried to lighten the mood, and it took a while, but finally he had her smiling again.

When the wine was gone and the plates cleared, he asked her what she wanted to do next. "You want to see a movie?"

She shrugged and bit her lip. Clearly she had another idea.

"What?"

"Emily said you usually go to your club on Fridays."

"I do, but tonight I'm with you instead."

"Could we go there?"

He hesitated, staring at her face. The way she tucked that damn lip between her teeth again made him shift in his seat. *Holy shit.* He swallowed the lump in his throat. "You want to go to Extreme?"

"Yes."

He narrowed his gaze. "I told you I would do vanilla."

"And I told you I would try your way. We did vanilla for dinner. Now, I think you should show me your other side."

Zane almost swallowed his tongue at those words. She had no idea how hard his already hard cock got when she tipped her head and spoke those words. "You sure? That wasn't my intention at all for this evening."

"Yes." She glanced down at herself. "Am I dressed okay?"

He smiled. "Anything goes at Extreme, baby. There will be regulars there in little or no clothes and newer members in something similar to what you're wearing."

"Take me." She smiled again, straightening her spine and lifting her face. "I want to know that side of you."

He stared at her for several moments. Was she for real? He wasn't kidding. He hadn't considered that option for a second. Was this wise?

"You're sure?"

"Yes." She glared at him through narrowed eyes. "Emily painted a way different picture than Lauren. I'm gambling on Emily's portrayal being more accurate."

"Oh, fuck yes. But that doesn't mean it's your cup of tea. Don't get me wrong, baby. The thought of having you with me at Extreme, on my arm, in my care, makes me...well, fucking hard." He leaned closer to whisper those last words.

She squirmed under his gaze, her hands gripping the edges of the table. "Let's do it then."

At that pronouncement, he groaned. "Woman..."

Two seconds later, he had the bill in his hand and was signing the statement.

Two seconds after that, he had her hand and was leading her to the truck.

CHAPTER 8

Abby was nervous. There was no denying it. She'd never done anything remotely close to what she was about to do tonight. A fetish club? But she liked this man. A lot. Zane was not only the sexiest heartthrob she'd ever been out with; he was also courteous, kind, doting, gentle.

She was in so much trouble.

She'd seen many sides of Zane while she'd been with him for two days. And she liked all of them. Now she needed to open her mind and take a chance. Trust Zane to handle her with care. She felt that trust, so the decision to go to Extreme with him was easy.

When they pulled up behind the club, Zane parked the truck and rounded to her side to help her down. With his hands at her waist, he pulled her close. "I really like you, Abby. A lot." He squeezed her, his fingers holding her tight.

"I like you too, Zane." She nearly choked up as she spoke. He seemed so serious.

He leaned in the last inches and kissed her lips sweetly before whispering against them. "It's been a long time since I've been out with a woman I didn't meet inside this club or at any other club. If anyone would have asked me a week and a half ago if I could give up D/s for a woman, I would have laughed in their face. But then I met you."

Abby swallowed. He was so sweet. "Zane—"

"Let me finish, baby." He stroked his hands up her sides until his thumbs brushed the edges of her breasts. "Dominance is just one part of me. And it's not the most important thing in the world. If you aren't comfortable, we'll leave. If you hate it, we won't come back. Whatever you do, don't force yourself to do anything just for me."

"'K." She nodded. Her nipples were hard pebbles against her bra and her sex was wet between her legs at the thought of his intensity.

Zane leaned down and furrowed his brow, making direct eye contact. "I mean it, Abby. I won't fuck up this thing we have over a BDSM club."

She smiled. "I don't think you could ever fuck up anything, Zane."

He chuckled. "Oh, trust me. I can. Wait until you see me lose a fight."

"Bet that doesn't happen often."

"Nope. But it isn't pretty when it does. I can get pretty intense in the ring."

"Emily told me." She smiled. "She said you were dubbed 'The Animal.'"

"Yeah, that's what they call me. I earned it. And I'm not too much fun when I lose, either." He nodded behind him. "You ready?"

She clutched his waist. "I am." God, she hoped she wasn't lying. She was nervous. She was beyond nervous. But Zane had a way of making her relax. She knew he would do his best to make her feel comfortable.

He took her hand and led her to the door where he nodded at a man outside. "Frank." Seconds later they were inside, and Zane greeted another man who seemed to be in charge. "Harper."

"Zane. How are ya?"

"Good. This is Abby."

"Nice to meet you, Abby. Harper Stevens." He took her hand and shook it. Nothing so far seemed remotely out of the ordinary. He turned back to Zane. "You need paperwork?"

"Not tonight. This is her first time. She won't be participating in anything."

"'K. You change your mind, come grab me, and I'll set you up." He turned to Abby again. "Safe, sane, and consensual here, Abby. If you plan to come again or decide to participate in a scene, you need to sign release forms. You need anything at any time, you come see me. Safe word in this club is always *red*. Got it?"

She nodded, grasping Zane's arm tight. *Deep breaths. It's just a club.*

"Have fun," Harper said as Zane led her past the front desk and into the main section of the club.

Zane took several steps into the crowd and then turned and faced her. He backed her against the wall at her side and cupped the sides of her face with both hands, his gaze grabbing hers and holding it tight. "Lord, I hope I'm not making a mistake. Do not leave my side. Got it?"

"Yes," she muttered.

"I might be bossy."

She smiled.

"It's one thing to disassociate when I'm not here, but inside this club, this is my stomping ground. I've never spent any time with a vanilla woman here. I'm used to being in command and having a submissive do my bidding."

A tight knot formed in the pit of her stomach, and her

pussy went from wet to soaking wet. She stepped her legs together and squeezed. She could feel her pulse beating hard under his thumbs.

Zane never dropped her gaze. Seconds went by.

Abby's mouth went dry. He was so intense, and her arousal skyrocketed. She hadn't seen the inside yet, but the mood was already beyond anything she'd ever experienced. His eyes alone were commanding, sexy, smolderingly hot. He wanted her. She could read his gaze. And not just sexually. She grabbed his waist to steady herself.

His grip on her face was firm as he lowered his lips to hers again and kissed her. Holy shit, the man could kiss. He angled his face to one side and consumed her. He didn't just kiss, he made it into an art. His tongue swept into her mouth and danced with her own just like he'd done when he picked her up. His lips were soft but demanding.

She heard a moan and recognized it was her own. Her body turned to mush. She thought her knees would buckle, but Zane had her. He wedged one leg between her thighs and held her pressed against the wall.

That didn't help keep her pussy from throbbing, or the moisture from building in her panties. And then she had the horrible thought that her wetness would get on his black jeans and mortify her. She squirmed, trying to stand straighter and keep her sex from touching his thigh.

Zane broke the kiss, but didn't move his face. "Stay still, baby." He resumed his perusal of her mouth while she froze on her tiptoes.

Every cell in her body came alive. She moved her hands from his waist to his biceps and held on tight.

By the time Zane pulled back again, she was putty. "God, Abby." He held her gaze again. "Sweetest kisses. I'll never have enough of them."

She gulped. His chest hovered inches from hers, and she wanted him to lean in the rest of the way and press against her breasts to ease the strain. Instead, she closed her eyes and took a deep breath. "Show me your world."

He hesitated, not saying a word until she opened her eyes. The smile on his face made her squirm more. She almost moaned when her pussy hit his thigh. There was no hiding the evidence.

Zane glanced down between their bodies. "My leg is getting very hot and wet."

Mortified, Abby ducked her head and looked away, lifting on her tiptoes again.

"Look at me, baby." His words were soft, patient, but demanding at the same time. And she was drawn to do as he said. When she met his gaze, he spoke again, "Love it."

She flushed, feeling the heat crawl up her face.

Zane shifted his hands toward the sides of her head, threading his fingers into her hair. "I'm gonna let you go, reluctantly, and show you around the club. I'm sure some of the other Fight Club members are here. Probably Emily and the other ladies too. I'll introduce you and give you a taste, but then I'm gonna need to take you home before I get carried away and do things to you I had no intention of doing tonight."

She licked her lips. "What if I want you to do them?" Her voice was deep, husky, not her own.

Zane groaned and stretched his neck back, pulling her face into his chest. "Baby. Stop that. Come on." He pulled away just as quickly, wrapped her arm around his bicep, and headed deeper into the club.

Abby didn't know how she managed to walk. She was so horny, every synapse in her body was firing messages. Her pussy was soaked. Her nipples were straining. Her lips were swollen.

Somehow she managed, holding on to Zane's arm and knowing if she didn't, she would fall to the floor.

The room was crowded and surprisingly noisy. People wearing all manner of dress, and undress, were laughing and talking to each other. Also surprising. She'd expected a bunch of somber quiet submissives bowing at the feet of their Doms.

"This is the main room, baby." He nodded across the space. "The bar is over there. They don't serve alcohol here, though."

"Oh." She hadn't thought of that.

"People have to be sober to make good decisions in this club." He pointed with his free hand to a group of tables and a lounge area to the left. "Most people hang out over there or wherever they can find space to talk and mingle."

"Other than a serious lack of clothing, I don't see anything unusual." She wasn't kidding about the clothes. Holy shit. Some women were naked. Some had on a collar and a leash. Some wore corsets, tight skirts, and high heels. Abby was indeed overdressed.

Zane glanced down at her and smiled. "Trust me. You haven't seen everything."

She didn't know what he meant, but she followed his lead across the room, relieved when she spotted Emily.

Emily grinned and jumped up from the booth she was sitting at with Rider and several other people. "Hey. You came." She hugged Abby gently. "I wasn't expecting you here tonight."

Rider stood and shook Abby's hand. "Don't bug them, baby," he said to Emily, tugging her back down. He rolled his eyes. "Let Zane handle this."

For some reason his words made the ball in Abby's belly tighten further. *Let Zane handle this.* She wanted Zane to handle *this* all right. And she didn't care how he did it.

Zane pulled Abby into the line of everyone else at the table. "Abby, meet several of the gang." He pointed, starting on the left and making his way around. "That's Rafe and his wife, Katy. Next we have Mason and his fiancée, Jenna. And you've met Gage and Kayla. Where's Conner?" He glanced around at the group.

Rider spoke. "Holding Sabrina's head over the toilet last I heard."

"Of course he is." Zane set his hand on Abby's around his arm. He turned his face to her. "You'll meet them later."

She nodded. There were so many of them, and there was no way she'd gotten a handle on their names. Not even half. The men were mostly wearing black. The women were all dressed in skimpy sexy clothes, the likes of which she had never seen, let alone owned.

She glanced around the room again and decided there were a few others like her, even a few in jeans. Probably most of them were new.

Zane turned to square his body in front of her, putting his back to his friends. He lifted her chin. "Eyes on me, baby."

She met his gaze and blinked. Every time he spoke, her pussy pulsed. Jesus. He had a way about him. And she was unbelievably surprised by her reaction.

"I'm going to show you around the club. You're going to keep your gaze down unless I say otherwise."

She nodded. Her mouth was too dry to lick her lips.

He leaned in closer. "I'm not trying to be an ass, although that's a general mannerism of submissives. My reasoning tonight is you don't need to see everything your first time here. It would be overwhelming. I'll tell you when to look up. Otherwise, your gaze stays on the floor or on mine. Got it?"

"Yes."

91

He kissed her lips briefly and sighed. "Lord, woman." He turned to tell the others what his plan was and then led Abby from the group.

She wanted to look back over her shoulder and see what their reactions were, but she forced herself to keep her gaze down instead. Perhaps he was right. He was certainly protective. If he didn't think she should absorb every aspect of the club this first time, he probably had good reason.

She had no idea what he'd meant when he said *Lord, woman*, but she hoped it wasn't something he'd been disappointed about.

Zane led her away from the crowd and the noise and into a wide hall behind the fray. The mood was considerably different there, and even without lifting her gaze she could feel it in the air. When he stopped and leaned his back against a wall, he pulled her back to his front and lifted her chin. His arms wrapped around her middle, and he leaned in to whisper in her ear. "This hall is a row of scenes. Each room has three sides. This side is open for spectators."

"Spectators?" she mumbled.

"Yep. That's the general idea. When people do a scene, others watch."

She had her face twisted to watch him speak, but he lifted a hand and turned her chin toward the room in front of them. "Watch, baby."

Abby stood very still while she absorbed her surroundings. The room had a large X in the middle. She'd seen pictures of them before on the internet. She knew it was a St. Andrew's cross. But seeing it live in a club was a completely different story. And seeing a naked woman attached to the cross made her entire frame stiffen. She faced the wood, so Abby couldn't read her expression.

Zane tucked both arms under Abby's breasts and held her close.

A man, presumably the woman's Dom, circled her several times. He wore jeans, but no shirt. He tugged on the ropes at her wrists and whispered in her ear. She nodded. He kissed her shoulder.

It was so sensual. Like a work of art. Like Zane's kisses. Art. It felt like she was watching the most amazing live painting while the man slowly stroked his hands across the woman's naked body. He gripped her ass and squeezed her cheeks. He even kneeled between her legs and caressed his palms down her thighs.

The lady moaned, setting her forehead on the cross section of wood.

Abby moaned also, quickly sucking in a breath to stop herself.

Zane didn't say anything, but his fingers teased the sides of her breasts.

She reached up with both hands to grip his forearms.

"Put your hands at your sides, baby." He spoke so close to her ear his warm breath made her shiver.

She released his arms and dropped her hands to her waist. She had no idea why he wanted her to do that, but again, her pussy gripped at nothing. She squeezed her legs together.

"Abby." He said that one word. Not a question. A statement.

She glanced at him. "Yes."

"Spread your legs, baby. Step out around mine." His lips landed on her neck, and he nibbled a path down to her shoulder as she complied.

Holy fuck. She'd never been this horny in her life.

A whoosh, followed by a slapping sound, made her jerk her gaze to the scene. She flinched with the woman on the cross as the Dom struck her with something in his hand. A flogger?

Abby cringed.

"He won't hurt her, baby. Not permanently anyway."

She wasn't sure she believed him. Even if he didn't hurt her physically, what about emotionally?

"It's freeing. Many submissives like to be spanked or flogged. It releases pent-up anxiety."

She couldn't grasp that idea, either.

Zane blew a breath against her neck. "Trust me. Just watch."

Abby did, barely blinking while the Dom performed some sort of organized ritual, swatting his submissive's upper back, ass, and thighs until pink lines were left in a crisscross pattern all over her. Abby relaxed marginally as the scene played out. It seemed as though she were in another dimension. The woman's moan increased as she took more and more of the flogging. She squirmed on the cross, bucking forward and backward as she endured every swish of the leather.

Suddenly the Dom dropped the flogger and stepped up to the woman. He flattened his body against hers, slowly stroked his hand down the welts across her back and ass, and then reached between her legs and fucked her hard and fast with his fingers.

Abby almost came the second the Dom shocked her with that move. She hadn't seen it coming, but her pussy flooded instantly with the most intense need.

The submissive moaned and ground her pussy against the man's fingers. And then she screamed her orgasm for everyone around to hear.

At the same moment, Zane swiped his thumbs across Abby's nipples and then pinched them fast and hard on the next breath.

Abby lost it. She came right there in the hall, her eyes glued to the submissive on the cross, her body held by Zane, who cupped her breasts now and kept her from collapsing.

It was quick and not nearly fulfilling enough, but Abby was still stunned by her body. And then it got worse.

"Baby, did you just come?"

She stiffened, squirming in his grasp, mortified once again and wishing she could slip through a fissure in the universe and disappear.

Zane didn't release her. Instead, he held her aloft with one hand under her breasts again and the other flattened on her belly. "Shit. You *are* going to kill me, aren't you?"

She said nothing.

Zane set his lips on her ear and whispered again. "Single sexiest thing ever, baby. Hands down." He kissed behind her ear and continued, "Stop squirming. Stop fighting me. Relax."

She did as he told her, loosening her stance, but unable to keep from groaning. She was that embarrassed. Clearly Zane was not. But that didn't change her feelings.

"I intended to show you more of the club, but after that..." He kissed her neck again. "Let's get out of here, baby."

She nodded. That was probably best. She was hot and shaky, and her legs weren't going to support her frame much longer. Even though Zane did the majority of the work, she felt unsteady. And on top of everything else, she'd just had a small orgasm in a public place. And Zane *knew* it. *Gah.*

CHAPTER 9

Zane didn't say much on the drive back to Abby's house. He was speechless. He didn't even say good-bye to his friends, who undoubtedly got the wrong idea and assumed they'd snuck out because Abby couldn't stomach the scene.

That was so far from the truth, and Zane gripped the steering wheel, completely unable to fathom what he was supposed to do with this new information.

Abby Burns was as submissive as they came. She didn't know it. Or hadn't. Hell, he hadn't suspected it, either. But seeing her in Extreme, seeing her reactions to everything around them, including him… His cock was so stiff it threatened to explode in his jeans.

Abby sat next to him on the ride home with her hands folded in her lap. Her knees shook.

Fuck me. The woman had an orgasm in his arms without him so much as touching her pussy.

Zane's knuckles hurt from his grip on the steering wheel by the time they arrived at her house. He rounded the last corner, jumped from the truck, and nearly jogged to Abby's side. Seconds later he had her in his arms, lifting her to the ground and then leading her to the house.

He still hadn't spoken, and he was probably freaking her out, but until he had her inside and had her undivided attention, he couldn't begin to communicate what he was thinking and feeling.

He took her keys from her hand when she pulled them from her purse, and he unlocked her door. Without asking if she minded, he pushed the door open, tugged her inside, shoved the door closed, and then turned toward her.

Abby's eyes were huge. "Zane…"

He stepped into her space, pressing her into the door. He lifted both her arms, clasped her hands above her head with one of his, and then lowered his lips to reenact the two kisses he'd already taken from her.

She didn't disappoint, either. Abby moaned into his mouth, her body squirming against the door as she licked the seam of his lips with her sweet tongue.

Zane's cock throbbed. He pressed into her, spreading her legs with one of his and jamming his knee between them. He needed her to stop wiggling before she made him come in his pants. He grabbed her waist with his free hand and spread his palm so he could touch as much of her as possible. It wasn't enough. Her blouse was thin, but he needed more contact.

Without pausing, he tugged her shirt out of her skirt and wormed his hand under it to flatten again on her bare belly.

Abby moaned louder. She was noisy. She bucked her chest toward him.

Zane smiled inside. His dream woman, and she hadn't even known she was submissive.

He was the luckiest man alive.

And he needed to pull himself together and step back

before he pushed her too far. He knew better. She was aroused and couldn't make good decisions, ones she might regret tomorrow if he didn't back away.

It took everything he had in him, but he released her and took a giant step back.

Abby slumped against the door, teetering. Her blue eyes were glazed over and wide. Her mouth was swollen and wet and open. She lowered her hands and set them flat on the door at her sides, as though that might keep her from falling. "Zane?" Her chest heaved as she took a deep breath.

"Baby." He ran a hand through his hair and let his gaze roam around the room, stepping back farther.

"Why did you stop?" she whispered.

Zane met her gaze again, only slightly less cloudy. He lowered his face to her chest. He could see her nipples, erect beneath her shirt that had somehow pulled tight across her chest. Her lace bra did nothing to hide them. And then he jerked his gaze back to hers. "Sorry. I didn't mean to get so carried away. You—you—" He was tongue-tied for the first time in his life.

"I what?" She looked confused, her brow furrowing while she fought to catch her breath. Her cheeks were pink. He needed to say something to erase that look of embarrassment.

He took a long stride back to her space and grabbed both her hands. "You're amazing. And I'm not going to fuck this up by screwing you against this door just because I can't control my cock around you."

She smiled. "We could move to the bedroom."

He shook his head. "Lord, woman. No, we cannot move to the bedroom. I like you a lot. Like a lot a lot. I don't take advantage of women I'm that into on the first date."

"But—"

He released one of her hands and set his finger on her

lips, shaking his head. "I know. I got you super aroused and then backed off. I get that. I get that you had an orgasm at the club watching the scene. I know it wasn't enough, and you're aching for more. But that doesn't give me the right to fuck you on the first date."

She spread her lips farther as if to say something else, but he cut her off, kissing her quickly and backing away. He pulled her into the room and dropped her hand. And then he reached for the door, his back to her. "Abby, I'm gonna say something I've never said to a woman before."

"What?"

"When I leave, I want you to finish yourself off."

"What?" Her voice squeaked that time.

He heaved in a breath, his shoulders rising and falling as he gripped the doorknob. "I'm sure you have a vibrator around here somewhere. Use it. But I'm gonna tell you something else." He paused, collected his thoughts. "This is the last time you will ever masturbate alone. My cock is going to protest the entire drive home knowing what you're doing. I don't like my women to touch themselves in my absence. But just this once, I'm going to let that rule slide because I know you need the release, and I also know you need time to think about what we're doing together before you see me again."

It took herculean effort, but Zane opened the door and walked out of the house. His hands shook as he jogged to his truck. How he would ever survive this night he had no idea.

∾

Abby stared at the door for a long time, heaving for oxygen after the intense play against the wood. The snick of the front door shutting reverberated through her head as if it had been much louder than it actually was. She heard his truck start and pull away. And then she shivered in the silence of her dark living room.

He left?

His words flooded back to her. *This is the last time you will ever masturbate alone...*

Shit.

He wasn't kidding, though. She needed to get her hands on her vibrator and finish herself off before she had an aneurysm. She turned on her heel and headed down the hall, her legs shaking. She should have taken her heels off before she moved, but she made it to the bedroom and leaned down to remove the straps.

My cock is going to protest the entire drive home knowing what you're doing.

When her bare feet were finally flat on the ground, she reached for the zipper on the back of her skirt and lowered it until the material fell to the floor. She didn't bother to pick it up. She simply stepped out and went after the buttons on her blouse.

Her fingers wouldn't cooperate. It took several attempts to get every button through its hole. When she finally shrugged out of the silky material, she popped the clasp on her bra and dropped it too.

With one hand, she tugged her panties down, while the other shot out to reach into her bedside table.

I don't like my women to touch themselves in my absence.

She couldn't shake his words from her mind.

She grabbed her favorite vibrator, shoved the comforter aside, and climbed onto the bed.

Her hand shook so badly she fought with the dial for several seconds before she had the vibrator turned on. And then she leaned back, spread her legs, and moaned loudly at the first contact.

Abby wasn't the kind of woman who had multiple orgasms. Hell, she wasn't the kind of woman who had *one* very often. But she'd never been as aroused as she currently was and had been for the last few hours.

And Zane was to blame. God almighty that man was intense. Hot. Sexy. And fucking incredible. She was ruined. She pushed the vibrator deep inside her, but then pulled it out and circled her pussy with the gathered wetness. The second she let the tip land at the base of her clit, she dug her heels into the mattress and lifted her torso off the bed.

Her other hand flew to her core of its own accord. She plunged two fingers into her channel while she let the vibrator do its job. It didn't take long. Less than a minute and she was at the peak and over the top, her clit pulsing against the rubber, a low hum filling the room. She was too far gone to scream.

And for the first time in her life, Abby left the vibrator there, kept up the pressure through the sensitivity. She needed more. Hell, she wanted more. It was never going to be enough. But it was better than nothing.

She circled her clit several times and then spread her legs farther as she rode to the top again. She scissored her fingers inside her, stroking across her G-spot.

Just this once, I'm going to let that rule slide because I know you need the release.

This time her orgasm was longer, deeper, more intense. She gasped as it took her out of this world, squeezing her eyes shut and letting her mouth hang open and her head tip back. When the pulsing finally subsided, she dropped the vibrator. It fell between her legs, making her flinch. It hummed loudly against the bed, but it took several minutes before she could recover it and turn it off.

It took several more minutes for her to gather the strength to set it aside. There was no way she would have the energy to brush her teeth. Instead, she grabbed the blankets, fumbling shakily, and curled up on her side. She fought to slow her breathing.

What the hell happened tonight? She couldn't wrap her mind around anything.

I also know you need time to think about what we're doing together before you see me again.

Tomorrow. Tomorrow she would sort out her craziness.

She closed her eyes and fell asleep before she could ponder things further.

CHAPTER 10

The sun filled her entire room when Abby finally lifted one eyelid enough to peek at her surroundings. She let her eye drift closed again as she slowly rolled onto her back. And then she relaxed into the mattress.

She was naked. She never slept naked. The second she realized it, the sheets suddenly seemed to abrade against her skin. She lay very still and thought about last night.

Holy shit.

Intense.

That's how she would describe the evening. She'd learned so much about Zane, and then she'd taken a step into his world. And his world had rocked hers to the core.

Holy shit.

Now what was she going to do? The man had her in knots last night. She'd freakin' come undone in his arms while watching some lady get flogged.

Holy shit.

Coffee. She needed coffee. And then she might be able to think.

She needed to get some writing done today. Everything

had been so confusing and hectic that she hadn't opened her manuscript the entire week. For at least a few hours, she vowed to put thoughts of Zane's sexy body completely out of her mind and focus.

She pulled herself from the bed, tugged a tank top over her head, grabbed a pair of clean panties, and then stepped into loose shorts. Needing caffeine, she made her way to the kitchen and started the coffee. While she stared at it, waiting for it to finish flowing, a knock sounded at the door.

Abby flinched. *What the…*

She glanced at the clock. It was already eleven. She was shocked. She padded toward the front door, spotted Emily, and opened the door. "Hey."

Emily grinned at her. "Can I come in?"

"Of course." Abby opened the door wider and stepped back.

"Did you just get up?"

Abby glanced down. She was a mess. "Uh, yeah. Not sure how I managed to sleep this late, but I did. You want coffee?" she asked as she shut the door and padded back to the kitchen. "I was just making a pot."

"Sounds good." Emily followed her and took a seat at the island on a stool. "How'd it go last night?"

Abby grabbed the pot and filled two mugs. She carried them both to the island and took a seat next to Emily. "Which part?" she asked as she dragged the cream and sugar toward them.

"Uh, start wherever you want?" Emily giggled. "Judging by your face, I'd say it went well. You look…"

"Well-fucked?"

Emily went white, her mouth hanging open before she started giggling again. "Okay. Sure. That."

Abby chuckled too. "Well, I'm not."

"What?" Emily glanced at Abby's hair and then back at her face.

Abby released her grip on her mug and reached up to tuck her hair behind her ears. "You would think, but not so much."

"What happened?"

"We had dinner, which was great. We got to know each other better, also great. And then you saw us at the club."

"And then you two disappeared, and we never saw you again."

Abby glanced down at her coffee and then lifted it and took a sip, moaning around the warmth. "Zane is, um—"

"Yeah, I know Zane. I warned you."

"You did. I think I might have fallen under his spell."

Emily clapped her hands together. "For real? Awesome."

Abby shivered. "I don't know about that. He yanked me home and immediately left me here." *Not even going to go there and tell her all the nitty-gritty details.*

"Oh my God. I was afraid something went awry since you left so early."

"You couldn't be more wrong." Abby smiled.

"What did he say?"

"That I needed to think about things."

"Uh huh. And? Have you?"

"Not yet. But there isn't much to think about." Abby lifted her gaze. "The guy is smokin' hot, his body is to die for, he rescues damsels and takes them home, *and* he can command a woman to heel with his voice alone. What's to consider?"

"So, you want to come with me and see him fight tonight?"

"Absolutely." Abby smiled. She wasn't kidding. There was nothing to think about. Whatever happened last night, she could only pray it happened again. The way the man made her insides turn to mush was not something she could say no to.

When she smiled, the stitches pulled on her forehead. They were starting to itch. She reached up and pressed on the spot. "Nothing like starting a new relationship with bruises and scabs and scars all over your face. And that doesn't begin to factor in my poor ass. It's still blue."

Emily laughed. "I don't think Zane cares. He sees far beyond skin deep, girl."

"Apparently. In any case, my doctor said he would take out the staples and stiches this afternoon. I'm so glad. They itch."

"Awesome. You'll feel so much better." Emily hopped off the stool. "Thanks for the coffee. I'll pick you up at six?"

"I'll just walk over to your place. Sounds good. And, Emily? Thanks. You've been so nice."

Emily shrugged. "Any time." She let herself out, leaving Abby to stare at nothing and think about everything.

Zane had many sides. She was about to add one more tonight. Fighting. Why did that make her skin tingle?

～

Abby followed Emily into the gym that evening, shocked by the number of people inside and the volume. A man greeted them at the door, but only because he happened to be walking by. "Emily." He took her hand in both of his. "Good to see you." He turned to Abby next. "You must be Abby."

Abby's eyes widened. How did he know her name?

"I'm Joe. I own the gym." He smiled broadly. "I've heard a little about you." He shook her hand.

"Oh."

He shrugged. "The guys talk when they work out. Well,

more precisely they harass each other. Whoever has the freshest relationship takes the brunt of the ribbing. This week it's Zane." He laughed a deep belly laugh as he walked away.

Emily took Abby's hand. "Come on. Let's wiggle through this crowd so we can see better. Kayla should be here somewhere."

"What about the others?"

"Katy and Jenna aren't super fond of the action. They aren't coming tonight." Emily pushed between people until she reached one corner of the ring.

Abby lifted her gaze to watch the ensuing fight. "God. They look like they're going to kill each other."

Emily smiled. "They won't. Most of them are friends. Even the ones they compete against. It's amateur. It's all good."

"Geez." She jerked as one of the men slammed the other against the fence a few feet in front of Abby. "Holy shit."

"Yeah. It happens. Don't worry. It's sturdy." She lifted up on tiptoes. "Hey, there's Kayla." She waved, and the gorgeous woman with long blonde curls headed their way.

"Hey," Kayla said as she arrived at their side. She leaned toward Abby. "I know we haven't had a chance to talk much every time we've met, but I'm so glad to see Zane with someone special."

"Thanks." Abby bit her lip. It warmed her to be so easily included with the other women.

"You got the stitches out," Kayla said as she took in Abby's face.

Abby stroked the spot on her forehead. "Yeah. I feel so much better. The stitches weren't so bad, but the staples on my scalp itched horribly."

"I bet." Kayla scrunched up her nose. "They did a good job. Already the red is fading."

"Thanks. So, what am I up against here?" Abby asked, glancing around Kayla.

"Gage is up next. And then I think Rider."

"Good. I was afraid we might be a little late," Emily said.

"Nope."

Abby kept her eyes glued to the ring. The two men inside were unbelievably buff and far more attractive than she would have expected for fighters. The African-American man with smooth chocolate skin swept out his leg and knocked the other guy to the floor. He was on him in an instant, straddling his torso and pinning his chest to the ground. It reminded her of wrestling.

"Shit."

"Yeah. Don't worry. Either the guy will tap out or the ref will call it. Either way, the winner is clear."

Seconds later, it was over. The referee announced the winner, and the sexy African-American man held up a hand. The two of them left the ring.

Instantly two other men entered with mops to clean off the floor for the next match.

Emily leaned in toward Abby's ear. "So, the area inside the fence is called the cage."

"Ah. Cage. Got it."

"It's always an octagon. They have three five-minute rounds with one-minute breaks. It might look like a free-for-all, but trust me, there are many rules."

Abby nodded.

"Here comes Gage," Kayla said. She lifted up on tiptoes and screamed for her man. "You got him, Gage."

Abby's heart beat faster. It was invigorating. She hadn't expected this sort of reaction. She'd never watched the sport in her life, but now that she was here, swept up in the excitement, she was intrigued.

The announcer spoke loudly, his voice filling the room.

"...and in the blue corner, we have Gage 'The Ranger' Holland..."

Before she knew it, the fight was on. A bell sounded, and both men danced around each other in the center. It didn't take long for punches to fly. Abby flinched at first, but then she got used to it. Each jab and hook forced one man back while the other advanced. For several minutes it looked like a boxing match, but then Gage threw out a high leg kick, knocking the other guy in the head. The man staggered back. Gage continued to advance. The referee said nothing. And the match ceased to seem like boxing.

When the bell sounded, Kayla screamed and jumped on her feet.

Emily told Abby the guy in the corner pouring water in Gage's mouth was Byron, their cornerman. The one-minute break was fast, and then both men were back on their feet.

Kayla moaned when Gage took a hard hit. She covered her face with her hands, peering through her fingers, still watching the action. And then Gage swept his foot out again, taking the other man to the ground this time. His opponent fell onto his knees, but jumped back up.

"Ugh," Kayla said. "Come on, Gage," she yelled. "You got this, baby." She cupped her hands around her mouth to make her voice carry.

Abby was mesmerized as she watched the rest of the match, which Gage won, and then the next one, which Rider did not win.

Emily was bummed, but she scrunched up her nose and shook it off. "Eh, it's rare, but you have to lose sometimes."

And then Zane was up. She knew they called him "The Animal." She was about to find out why.

When he entered the cage, he was already on his game.

His face was fierce. He didn't look her direction. Hell, he didn't look any direction except at his opponent.

The guy he fought visibly cringed as he stepped to the center.

Abby bit her lip. They weren't kidding. He did look like an animal. The tattoo on his left arm was a giant claw. The word *one* was inked under his bicep. And across one pec was the tattoo of a set of claw marks as though he'd been attacked.

Lord this man had many sides. She watched as he came at his opponent fast and hard right after the bell rang. She thought he even growled.

He wasted no time. He threw a left hook and followed it immediately with a right jab, backing his opponent toward the fence.

Abby held her breath, reaching up on tiptoes as the other ladies had when their man was in the cage. She could see somewhat better, but there were still a few heads in front of her blocking her view.

Zane swung around quickly and kicked the other man in his butt. The guy lurched forward but managed to stay on his feet. When Zane grabbed the man around the neck and held him in a chokehold, Abby cringed. It was scary, but it was invigorating at the same time. That guy was the same man who had laughed over dinner with Abby and then managed to command her every cell in a sexual tug-of-war after. This new side, the fighter in him, was awesome.

The two men struggled for several seconds, both trying to get the upper hand, but Zane didn't release the guy's neck. He tugged hard, bringing the man to the ground. And then he grappled to get the guy on his back. When the bell sounded, Abby was shocked it had been five minutes already.

Zane did not look pleased, probably because he'd been so close to winning. At least she assumed he would win if he pinned the guy to the ground. He stalked toward his corner and tipped his head back while Byron wiped his face and gave him water. And then the minute was over and Zane jumped back onto his feet as though not an ounce of exhaustion had driven him to sit down.

The fight commenced again. The other guy still heaved for air, his chest and shoulders rising and falling rapidly. Zane didn't appear nearly as winded. He blocked several jabs, advancing on his opponent until he had the guy pressed into the fence. When the guy swung at Zane, Zane ducked. Instead, he plowed headfirst into the man's torso and lifted him completely off the ground, pinning him to the fence on a loud growl.

Abby covered her mouth with both hands, trying to keep from calling out. She didn't know Zane well enough to scream for him or encourage him. She didn't know if he liked that sort of thing or preferred to be left alone in the cage.

Zane grabbed the man with both arms and flung him to the ground like he wasn't even in the same weight class. And then Zane was on top, grappling as he had been when the bell sounded to end the first round. Zane threw himself into the fight, leaning forward and pinning the man's arms with both of his knees. A long standoff ensued while the referee danced around the two of them. They were frozen in place like a sculpture. A glorious stone carving.

And then the referee blew a whistle and it was over. Both men got to their feet, Zane lifting one arm in victory. He spun around in a quick circle, waving at the crowd, but he still didn't make eye contact with Abby.

Abby felt like she'd been the one fighting, as hard as her heart pounded and as fast as she was breathing. Plus she was exhausted. If she was going to keep up with Zane "The Animal," she was going to have to work out more often.

Emily grinned as she took Abby's arm and tugged. She nodded behind her. "Let's get out of the center. We can wait in Joe's office. It's quieter there."

Abby followed Emily and Kayla through the crowd and into a small office in the back. Emily wasn't kidding. Abby hadn't realized how loud it was out there until they shut the door and sat. "That was exhausting."

Kayla laughed. "Yeah, I always feel that way. I'm not sure who works harder, Gage in the cage, or me stressing next to it." Kayla leaned forward. "So, what'd you think of Extreme last night?"

"It was interesting." Abby clenched both knees with her hands.

Emily chuckled. "It was more than interesting. This girl had just-fucked hair this morning, and she didn't even get any."

Kayla's eyes went wide. "What? From Zane?"

Abby shrugged. "He was trying to be a gentleman."

Kayla's eyes widened farther. "That's so fucking hot. And you let him?"

"He didn't give me much of a choice. But I hope he caves tonight, because I don't think I want to spend another night wound up as tight as I did last night after he left me high and dry."

"Shit. How romantic." Kayla leaned back. Her long hair hung in ringlets behind her. She lifted her head back to center after a second. "Was that your first time at a fetish club?"

"Yeah."

"Did you like it?"

"A little too much." Abby bit her lip to stifle a giggle. "I had no idea."

"Yeah, neither did we initially. It's hot, though. Can't deny that." Emily turned to face the door as it opened.

Abby twisted her torso also.

Rider stepped inside, closing the door behind him. He leaned over Emily and kissed her soundly. "Hey, baby."

"Sorry about the match," Emily said.

Rider shrugged. "I'll get over it." Rider tugged Emily out of her seat, plopped himself down in her vacated spot, and pulled her onto his lap. He lifted his gaze to Abby. "Did you like the fight?"

"Yes. Surprisingly."

Rider gave Emily a squeeze. "There you go, baby. Another woman who likes to watch us fight. Your numbers are increasing." He wove his hand into the back of her hair and angled her head so she faced him. And then he kissed her again.

Abby squirmed. The man oozed testosterone. Zane did too, but seeing another of The Fight Club with his girlfriend made her clench her legs together. She wanted that. She wanted it bad.

A few minutes later, Gage entered the room. He swept Kayla off her chair and buried his nose in her neck, her feet completely off the ground. "Mmm." He turned toward Rider, letting Kayla slide down his body. "Sorry, man. Guess I was the better guy tonight." He smirked.

Rider swung out a hand, but Gage jumped back, taking Kayla with him.

They were all smiling, which made Abby warm to witness their close friendships.

When the door opened the next time, Zane stepped in, closing it behind him.

Abby tipped her head back and grinned.

Zane leaned over the back of her chair and kissed her lips upside down. "What'd you think?" He set his hands on her shoulders and then ran them down her arms until he tangled his fingers with hers.

She wanted to close her eyes and breathe in his clean scent. His hair was damp and spiked. His chest was rock solid against the back of her head. The bulging muscles of his arms wrapped around her made her forget to speak.

Finally she let a slow grin spread across her face and recovered her senses. "Awesome. Loved it. The testosterone in the room was palpable. How do you keep the women from fawning all over you?"

He chuckled. "I race from the room as soon as it's over." She loved the sound of his teasing. His skin was warm, and the way he enveloped her blocked out the room for a moment as she held his upside down gaze.

Someone cleared their throat, and both women giggled.

"Let's get out of here." Zane winked.

CHAPTER 11

Zane pulled in front of Abby's house and turned to face her as he shut off the engine. "Did you really enjoy it?"

"I did. You're fierce. The girls weren't kidding."

"Yeah, I'm kinda competitive in the cage."

"I see that."

He took her hand and turned it over, staring at her palm while he stroked it with his thumb. Every single touch ignited a fire inside her. "You want me to come in?"

"Of course."

He lifted his face to hers. "Here's the thing, Abby." He set his head against the headrest as he continued while her breath caught in her lungs. "I want you."

She smiled. "You say that like it's a bad thing."

He looked at her seriously. "Depends on how you look at it. Last night…" His voice trailed off, and his eyes shifted to look out the windshield.

She waited, her fingers still in his hand, the rest of her stiff.

"I haven't had an actual girlfriend for a long time. High school. And that's because as soon as I started fighting with these guys and joined Extreme, I knew I couldn't do vanilla again." He turned to face her. "It's hard to explain, but once I had a taste of D/s, I was hooked. I've been a practicing Dom for several years. Until you came along."

"You aren't that old."

He smiled. "Twenty-four. I was already with The Fight Club when I turned twenty-one and they took me to Extreme for my birthday. It was my first experience. I've never looked back."

"And you don't think I can be what you need."

"No. I didn't say that." He hesitated. "Hell, I'm actually thinking you can be more than I ever dreamed. You might not quite realize it yet, but you have a splendid submissive demeanor. I was speechless last night inside the club." He leaned closer, releasing her hand to cup her cheek and draw her toward him. "Best night of my life, baby."

She shivered.

"But I don't want to push you."

"You said that last night. I don't feel pushed, Zane."

"And I like you enough to do vanilla, or at least try it. But I don't want to hurt you, either."

Ah, so that's what this is about. "How about you let me worry about me. I'm a big girl. I can make my own choices in men."

He closed the gap and gave her a quick kiss. "How about you let *me* worry about *you*. If I go into your house with you right now, I'm going to have sex with you."

"Thank God."

"I'm serious, Abby. This is a big deal to me. After I sleep with you, I'm going to want to do it again. And then," he paused, waiting for her to pay close attention. "Again."

Her pussy grew wet. Her jeans felt too tight rubbing against her crotch. She wished she hadn't chosen the particular lacy thong she wore as it currently made her far too aware of her clit. She squirmed.

Zane glanced at her lap and smiled. "I'm demanding in the bedroom."

Her heart beat faster. Her nipples rubbed against the equally annoying lacy bra. She swallowed. He was not intimidating her. He was making her hot. "Zane."

"Yeah, baby."

"Let's go inside."

"Okay." He let her go and opened the door to the truck. She twisted to her side, grabbed her purse, and was opening her door when he met her. He wrapped his hands around her waist and lifted her to the ground. Before he shut the door, he flattened her to the side of the truck and cupped her face. "The doctor did a good job. The scars are healing nicely."

She nodded, not the least bit interested in her stitches right then. His eyes bore into her, the blue deep and penetrating. And then he took her hand, shut the truck door, and led her to the house.

Like last night, when she pulled her keys from her purse, he grabbed them and unlocked her door.

Like last night, he shut the door and turned to press her against the wood, taking her mouth in a kiss as though he couldn't possibly wait another moment.

Like last night, she was glad. Now, if she could just get him to stay…

Zane didn't break the kiss, but he cupped her face again and tipped his head to one side.

Abby moaned against his mouth, her tongue stroking his, tasting him and loving his personal flavor. By the time he pulled back, she shook with need. Her jeans pressed too tight against her pussy. Her cotton shirt was too tight against her chest. She wanted her clothes gone, and more importantly his.

She cleared her throat. "Do you think we could maybe make it farther into the house this time?"

"Mm, baby, we can try." He didn't bother flipping on any lights. But he shocked her when he bent down and lifted her into his arms.

She gave a brief squeal as he headed down the hall, directly to her bedroom. He was familiar with the place. He'd been inside and helped her get settled when he'd brought her home after the car accident. But the man had an unbelievable memory because he didn't lose her gaze as he made his way through the house and directly into her room.

In fact, he didn't break eye contact as he approached her bed and then set her on her feet next to it. He was still staring as he tugged her shirt up and flung it behind him. Finally, he lowered his gaze to her chest. He gripped her waist with both hands and then stroked them up to cup her breasts, barely encased in the lace bra.

"God, you're sexy." He flicked his thumbs over her nipples and then dipped both index fingers under the top edge of pink lace to tease them some more.

Abby hitched her chest forward into his hands, her head falling back.

"Baby, look at me." His voice was deep, commanding. She'd heard it before. Last night. It seemed to be reserved for dominance and the bedroom. Or perhaps those two things weren't mutually exclusive.

She lowered her face to his.

"You okay?"

She nodded. "Please... Zane..." Her voice was weak, barely a whisper.

Zane reached behind her and popped her bra clasp.

Immediately she shivered as the lace fell away and he tossed it toward her shirt.

"Watch me, Abby."

She wasn't sure what he meant until he dipped his head again and fondled her breasts. She let her gaze follow his and was mesmerized by the way he cupped her and then squeezed. She went up on tiptoes when he grasped her nipples between his thumbs and pointers and pinched, just hard enough to shock her. Watching him learn her was heady. Her nipples stood at stiff points before he was done. Pink splotches spread across her chest.

"So responsive, baby. Are you wet for me?"

"Yes." The word came out on a breath.

Zane released her breasts to lower his hands to her jeans. With ease, he popped the button and lowered the zipper. And then he tugged the denim over her hips. He kneeled to pull off her sandals and then grasp the bottom of her jeans. Seconds later, he rose back to his full height, his fingers grazing up her body from her shins to her chest. "Your skin is flawless."

"With the exception of multiple new scars." She tried to smile, but he ignored her and continued to stare at her body until goose bumps rose across her skin.

He made lazy circles around her nipples, avoiding the tips. She would come without him touching her again if he kept up this languid pace.

Abby reached for his shirt, wanting to see his chest and even the playing field. She also wanted to explore his tattoos close up. What she'd seen in the cage had made her crave a closer inspection.

"Hands at your sides, baby."

Abby paused a second, her hands on his T-shirt. She took a breath.

"Hands at your sides, Abby," he repeated.

New moisture flooded her pussy. She released his shirt on a whimper.

"That's a girl. Let me direct, baby. I promise you'll like the results."

She already liked the results. And she wanted him to speed up the process.

Zane took a step back, releasing her to pull his shirt over his chest and drop it on the floor.

Lord, his pecs were huge. Firm. Not an ounce of fat on this guy. The intricate designs inked on his body suited him perfectly. She lifted her fingers to explore his chest when he shook his head. "Hands, Abby."

She dropped them to her sides, but shifted her weight, fidgeting at the command. Her desire to stroke his skin increased. Why didn't he want her to touch him?

"Good girl." He reached for the sides of her thong and lowered the scrap of material to the floor.

She lifted her feet one at a time to step out. One second later, she was on her back on the bed, and Zane had a hold of her thighs.

He spread them wide with his huge palms, his gaze landing on her pussy. He stared for so long, she squirmed. It was so fucking sexy the way he looked at her, but unnerving at the same time. "Stay still," he admonished.

She didn't think she could, but she tried. She'd groomed this morning in anticipation of sleeping with him, but had she done a good enough job? She felt like he was judging her work. Would he find the small strip of hair she kept trimmed sexy? Or maybe he didn't like a shaved woman.

Zane hesitated. "I just tossed you on your ass. Did I hurt you?" He winced.

She shook her head, wiggling her butt against the bed. "No. The wound is almost healed. I barely notice it."

"Good." Zane lifted his gaze to hers. He closed his eyes

for a second and exhaled. "I want to remember this moment. The first time I laid eyes on you." And then he met her gaze again. "You're the sexiest woman I've ever seen." While he spoke, he moved his hands closer to her center, still holding her open, but inching to her core. Without looking down, he stroked one finger through her lower lips. "So smooth." And then his head dipped back down and he explored her further, gradually drawing out her moisture to circle her pussy, her lower lips, and finally her clit.

Abby bit the inside of her cheek to keep from screaming. She shot so close to an orgasm in such quick order her mind was spinning. When his finger danced over her clit, she bucked upward.

Zane removed his touch. He released her legs and stepped back.

She lifted her head to look at him.

Zane unbuttoned his jeans and tugged them and his underwear off his body. His fucking fine body. His cock bobbed in front of him. Thick and long and delicious.

Abby licked her dry lips, hoping she would get a chance to taste him before the night was over. He'd said again, and again, and again. She prayed he wasn't exaggerating. It would take that many agains to get him out of her system this first night.

Before Zane dropped his jeans, he reached in the back pocket and pulled out a condom. He set it on the bed next to her. How many did he have on him? Hopefully more than the one, because protection wasn't something she kept lying around the house. She hadn't been with a man for a while and certainly not since she'd moved.

"There's more," he stated as though he read her mind. "And there's always a box in the truck."

She flushed.

"Now," he said, "I'm going to give you a choice. Don't get used to it because it won't happen often. But I want to make this first time exactly how you envision it." He stroked his hand up his cock from the base to the tip and then back down.

Abby watched him, scooting back on the bed, hoping if she made room for him...

"I'll learn quickly what you like, what gets you off, baby. But while I'm gathering that information, I need a little help."

She lifted her face to him. What was he talking about? She took deep breaths, her eyes glazing over.

Zane's face changed from serious to smiling. "Baby, you don't give a fuck how I take you as long as I do, do you?"

She shook her head. "Please, Zane."

"Scoot back farther, baby." He came toward her, climbing onto the bed as she squirmed to back up. Her legs came together in the effort, and she waited, anticipating his frame coming over her. Fast or slow, hard or gentle, she didn't care. She just wanted him over her.

But Zane had other ideas. He never made it that far. He stopped before he hovered over the top of her. Instead, he grasped her thighs again, spread them wide, and before she realized his intentions, he lowered his mouth to her pussy and stroked his tongue through her folds.

Abby screamed. Her legs struggled against him involuntarily, but he held her steady.

And then he did it again. Without the initial shock, his stroke wasn't as intense, but her vision clouded. She reached forward to grab his head, weaving her fingers into his hair. She couldn't take more. She would come any second, and she really wanted him to be inside her when she came.

Zane was relentless, though. He didn't climb up her

body as she willed him. He sucked her clit into his mouth and then pinched it gently between his teeth.

"Zane," she yelled, her hands either pushing or pulling on his scalp. She didn't know which.

He didn't acknowledge her, neither her word nor her grip. Instead he sucked again and then released her clit and dipped his tongue inside her.

Abby dug her heels into the mattress and lifted her torso, or tried to. His grip was firm.

She was so close. Just as she was about to fall over the edge, he stopped. He tilted his face up. "Put your hands over your head, baby."

She didn't register his request at first. And then she caught on and released his head. Her hands lifted, but she held them in front of her for a moment, unable to give them the proper command.

"Set them over your head, baby." He waited. His voice was patient.

She dropped them beside her ears. It felt strange, not participating in this game. But it was also sexy as hell. Her thighs quivered where his fingers gripped them.

"What do you need, Abby?"

She swallowed. *Huh?*

"Abby, tell me what you need, baby."

"To come. Please."

"I want to swallow the first one. Okay?"

Now he asks? She nodded.

He ducked his head again and went at her like a starving man, sucking and licking every inch of her skin. When he tugged her clit back between his lips and set his teeth on the little bundle of nerves, she shattered. Her pussy and clit spasmed, the pulsing continuing for longer than she'd ever experienced, even last night alone in this bed with her vibrator.

Zane didn't let up just because she came. He gentled his strokes, but kept his tongue engaged with her pussy.

Finally, she winced and he released her. "Gorgeous."

She stared at him. Stunned. Generally, in her experience, men didn't enjoy going down on women with quite the level of obvious desire Zane exuded.

He climbed up her body, his mouth trailing kisses up her belly until he sucked a nipple between his lips. He lapped at the distended tip over and over, and then he switched to the other one. By the time he was done torturing her nipples, she was fully aroused again.

He crawled up the rest of the way until he faced her, and then he lowered his lips to hers and kissed her. She tasted herself on his lips, but she didn't care. It was intoxicating the way he worked her over.

When he broke the kiss, he muttered against her lips, "You good, baby?"

"Better than."

He smiled, reached down to grab the condom, and then kneeled between her legs to rip it open with his teeth. In seconds, he had it out of the package and rolled onto his cock. When he slid back over her body, he smoothed his hands up her arms and held them higher above her head, his fingers entwined with hers. He set his forehead against hers. "Eyes on me, baby."

She met his gaze, finding it difficult to concentrate with his body pressing her into the bed and his cock lodged at her entrance. She wanted him inside her with renewed urgency.

Zane held her gaze while he pressed forward, languidly, as though he wanted to savor every second.

Abby wished he would thrust hard and fast, but he wasn't having it. And besides, the slow torture might have been even better. Her walls parted for him, every nerve ending alert to the sensation. And then he gave her the last few inches, plunging deep until he was fully seated.

A long moan escaped her lips, or maybe his. Probably both. She blinked. His gaze was still on hers, but his face was tense.

Zane pulled partway out and thrust back in hard. His hands gripped hers tighter. And he definitely groaned that time. "Abby… Jesus…" His head slid to the pillow beside her, his lips landing on her neck as he continued to pound into her, rougher now that the initial entry was over.

She loved it. He was all-consuming. The way he held her body against the bed made her lose control. Every time her clit hit the base of his cock, she rose higher. She lifted her knees to plant her feet alongside his hips, needing the traction, bracing herself for every thrust, arching her ass off the bed to get the best contact.

When she wrapped her legs around his torso, he lifted his face and smirked, shaking his head, but he didn't say a word. In fact, he tipped his head back and opened his mouth, "Come with me, baby."

Abby closed her eyes, concentrating on the sensation at her core. She was close.

"No, Abby. Come." His command made the hard ball in her belly burst. He plunged deep and held himself firmly against her clit. And she shattered for the second time, her channel gripping Zane's cock as he followed right behind her, his grunt filling the room, echoing off the walls as she pulsed around him.

Zane held steady as they both came down. She opened her eyes to meet his gaze, his brow furrowed, his look intense. He released her hands and caressed one down her arm to cup her face. He looked like he was about to say something. His lips parted, but then he closed them and let his face relax. A smile spread slowly, easing her tension.

She was dying to know what all was going on is his head, but decided to keep quiet and wait for him to speak.

Finally, Zane pulled out of her slowly, eased the condom off his cock, and wrapped it in a tissue. He flopped onto his back next to her, dragging her body so her chest pressed into his side. He even tugged her top knee until it rested between his legs.

Abby set her palm on his firm chest. Her cheek lay on his shoulder. She could see his tats, and she traced a finger around the outer edge of the large claw on his bicep.

Zane's breaths slowed gradually until he took a long deep inhale and blew it out. He squeezed her shoulders with his arm wrapped around her. "You're amazing."

She grinned against his chest. Those weren't difficult words to hear. "You're not bad yourself," she added against his pecs.

Suddenly Zane flipped her to her back again and leaned over her from his side. Every time he made eye contact, she found herself holding her breath. He was that intense. "Baby, I need to tell you something."

She hesitated. This couldn't be good. Nothing good ever came from "I need to tell you something." And she'd just had the best sex of her life. She bit her lip between her teeth and stared at him, fighting the panic welling inside her.

His face grew more serious as he let his gaze roam all over hers. "You're mine."

What? She released her lip, and her mouth fell open.

"You're mine," he repeated as his lips lowered to meet hers. He kissed her briefly and then muttered some more, "Mine, baby." He angled over her farther, his forearm landing on the other side of her head as he suffocated her with his presence.

She couldn't speak. She'd had two glorious orgasms,

and her pussy already jumped to attention. She should be ticked he spoke to her like that, claiming her. Demanding what he wanted. Instead, her body betrayed her, accepting and celebrating his announcement.

"I'm gonna get cleaned up, baby. Be right back." He lifted off her and padded to her adjoining bathroom.

She listened as the sink ran and he moved around in her space. She didn't move. She was both sated and once again needy, but there was no way she could lift a limb at that point.

She knew one thing for sure.

She wanted to be his. She wasn't entirely sure what he meant with his proclamation, but she wanted it.

CHAPTER 12

Zane stepped back into the room carrying a warm washcloth. He'd needed the moments alone to pull himself together, but now he needed Abby's body pressed against him even more. His two-minute absence hadn't changed that.

When he reached her side, she stared up at him, her face unreadable. She hadn't spoken, but that was okay. He hadn't expected her to react to his words. It was essentially their second date. Men didn't usually lay their cards out like that so soon. It was dangerous.

But Zane didn't play those games.

He knew what he wanted. And he wanted Abby. She needed to know his intentions up front. He would give her anything in the world. But after the last few days, he knew she was perfect just the way she was. If she had needed vanilla, he would have given it to her. But she fell somewhere in between. And Zane had the confidence they could dip their feet into both worlds and be beyond happy.

He spread her legs farther apart and cleaned her up. She reached for the cloth to do it herself, but he set her hand aside. "Let me, baby," he muttered. He could feel her gaze on the top of his head as he wiped her pussy. She winced when he brushed over her clit. Sensitive.

He set the cloth on the bedside table and climbed up beside her again, drawing the covers over them and pulling her shivering frame into his warmth. He kissed the top of her head as she relaxed and snuggled into his embrace, her front to his chest, her head resting on his arm.

He made lazy strokes across her back until she shuddered, a small giggle escaping her lips.

"Tickles," she whispered.

He smiled at the top of her head and held her tighter. Eventually her breaths slowed and he knew she was asleep. In his arms. In his life. He'd never been more content.

Abby Burns had rocked his world, and he intended to keep her.

With that thought, he closed his eyes and let sleep drag him under with her.

∼

He was having the best dream ever. He was warm and relaxed in bed, and the hottest dream woman was stroking her palms down his torso. When they met his turgid cock, he moaned but willed himself not to wake up yet. No man alive wanted to wake up from a wet dream like this one.

Suddenly, the scene changed and she was farther down his body, her dainty palm grasping his cock, her tongue licking through the slit on the head. The fucking best dream...

And then her mouth engulfed him, sucking him deep and sending every blood cell in his body to his dick. He fought against nature to remain asleep and not miss the ending, but he was losing. When the woman drew off and let his cock fall out of her mouth with a pop, he could feel himself surfacing. The second she sucked him back in, deeper and firmer than the first time, his eyes shot open.

For a split second he was aggravated. And then his attention shifted to his cock, and he found himself staring down at a mess of thick black wavy hair. He feared hallucination, and then he smiled. Abby. Jesus. That woman had burrowed into him and taken him unaware. He would get her back for this.

But first he would let her explore and enjoy the fucking hot morning blow job.

Her teeth gently grazed the thin skin of his cock as her head bobbed up and down. He was so close. How long had she been sucking him in his dream? He had no idea. But he was rock hard, and he hadn't even managed to send a message to his arms to reach for her.

When she moaned around his length, the vibrations enough to drive him out of his head, he went into action, lifting both arms and threading his fingers into her hair, careful not to tug the locks where she would be sore from the staples. He didn't stop her. He was too far gone to have that kind of willpower, but this little game of hers where she'd managed to top him wouldn't go unnoticed. He would let her finish, suck his cock dry, and then he would teach her a beautiful lesson about submission. One she would not soon forget.

Abby sucked.

Zane gripped her head.

Deeper.

Harder.

And then he came, shooting down her throat on a long deep moan, her body tensing from top to bottom. All he knew was his cock and how good her mouth felt wrapped around him.

He wasn't a man who usually lost control of a situation, but Abby pressed buttons in him he didn't know he had.

When he was completely spent, she lifted her face finally and set her chin on his torso, grinning at him like she'd won the lottery. "Morning."

Zane stared down at her, knowing a smile was also spreading across his face and unable to stop it. He was losing his Dom status quickly. Abby was tearing it to shreds. He needed to regroup and flip this woman onto her back. And he would, after he gave her another moment to relish her accomplishment.

As his blood returned to his limbs, he caught his breath. And then he pounced, jerking down to haul Abby up the bed and flipping her onto her back. He didn't give her a moment to think before he had her hands above her head and yanked the sheet up from the side to secure her to the spindles.

"Zane…" She whispered his name, but not in fear. Good. He didn't want to scare her. He just wanted to show her more of what being with him would mean, both to him and to her.

When he had her hands completely bound, he finally lowered his gaze.

She was shivering. Her nipples were hard pointed peaks. And he shifted down her frame immediately, spread her legs wide, and speared a finger into her tight warmth. Eureka. She was soaking wet. It could have been from the blow job. Some women were aroused by sucking on their partner. But he was confident her reaction had more to do with his dominance.

Abby squirmed, small sounds coming out of her mouth as she wiggled around his hand.

Zane gripped her thigh and held her steady while he continued to fuck her with that one finger.

Her belly dipped and her breathing became erratic.

Fuck me. She was close to coming. He didn't want her to come yet. That wasn't in the plan. He pulled his finger from the sheath and lifted it to circle her stiff nipple, spreading her wetness on the distended tip.

Abby bucked her chest. She tipped her head back, elongating her smooth neck and pressing her breast up into his finger. Her glorious body hummed.

Zane dipped his finger back into her pussy and drew out more of her moisture to lavish on her other nipple.

Abby panted. He knew she was responsive. Hell, he'd seen her come from watching a scene. A woman didn't get more responsive than that, but this squirming, gasping, gorgeous creature was a sight to behold.

Zane released her and stepped from the bed, leaving her staring at him with her eyes wide and her mouth open. He narrowed his gaze at her. "Don't move. Don't speak. And keep your legs spread wide." He left her there, padding from the room. He had no choice. For one thing, she was too easy. If she always came that easily, how would he ever control her?

For another thing, he was so fucking horny, he needed to get a grip on his own arousal before he continued. He'd just had a fantastic blow job and already his cock stood at attention.

Coffee. He padded naked to her kitchen and rummaged around in her cabinets until he located everything he needed and had the Keurig brewing. He wiped a hand down his face while he waited and commanded his cock to stand down.

Steaming mug in hand, he returned to the bedroom.

Abby lay exactly where he'd left her. Good. He wasn't sure how far she would test him at first. He suspected the next few weeks would be filled with him fighting for dominance and her testing the boundaries. What he knew for sure was she was submissive. She would cave. And she would enjoy every minute of it and look back to wonder why anyone would choose a different path.

Zane climbed between her legs, careful not to spill his cup. He spread her wider and met her gaze while he took a sip. Her lips were pursed, probably to keep from speaking. "Ah, baby. You're so submissive." He stroked her thigh. "You tried to top me." He lifted an eyebrow. "Hell, you did top me." He took another sip and then grinned. "It was fucking hot. And I loved it. And you can do that again anytime you want. But…" Another sip of his coffee while she waited.

She opened her mouth, but he set his finger over her lips. "Uh uh. Not a word. My show now. You had yours." He glanced down at her pussy. Still soaking wet, a trail of her arousal leaking between her legs toward her ass.

Her nipples stood erect. She thrived under his direction.

"Here's the deal. Payback. You can have your fun. I enjoy your fun. But now I'm going to have mine. My way." He reached across her to one side and set his mug on the bedside table. When he came back to center, he hovered over her, his face inches from hers. "You're so fucking sexy when you're aroused. And I don't know where you've been hiding, but you're a natural submissive, baby."

Her mouth opened again.

He halted her with a quick kiss. "No words. My show. My rules." He sat back. Just staring at her made her squirm. He wanted to explore her, taste her, touch every inch of her skin, but if he did so, she would come. And he wanted her to know what it felt like to stay on the edge. "If you speak a word, I'll make this take longer."

She closed her mouth.

"Good girl." He pinched both her nipples without warning, sharp and brief.

She yelped and then her eyes went wide, thinking she'd be in trouble for breaking the silence.

He smiled. "You can moan and scream all you want. But no talking."

She relaxed her body marginally against the bed.

Zane trailed a finger up the inside of her thigh and circled her lower lips. He added two other fingers and danced them across her pussy until he tapped the hood of her clit. "Love this little strip," he said as he toyed with the hair trimmed short above her clit.

Her torso lifted. He chuckled. "My girl is so responsive. You make it very difficult to play." He stopped touching her to watch her face again. "You're a quick learner. I wouldn't have expected you to go this long without talking. I'm proud of you." He set a hand spread open on her belly. "I know there's a tight bundle of need ready to explode in here, and when it does, it's going to be epic. Your obedience will reap this reward."

She panted again, her gaze hazy.

Zane stroked her tits again, circling her nipples in spirals without touching the tips. They were so stiff. He knew if he pressed on them, she would come. He leaned over finally and flicked his tongue over them one at a time when he thought she could handle it. And then he hovered over her farther and licked the seam of her lips.

Abby reached out her tongue, but he pulled back, stroking his thumb across her bottom lip. She whimpered. *So fucking sexy.*

When he dipped his thumb in between her lips, she curled around it and sucked. She stared at him, her eyes watery and dilated.

It was time to let her come. Zane popped his thumb

out of her mouth and kissed a path down her chin, her neck, her shoulder. He nibbled his way across her chest, carefully nipping each nipple while she bucked into his mouth. He made his way down her belly until he reached her pussy. He flicked his tongue over her clit, and she dug her heels into the bed again to lift her torso.

Her arms jerked, but she was well secured. He didn't want her to hurt herself, but the sheets were soft enough to protect her.

Zane used one hand to lift the hood of her clit, holding it tight. And then he simultaneously sucked her nub into his mouth while fucking her hard with three fingers from his free hand.

Abby screamed, instantly rigid.

Zane sucked, fucking her pussy rapidly, reaching as deep as he could so his palm flattened against her lower lips with each thrust.

Her scream turned to a whimper as she froze. He felt the swell of her channel just before she came. He swore she came both clitorally and through her G-spot. The inside of her pussy gripped his fingers. Her clit pulsed around his lips.

When she finally collapsed onto the bed, he eased off her, kissing her mound reverently before lifting to hover over her and untie her hands. Her face was flushed. Sweat beaded on her forehead. Her lips opened and closed several times, her eyes seeing nothing. And then she met his gaze. "Oh. My. God."

He chuckled.

"Zane."

"Yeah, baby?" he asked unnecessarily, leaning on one elbow to the side of her and stroking his fingers across her breasts.

"I—" She didn't finish. A tear escaped her eye and ran down toward her ear.

"Just relax. Catch your breath, baby." He wiped the tear away and then pulled her closer. She was shaking. He pulled the covers over them both and held her tight, kissing her temple. His mouth to her ear, he whispered calming words. "Shh, baby. It's okay. I've got you."

It wasn't okay, though. He was falling. So hard he couldn't see the ground below.

Abby slowly relaxed in his arms. Her breathing slowed. When she finally spoke again, she made him laugh. "You drank coffee without me."

"You were naughty."

She lifted her face off the pillow. "I gave you a blow job. Men like to wake up with their cocks in a woman's mouth."

"Mmm. This is true. But Doms like to direct things. Sweet sexy women who think they can control their Dom will find themselves in a heap of trouble."

She flopped back down, a smile on her lips. She was not in any way mad. "You do realize I have not been thwarted."

"Yep." He kissed her temple. "You do realize my arsenal is huge."

"I'm counting on it." She twisted to face him. "I hope my heart can stand it."

CHAPTER 13

An hour later, Abby was reaching into the cabinet to get a mug when Zane came up behind her and wrapped an arm around her under her breasts. He kissed her neck. "My shirt rides high when you lift onto your tiptoes." He nibbled behind her ear. "I'm going to move all the dishes up that high. I like to see your ass peeking out."

She giggled as she flattened her feet. "Maybe I need a longer shirt."

"Maybe you need no shirt at all." He reached for the hem and lifted it above her hips, setting his hands on her waist and pressing her into the counter.

Her breath hitched. How the hell could she be aroused again? Her bare ass and pussy in the kitchen made her shiver.

A knock at the door made Zane groan against her neck.

Abby wiggled around until she was facing him. "Probably Emily wanting to make sure we're still alive in here."

"Nosy."

Abby grinned as she moved to separate herself from his clutches.

He held firm. "I'll get it. At least I have pants on. You stay here." He padded across the room. His jeans were all he had on. His feet were bare and his fine smooth back took up the entire room. She wanted to freeze the moment with her eyes permanently open, pinned to that view. Even his ass was fucking hot inside his jeans.

Instead, she turned to pour herself a cup of coffee. She'd been hampered in the bed and then hampered again in the shower. Finally, she was going to get a sip. She waited, expecting to hear Emily's voice filling the room any second.

Instead she turned around to find Zane pulling someone into the house and shutting the door fast, his hand twisting the lock.

Lauren.

Abby set the mug back on the counter and raced across the room. Before she got there, Zane had Lauren in his arms and had taken a few long strides to reach the sofa. He laid her down on the cool leather and kneeled at her side as Abby reached them.

"Lauren? What the hell happened?" Someone had punched her in the eye and her lip was cracked.

Lauren moaned. She turned her head toward Abby. "Sorry," she muttered, wincing. "Nowhere else to go."

Abby wondered how she'd even arrived here. "It's okay, honey. Stay still. Let me get you a blanket." Abby raced from the room and returned with a comforter from the guest room.

Zane grabbed it from her and tucked it around the shivering Lauren. "Did Yenin do this to you?"

Lauren's good eye opened wide. "How did you know—" Her gaze shifted to Abby. "Right. Abby told you." Tears formed in Lauren's eyes and fell down her face. One eye was swollen almost shut, the black ring of a new injury beginning to form. Her lip was cut in two places, dried blood already forming in the corner of her mouth. And those were the injuries Abby could readily see.

"Grab some ice, baby," Zane instructed. "Two bags."

Abby hurried back to the kitchen and pulled out two Ziploc bags to fill with ice. When she returned, Zane was prodding Lauren all over, watching her face for signs of pain.

Lauren winced when he pressed on her belly. "He kick you?"

She nodded, biting her lip and holding back tears.

"We need to call the cops, honey." Abby's heart beat fast as she considered what needed to be done. "And probably an ambulance."

"*No*," Lauren shouted. She jerked her gaze to Abby. "Please. No cops. No doctors. I just need to rest a bit."

"Lauren, honey, that's crazy. If that bastard hurt you, you have to report it."

Lauren's free eye went round and huge. "He'll kill me."

Zane wrapped one bag of ice with the washcloth Abby handed him and held it to her eye. He held the second bag to her lip. "Sit down, Abby. Please, baby."

Abby was stunned. What was the matter with him?

Zane lifted his gaze to her and raised an eyebrow. "Baby, you're shaking. Sit. Let me talk to Lauren."

Abby lowered herself into the chair next to the couch and pulled her legs under her. She was still naked beneath the shirt. She needed more clothes. She tugged the shirt lower on her thighs, trying in vain to cover more of her skin.

Zane spoke gently. "Talk to me, Lauren. Where does it hurt?"

"Everywhere."

"I know that, honey, but where does it hurt the worst?"

"I don't know."

"Do you think anything is broken?"

"No." She winced.

Zane let up on the pressure over her eye. He pulled the ice pack away for a minute and examined her face. He pulled her eyelid back and looked at her closely.

Abby was relieved when he set the ice back down. How lucky could she be to have a paramedic for a boyfriend all the sudden when her only friend in town, or at least the only friend she'd had before Zane came along, came to her doorstep beaten to a pulp?

"Can you get us a glass of water, baby?"

Abby jumped up and headed back to the kitchen, glad for the distraction and something to do. She returned with the water and watched as Zane lifted Lauren's head and helped her take a drink.

Lauren winced again as her lips hit the glass. "Hurts."

"I know, but you need the fluids. Try to drink it all."

Lauren nodded and did as he said. Seemed Abby wasn't the only one who fell under Zane's spell and did his bidding. He had a magnetic way about him that commanded everyone around.

Thank God both of them had the day off. Lauren was in bad shape.

Zane sat back and stopped poking and prodding. "Tell me what happened."

Abby resumed her seat in the chair, leaning forward to listen to Lauren.

"I told him I was leaving him."

Zane took a deep breath. "Anton?"

"Yes."

Zane pulled out his phone.

Lauren lifted her head. "What are you doing? You can't tell anyone. I'm not kidding. This is serious. I think he'll kill me. And," she glanced at Abby and then returned her gaze to Zane. She licked her lips. "I think Abby's in danger too. That's why I came here."

Abby jumped from her seat. "What?"

Zane reached for her and pulled her to his side, settling her on the coffee table next to him. "He was the one who ran her off the road, wasn't he?" His gaze never left Lauren.

Lauren nodded. A tear ran down her cheek. "I think so. I overheard him talking to his men about it."

"But how? Why?" Abby stuttered.

Zane's grip tightened on her waist.

Lauren leaned back onto the couch, defeat clear on her face. "I don't know. One of the women in the break room must have ratted on us after we spoke Monday. Either that or he has the break room bugged. I wouldn't put either idea past him. He's dangerous. He decided he wanted me, and he doesn't take *no* for an answer."

Zane leaned forward again. "Lauren, I need to call Rider. He's a good friend and he lives two doors down. I'm not asking you to go to the station right this second, but I need to look into it." He glanced at Abby and then back. And then he played his trump card. "You don't want Abby to get hurt."

Lauren shook her head. More tears fell. "I'm so sorry, Abby. I had no idea."

"I know, honey. It's not your fault. Let Zane talk to some people. We'll figure out what to do."

She nodded.

Zane stood, squeezing Abby's hand, and lifted her with him. "Put some more clothes on, baby. We're gonna have company."

Abby took one more look at Lauren and then left the

room. She couldn't think. She was glad she'd already had a shower. She opened her underwear drawer first and grabbed panties and a bra. As she shrugged into her panties, she headed to the closet. Jeans. A T-shirt. She was presentable before the doorbell rang. Rider was fast.

As she reentered the living room, Rider stepped inside in uniform. "Hey." He nodded at Abby and turned to Zane. "I was about to start my shift. Called and told them I would be late. They're sending someone out."

Zane motioned Rider farther into the room.

When Rider saw Lauren, he winced. "Shit."

"Yeah. This would be the work of Anton Yenin," Zane said.

Rider nodded. His phone beeped, and he snagged it from his waist to read a message.

Jacobson will be here in a few.

Abby crept up to Lauren and sat on the edge of the couch in front of her to take her hand. Lauren's face was swollen worse already, and she was white as a sheet. Her lip trembled.

"Seems he was probably also the guy who ran Abby off the road, or one of his men." Zane headed for the kitchen.

Rider cringed. "Fuck."

"Yeah, that's what I thought. Coffee?" Zane asked over his shoulder.

Rider shook his head. "No, thanks."

Zane came back into the room carrying two mugs. He handed one to Abby, making her stomach dip at the gesture. He'd even added cream and sugar, just how she liked it.

Lauren got nervous. "Another cop is coming?" She pushed to sitting.

Zane stepped in front of her. "Lauren. You said yourself the guy was going to kill you. Why don't you want to report it?"

"He threatened worse if I talked."

A knock sounded at the door, making Abby flinch. She took a deep breath as Rider opened the door and let another police officer in.

Rider shut the door and introduced him to the room. "This is Jacobson. He's been working the case tracking Anton Yenin for over a year." Rider nodded at Zane. "You've probably met Zane Randolf. He's a medic with the fire department."

Jacobson shook his hand.

Rider turned to the group. "Abby Burns is with Zane. She's renting this house."

Abby sucked in a breath at the way Rider introduced her. *With Zane.*

"And the woman on the couch is Lauren. What's your last name Lauren?"

"Schneider," she mumbled.

"Lauren was with Yenin until this morning. It didn't end well."

Jacobson narrowed his gaze. "Honey, if you were with Yenin, it ended fantastically. You're still alive. How did you get away?"

She glanced down at her lap. "When I told him I was leaving, he was irate. But he was also busy. And he said he was tired of my whiney ass. He had two of his men hold me while a third beat me." She heaved in a sob. "Then he told them to toss me out. Before they dragged me out the door, he looked me in the eye and warned me to keep quiet or I would be sorry. He said I was lucky he didn't just kill me. If I wanted to stay alive, I had better go nurse my wounds and forget I ever met him."

Jacobson crouched in front of her and set a hand on top of one of hers. "You did the right thing."

Her lip trembled. "Doesn't seem like it. I've put my own life in danger. And Abby's too."

Abby squeezed Lauren's leg through the blanket. Part of her wanted to scream in fear. The other part saw this woman she'd befriended hurting and desperate for a shoulder to lean on.

Jacobson asked Lauren dozens of questions and took notes on a pad he pulled from his pocket. When he finished, he stood. "You need to consider pressing charges. We have ways of keeping people safe."

Lauren shook her head. "I'm done. I just want it to be over."

"Honey," Jacobson began, "with Yenin, it's not over until he says it's over, and it usually includes a body bag." His words were harsh, making Abby cringe, but she was also sure he spoke the truth.

Lauren shook her head. "I can't do it. I need sleep. And I need to pull my life back together. I don't need to stir this pot and bring more trouble to myself."

Jacobson hesitated and then nodded. "If you change your mind, call me." He laid a card on the coffee table.

"That's it?" Abby asked. She twisted around, wondering what in the hell was going to happen next.

"Afraid so. If Ms. Schneider doesn't want to press charges, there isn't much I can do. I will suggest that both you and Lauren find someplace else to stay and lie low for a while. Probably not the same place. And I would do that fast."

Zane followed Jacobson to the front of the house. "We'll sort that out. Thanks for your help." He held the door open for the officer and then waited until the guy was back in his cruiser before he turned around.

Abby stared at him. She thought she would vomit. She totally understood where Lauren was coming from, and she wasn't at all sure it mattered one bit whether she reported the incident or not. Neither option would alleviate her unease.

Rider turned to Lauren. "I think the best plan would be for me to take Lauren to my house. And you," he pointed at Zane, "to take Abby to your place. Hopefully Yenin didn't have her followed here. But in case he did, this isn't the safest location."

Lauren sat up straighter. "I can't put you out like that."

"Honey, if my fiancée found out I left you high and dry, she would have my balls. You're coming with me." He turned on his heels and walked outside. Two minutes later, he came back in. "I don't see anything that would suggest you were followed. How did you get here?"

"Cab."

"Okay, then." Rider helped her to stand and grabbed her purse. When it appeared she wasn't able to walk easily, he lifted her into his arms and carried her. He turned back at the door. "Zane, you and Abby get gone. I'll text you later." And then he left, tugging the door shut behind him with one hand.

Abby's legs collapsed, and she sank onto the couch, putting her head in her hands.

Zane was at her side in an instant. He sat next to her and wrapped his arm around her shoulders. "Babe." He lifted her chin with a finger. "It's gonna be okay."

"How exactly?"

He smiled. "Look at the bright side, I get you in my bed."

She rolled her eyes. "I don't think I can do that on a daily basis. I didn't get enough sleep."

He wiggled his eyebrows. "Good. Then I did my job.

Come on. Let's get some stuff packed and get out of here before the Russian mafia come in and ransack the place."

"That is so not funny, and if Mrs. Lamphry's roses get damaged..."

Zane laughed as he hauled Abby to her feet.

Surely he didn't really think some Russian thugs would come to her house. Right?

CHAPTER 14

Before heading to Zane's house, Abby went with him to the gym. He needed to work out, and she readily agreed she didn't want to be left alone while he did so.

Zane introduced her to Conner, the only member of his group she hadn't met. As Zane headed for the locker room to get changed, he left her with Conner. The man was tall, like unbelievably tall. Six four, she would guess. And he seemed far mellower than the other guys. He was also significantly older than the rest. She liked him immediately. After acquainting herself with a police officer, a K-9 trainer, and an EMT, it was a relief to find out Conner was a college lit professor.

She also learned from him that Rafe and Mason were attorneys.

"So, how do you put up with this guy?" Conner asked loud enough for Zane to hear as he returned dressed to spar.

She smiled. "I haven't had a choice really. I keep getting injured, and he keeps showing up to rescue me. In fact, both times I was pinned and had to be extricated."

Conner chuckled as he walked away.

Zane kissed her forehead and nodded toward Joe's office. "You can hang out in there if you want some peace and quiet. Or you can watch Conner kick my ass if you like that sort of thing." He winked.

"How do you know he's going to kick your ass?"

"Baby, he kicks everybody's ass. He's undefeated in the ring."

"Wow. Why doesn't he go pro?"

Zane shrugged. "Doesn't want to. Same as the rest of us."

While Zane headed for the ring, Abby sat in a folding chair along the wall.

Joe took a seat next to her as Zane and Conner stretched in the cage. "How are you holding up?" Joe asked. "I heard about what happened with your car accident and your friend."

"Yeah, it's a little crazy, that's for sure. I'm doing okay, though." She smiled.

"If you need anything, let me know. I think of all my guys as sons, and their women become my daughters."

"Thank you, Joe. That's really sweet. I'm glad Zane has had all of you in his life. He's a lucky guy."

"That he is." Joe winked at her as he stood. "I better go help these guys before they start swinging punches."

Abby leaned her head against the wall and watched as Zane and Conner went through several types of take downs. She winced when they began to grapple on the floor. It really did look like they would kill each other. No wonder Zane and Conner preferred to remain amateur. She couldn't imagine what the pros must look like. And she didn't even want to ponder what the underground fighters did to each other.

Two hours later, Zane emerged from the locker room

and grabbed both her hands to haul her to standing. "I'm sure that was boring as hell. Thanks for waiting for me."

"It was interesting, actually. Now that I've sat through a practice, I feel like I understand the sport much better."

Conner came up behind Zane, shrugging his gym bag onto his shoulder. "Get your woman out of here before she kicks your ass to the curb, Randolf. You're a lucky bastard she even agreed to enter this building." Conner chuckled as he left.

Two minutes later, Abby said good-bye to Joe and they headed for the parking lot.

Abby had her arm draped through Zane's and her face tilted up to look at him when he suddenly came to a stop. She followed his gaze to find a man leaning against Zane's truck.

Zane took the last few steps toward the man she didn't recognize. "Dmitry. What brings you to this side of town?"

The man smiled and spoke in a heavy Russian accent. "I was hoping to have a word with you." He glanced at Abby, making her wince inside. This couldn't be good.

"Go ahead. What's on your mind? I don't have secrets from Abby."

Dmitry lifted one brow and glanced at her. "Ah, so this is Abby Burns."

Abby stopped breathing. How did he know her name?

"It is. Why do you know her?"

"I don't. But I've heard the name."

"Where?"

"Around." Dmitry shrugged. "We Russians may be a group divided, but word spreads quickly amongst us."

"What sort of word are we talking about? Is Abby in danger?" Zane stiffened. His voice was deeper, almost threatening.

"Not that I'm aware of." Dmitry chuckled as though to

defuse the tension. "I heard her gal Lauren was in a bit of trouble with Yenin."

"She was. I hope that's over now."

"I hope so too." Dmitry shifted his gaze to Abby. "Tell your friend to lie low for a while. Anton is pissed."

Abby didn't move. She was completely unsure what to make of this crazy confrontation.

Dmitry turned back to Zane. "You change your mind and decide to make some extra bucks under the radar, you call me."

Zane nodded. "Not gonna happen. But I have your number, Volikov. Was there anything else you needed?"

"Nope. I was just in the neighborhood. Saw your truck. Thought I'd stop and say hi." Dmitry righted himself from the side of Zane's truck and sauntered away.

Abby didn't take her gaze off him as he casually folded himself into a black Camaro and sped away from the gym. "What the hell was that all about?"

"I don't know. But I don't like it." Zane opened the passenger door and helped Abby climb in. He rounded the hood, started the engine, and then turned to face her as the air conditioning kicked on.

"What did he mean about changing your mind?"

"Fighting. He's the guy who has made numerous offers to introduce me to the underground."

Abby shivered. "Oh. Yikes. Why do you think he came here? I'm no expert, but even I'm smart enough to realize he had a message hidden in that little chat. Do you think it has to do with Lauren?"

Zane shook his head. "Damned if I know." He turned toward the front and put the truck in gear. "Guys like Volikov fight for the money and the love of the sport. They're basically good guys. I've sparred with many of them on occasion. Sometimes they come to the gym. I don't believe Dmitry or any of his close friends are much fonder of Yenin than the rest of us, but they're stuck. It's a fine line for the Russians to keep their noses clean while living under the Yenin radar. Yenin is bad news all the way around. Dmitry knows it. If he's heard some things and my name or yours came up, he probably just wanted to warn me."

"Do you trust him?"

"I do. Do I want to fight dirty? No, but like I said, I've sparred with him. He fights fair when he's above ground."

Abby didn't say a word on the way to Zane's house. She knew he was undoubtedly processing what Dmitry had said all the way home.

She pulled out her cell phone and sent a quick text to Lauren to continue to lie low and not take any chances.

But what about herself? Why on earth had Anton Yenin sent someone to bully her at the casino, and why would he have someone run her off the road?

～

Later that evening, Zane poured Abby a glass of wine and put it in her hands. He'd fed her dinner, entertained her with his wit, and settled her on his couch. "Drink. Your nerves are frayed."

"Yeah, 'cause there's this Russian guy who ran me off the road and then beat the hell out of my friend and warned her he would kill her if she told anyone, and then she told me." She didn't breathe while she spewed that out. And then she turned toward him. "Now I'm putting *you* in danger too. And on top of all that, some other Russian guy just gave us a loaded message in a parking lot that made no sense."

Zane sat beside her and set his wine glass on the coffee

table. He took her into his arms. "Baby, slow down. Nothing's going to happen to you in my house. Nor me. We're good. Rider didn't notice anyone around your house, either. This is just a precaution. And I for one am not sorry. If it means I have to keep you for a while, tied to my bed, I'm all over it." He paused and tipped her chin up. "As for Dmitry, we've been acquaintances for a few years. I can't imagine him doing anything to harm me or you. He may fight for the underground, but he's not one of Yenin's minions and he isn't mafia. He probably just heard the gossip and wanted me to be aware that your name and Lauren's were being tossed around in his community."

"Yeah, but why? Why me? I don't have anything to do with this."

"If Anton even suspects you had anything to do with Lauren rebelling against him, he would hold a grudge."

"Forever?"

"I don't know, baby." He took her hand and held it tight, pulling it up to his face to rub against his cheek. "Let's put it out of our minds for tonight. I'm still pondering the idea of tying you to my bed."

Abby glared at him, her eyes twinkling with laughter. "Anything for a fuck."

"Mmm hmm." He kissed her nose, hoping she knew he was teasing. She must. She didn't seem angry.

Abby took a sip of her wine. "I have to go back to work tomorrow."

"And you'll be careful. Nothing can happen to you at work. The Crystal Palace is filled with cops."

"Sure. The last time I was there, someone apparently listened in on my conversation and then turned me in to the fucking mafia." She twisted toward him again. "And that asshole, Anton. He sent a man to my table to warn me against Lauren. And since that wasn't good enough for him, he also ran me off the road. I could have died."

"But you didn't."

She slumped.

Zane tipped her glass toward her face. "Another sip, baby. Let's change the subject."

"Let's." She humphed and drank her wine. "Let's talk about us."

Zane tried not to choke. He grinned at her. "It's never a good thing when a woman wants to talk about 'us.'"

She rolled her eyes. "This is happening so fast." She sat up straighter. "One minute I'm under my porch pinned by a rusty nail, and the next minute I've practically moved in with the paramedic who dragged my ass, literally, out from under the porch. I've been to an MMA fight, a BDSM club, and I've had the best sex of my entire life. *And*, I got run off the road by a maniac Russian mob guy who wants me dead. My head is spinning."

Zane set his finger on her lips, silencing her. "Best sex of your entire life?"

She rolled her eyes again. "Don't get a big head," she muttered past his finger.

"Oh, baby, my head is big all right. And hard." He leaned in to her face as her eyes shot wide. When she opened her mouth, he covered it with his own, whispering against her lips. "I think I liked you better this morning when you were silent and obedient. Let's play that game again. You need to take a chill pill, and I have the perfect pill for you."

When she opened her mouth again, he raised his brows. "Baby, don't do it. I'm warning you." He took her wine glass from her fist and set it on the coffee table. Then he tugged her around so she was lying on his couch. He leaned over her and got in her face again. "Here's how this is going to go."

She pursed her lips and rolled her eyes yet again.

"Oh, baby, you have got to stop rolling your eyes at me. If you do it again, I'm going to take you over my knee. And I'd rather not do that until your ass is fully healed."

Her eyes went wide, but her breathing also got loud and ragged. His words affected her. In a good way.

"Good. So we're clear on that. Now, for the rest of the night, I want you to submit to me. You do as I say, and you'll find yourself well rewarded. You fight me on this, and you'll go to sleep very needy. Got it?"

She inhaled slowly and then nodded.

He smiled. "She's catching on." He lifted off her and hauled her to stand in front of him. "You don't speak unless I ask you a direct question that requires an answer. Your job is to do as you're told. My job is to make your body hum."

She visibly shuddered. He liked that.

Zane leaned back against the couch. "Please take off your clothes."

She tucked her lips inside her mouth and stared at him.

"Don't think. Don't hesitate. Just obey."

Her hands shook as she lifted her T-shirt over her head and dropped it on his coffee table. When she popped the button on her jeans, he watched her closely. Her cheeks were red. It embarrassed her to strip for him, even though he'd seen her entire body already. Her timidness made him rock hard.

He almost moaned when she wiggled her hips back and forth to shrug off her jeans. He gripped the back of the couch where he'd spread his hands as she squirmed out of her panties and then popped her bra and let it fall from her arms.

"Turn around."

Abby slowly shuffled her feet until she faced away from him.

He wanted to see her wound, make sure she wasn't exaggerating when she said it didn't hurt any longer. A small red line marked the spot that had been stitched. Except for about an inch of pink surrounding the mark, it looked good. Zane set his hands on her hips and stroked his thumb over the wound.

Abby didn't flinch.

"It looks good. No pain?"

She shook her head, twisting around to look over her shoulder. "No. And I kinda forgot about it after my car accident."

Satisfied, he spun her back around. "Sit on my coffee table, baby. Tall. Hands behind you, shoulders back, legs spread."

She eased her ass onto the table and followed his directions. Her gaze even lowered to the floor. Fuck she was submissive. She was so fucking perfect, he had to pause before he could speak again.

Her tits stood out in front of her when she pulled her shoulders back. Her nipples pebbled even though he hadn't touched her. And her pussy… "Baby, you're wet."

She flinched, but that was all.

"You might note you're always wet when you submit to me. I know you didn't previously consider yourself submissive, but you are, baby." He leaned forward, forcing himself not to adjust his cock as he put his elbows on his knees. "It comes natural for some people." He stared at her for a long time, taking in her gorgeous body. Her skin was smooth and pale. Delectable. He wanted to run his tongue over her. He *had* done so. He wanted to do it again. "It comes natural for *you*. And it turns me on more than you can imagine."

She made a soft sound. Maybe a moan. His cock pulsed against his jeans. He wanted her lips wrapped around him again. Was it too soon to command her to suck him? She'd done it this morning on her own and seemed to love it. But taking that last step and directing her to suck his cock was huge. Not every woman found it fulfilling. Few did in fact. However, a submissive by nature sometimes could do anything and find it arousing simply by pleasing their Dom.

He decided against it. He didn't want to push her.

Another tactic.

Zane stood. "Let's move to the bedroom." He headed down the hall, hearing her soft footsteps behind him. When he reached the bedroom, he tugged the comforter off his bed and pointed at the sheet. "Climb up. Lie down. Spread yourself open for me."

Abby did as he said, situating herself sideways on the bed so he had the perfect view of her from his stance at the side.

"Touch yourself, baby."

Abby sucked in a breath.

"Show me how you masturbate when you're alone."

She lifted her hands from her sides and cupped her breasts. That wasn't entirely what he had in mind, but it was smoking hot, and for all he knew she always stroked her tits first.

Abby bucked into her own hands when she pinched her nipples. She moaned. Zane fought to keep from doing the same.

"That's enough nipple action, baby. Lower your hands. Stroke your clit."

Her hands shook as she spread them down her belly toward her pussy. When her fingers tentatively landed on her clit, she held the hood back with one hand and flicked a finger from the other over the distended nub.

Zane leaned against the side of the bed, pressing his cock into the mattress as he watched the best porn ever. "That's so sexy, baby." His voice sounded foreign to him, deep, too low. "Reach inside now. Gather your wetness. Spread it around."

Abby released her clit and dug her heels into the bed as she stroked one finger through her folds.

"Pull your lips apart. Let me see your pussy better, baby."

She used both hands to do so, and the view of her pink parted lips, her arousal nearly dripping from her core, made him inhale sharply. He'd meant to command her to orgasm for her benefit, not his. But at this rate, he might come inside his jeans before she ever got off.

"What gets you off, Abby? Clitoral? Or G-spot?"

She tipped her face to meet his gaze. "I— Um, I—I've never come with my fingers. I use a vibrator."

Zane smiled. He set his hands on her ankles and held them open wider. "Until now."

She stared at him, her mouth agape. She let her head fall back finally, her fingers dangling between her legs, wet with her juices, no longer touching herself.

"I'm going to direct you. And you're going to come."

She didn't acknowledge him. If she didn't believe him, all the better. It would make her orgasm that much sweeter in the end.

"If I can make you come with my fingers, I know you can do it with yours. Hell, you know better than me what you like and where you need the contact."

Her belly dipped. He loved when she did that.

"Drag your wetness from your pussy to your clit and flick your finger over the bundle of nerves, baby."

Abby stroked two fingers through her lower lips and did as he told her. When she flicked her clit, her legs shook.

Zane moved his hands from her ankles to her shins and held her steady. "Lick your fingers, baby."

Abby stopped touching herself and met his gaze. She hesitated. But only for a moment. And then she sucked two fingers into her mouth, sticking out her tongue and teasing him. Her gaze held his.

Zane leaned forward, making sure she heard him well. "Abby, I'm the Dom here, not you. You will not tempt me with your sultry looks or your tongue when I'm instructing you. Understood?"

She froze, her tongue sticking out to swipe over her pointer. Her gaze lowered, and she released her fingers.

"Good girl. Use them on your clit."

Her face turned red, as though she'd been caught doing something she shouldn't have done. And essentially she had. She just didn't know it. She would learn. He would teach her everything there was to know about pleasing him, submitting to him, making herself complete. Because in the end, that's what this was all about, ensuring his sweet submissive was fulfilled. Her needs would be met. Her needs would be way more than met. And getting to that place... Getting to the point where she was a true submissive... Zane could barely contemplate the course of travel—it made him so fucking horny.

Abby set two fingers once again on her clit, but she watched Zane while she touched herself.

He knew what she was doing. She was showing him she couldn't get herself off. She thought she might prove the point so he would give up the battle.

She thought wrong.

"Abby, baby." He met her gaze. "You won't win."

She looked shocked, as though not realizing he was on to her.

"If you want me to fuck you at some point tonight, you will orgasm first at your own hand. And don't even consider faking it. I'm way too astute for that, baby." He smoothed his hands up over her knees and grasped her thighs. That might help. It would at least give her the impression he was participating. The pressure on her thighs would keep her from having to concentrate on anything besides getting herself to orgasm.

Abby hesitated and then pressed her thumb against the base of her clit. Hard. She held it there while she lifted her hips off the bed and moaned.

Ahh, so that was the caveat. "That's it, baby. Do what you need. Show me your gorgeous pussy when it pulses with your orgasm."

Still pressing on that spot, she wiggled her finger back and forth. Her other hand came down to reach inside her. She pressed two fingers in as far as they would go and thrust them in and out. He could see they were curled upward. They would be stroking across her G-spot with each pass.

Zane pursed his lips and pressed his cock firmer into the bed. He watched closely, his gaze switching between her pussy and her face. When her mouth opened, her ass lifted, and her finger stilled at the base of her clit, he knew she was close.

Her thighs stiffened. Her head tipped back. And the sound she emitted as she came was so raw and beautiful, he needed to be inside her.

Before she was done, he halted her. "Stop."

Abby froze.

"That's enough, baby. Move your fingers."

She didn't move fast enough. Her expression was stunned. "Zane... I..."

Zane grabbed her wrist and pulled her hand from her clit. "I know, baby. But this is my show. My rules. You aren't to question me."

Her legs quivered. She swallowed hard. Her eyes were wide. She licked her lips. She whimpered.

"Flip over. Get on all fours."

Abby struggled to follow his direction, but he watched as she found her arms and legs and did as he commanded.

Zane shrugged out of his jeans. He'd never needed to come so badly in his life. He yanked open the draw of his nightstand and grabbed a condom, not bothering to shut the drawer. He tore the foil with his teeth, tossed the wrapper to the floor, and donned the condom in record time. Seconds later, he was behind her, holding her by the hips and nudging her across the bed some. He needed more space. Her ass was so fucking sexy. The spot on her upper cheek where she'd been impaled was barely noticeable.

"Lower to your forearms, baby. Rest your head."

She complied.

He separated her knees with his and lined his cock up with her entrance. "Brace yourself, baby." And then he plunged into her, spreading her thighs wider with his hands. He wouldn't last long. And he wanted her to come hard.

Taking her lead, he reached around her body and planted his thumb below her clit. He pressed into her while he thrust with his cock.

Abby moaned, her body rocking forward and backward with each thrust.

"That's my girl. Let it go, baby. Give it to me."

Abby came, her clit pulsing under his finger, her pussy

gripping his cock. He wasn't there yet himself, but he didn't care. He wanted to witness this, watch his submissive swaying beneath him totally out of control. She needed that. And he loved seeing it.

When she was finished, he released her clit and gripped her hips again. He increased his pace and closed his eyes as he brought himself to his own orgasm.

Pure bliss. Sweetest pussy ever. And the woman attached to it was a dream come true.

Abby collapsed.

Zane landed half on and half off her, his leg between hers, his hand on her back. His heart beat rapidly. He kissed her shoulder.

Minutes passed before he could speak or move. "Have I told you how amazing you are?" He brushed her hair off her shoulder to give his mouth better access as soon as his hand was able to move.

"You might have mentioned it," she mumbled into the pillow.

Zane rose above her and flipped her onto her back. "I mean it."

She gazed into his eyes. "I thought you wanted to watch me masturbate. You cut me short."

He grinned and then shrugged. "I did, but then I wanted to make you come myself even more. I'm allowed to change my mind. The important thing is, you were right there. Now I know two things."

"What are those?" She grinned.

"You indeed *can* make yourself come without the aid of a vibrator." He kissed her nose. "And that spot right below your clit is the key to everything."

She moaned and tossed her arm over her eyes. "It's not good for you to know so many of my secrets."

"Oh, baby. It's fucking awesome. I want to know all of your secrets. Tell me another one."

∽

Abby stared into Zane's face, seeing a truly deep interest in knowing everything about her.

Should she tell him? She had told so few people about her little side project working on the next great American novel. "Hmm. I think I should save a few for another day."

He shook his head. "One more." He wrapped his fingers in her hair and held her gaze.

She had hardly caught her breath, and he wanted to chat. He meant it.

"I'm a writer," she blurted.

"A writer?" His eyebrows rose high. "Like books?"

She grinned. "Well, I guess. If you can call a person who hasn't published anything but indeed taps on a keyboard in her spare time a writer, then yes."

"Awesome. Conner's fiancée is a writer also. And an editor."

"Really? Can't wait to meet her." Though the idea of letting anyone see her words yet was daunting.

"Hopefully she'll be able to get out of the house more soon. Apparently after the first trimester, she's supposed to feel better. Though I think Conner has his doubts at this point."

"What does she write?"

"Romance is what I hear. That's what she edits. Their house is covered with books."

"That's so cool. I don't know anyone who writes. I've been an island so far."

"Why haven't you joined a writing group?"

She shrugged. "I've only been here a month, and I'm

still a little embarrassed to show anyone my work." *A lot embarrassed.*

He leaned down and kissed her lips, taking her by surprise. "I'm sure it's wonderful. When can I see it?"

She shook her head. "Not in the near future, so don't even ask."

He rolled his eyes. "Have a little faith. I bet it's excellent. What's it about? What genre?"

She swallowed and thought about how much to tell him.

His look was eager and sincere. Two minutes ago, she'd been ready to pass out after the best fuck of her life. Now, she was perking up as the man she'd just had sex with showed a genuine interest in her passion. A warm feeling spread over her body.

"It's a mystery."

"How much is written?"

"A lot. I'm almost done with the first draft."

"Awesome. That's so cool. Then what do you plan to do? Do you have a publisher?"

"God, no."

His brows furrowed.

"I was planning to sit on it for about ten years and talk myself out of humiliating myself."

Zane sat upright, threw one leg over her body to straddle her. He grasped her hands and held them over her head. His gaze was serious. "You can't do that. What's the point in doing something you love if you aren't willing to share it with the world?"

"You haven't even seen it, Zane. For all you know, it's awful."

"I don't believe that for a minute. You're smart, funny, witty... I bet it's the bomb."

A flush stole over her cheeks. It felt good for someone

to have a little faith in her. The truth was she hadn't really talked to very many people about her writing because her parents had mostly poo-pooed the idea, and her high school friends had thought she was crazy to entertain such a far-fetched dream.

In fact, Zane was the first person to light up and show interest without insinuating she was completely fucked in the head to think she could ever make it as a writer. Her feelings for him went up ten notches.

"So, when do you work on this novel?"

"Whenever I'm not at the casino. And when my head isn't concussed. I'll get back into it this week."

"So what's the goal?"

"To become rich and famous and quit my day job, of course? What's everyone's goal?" She grinned and tugged on her wrists.

He held her steady, glancing at his hands. "So, I should hang on to you and become a kept man as soon as you get rich and famous."

She gave a sharp chuckle and rolled her eyes, tugging on her hands again. She felt exposed, trapped in his grip with him hovering over her naked body so intimately now that they were no longer having sex. "I wouldn't hold your breath."

"Stop pulling. I like you pinned beneath me."

"Why?"

"Captive audience." He glanced at her chest.

Her nipples jumped to attention as he let his gaze linger over them. "You're staring."

"You're gorgeous."

She lifted her gaze from her own chest to his. Now, *that* was beauty. Incredible. Impossibly solid male pecs that made her want to groan. The claw marks on his pec were stunning.

Next thing she knew, his lips were on hers, scrambling her brain as he devoured her. Her unease quickly evaporated as he flattened himself on top of her and scooted down the bed to take her nipple into his mouth.

CHAPTER 15

On Monday morning, Abby rode to The Crystal Palace with Zane. He'd insisted on driving her and picking her up. They hadn't heard a peep from Yenin or anyone else, so Abby figured the man was done bothering her. After all, he'd let Lauren go. Why would he care about either of them anymore?

Zane grabbed her wrist and hauled her to him before she got out of the car. "I'm growing rather fond of you. Please be careful. I don't want to pick you up in my ambulance again." He grinned. "Don't leave the casino. Got it?"

"So bossy."

He narrowed his gaze.

She rolled her eyes. "All right. Fine. I won't leave until you come to get me."

"If I'm not free, I'll send one of the other guys." He wrapped his palm around her neck and pulled her in closer to kiss her lips.

Things happened to her body that shouldn't have occurred from a simple kiss. She was in so much trouble when it came to this man. He ruled her. She wasn't sure how she felt yet about his ability to command her so thoroughly, but there was no denying it. "See you tonight," she mumbled against his lips.

He let her go, and she felt his gaze on her back as she walked in the front doors. She glanced over her shoulder and rolled her eyes again at his overprotectiveness.

Thankfully, the day was uneventful. Her boss was extremely understanding and concerned about her wellbeing. He pulled her into his office first thing to make sure she was feeling okay. The police had spoken to him, so he knew there was a good chance Anton Yenin had run his employee off the road after work, and he felt a responsibility to his employees that extended way beyond the front doors.

Abby felt much better after the discussion. She was grateful her mind was back one hundred percent, and she had no trouble dealing blackjack all day without slowing down. She knew no one would fault her if she wasn't quite up to speed, but she had a work ethic and years of experience that kept her on her game.

Lauren was still a mess, emotionally and physically. She was hiding out at Rider's house for the near future. She had refused to go to the hospital, but the police had taken pictures of her and noted her condition for the record just in case. She hadn't pressed charges, but Abby hoped she was recovering. The fact that she was safe was what mattered most.

Neither Yenin nor any of his cronies showed their faces inside The Crystal Palace all day. Thank God. Abby didn't let herself think about the Russian mafia while she worked and only gave their absence a sigh of relief when she took her hourly breaks and ate lunch.

She could do this. She felt stronger by the hour, and

when six o'clock rolled around, she was almost completely relaxed.

It was with this confidence that she walked out the front door of the building after her shift and rounded to the side to sit on a bench and wait for Zane to pick her up. He'd texted to let her know he would be there, but it would be closer to six-thirty. Fine with her. The weather was perfect. No way was she going to sit inside and wait. She tipped her head back and lifted her face toward the sky, closing her eyes and letting the late afternoon sun stream across her face.

She never managed to open her eyes again. The next thing she knew, a cloth covered her entire face, suffocating her with a horrible smell, and someone enormous had one hand covering her nose, mouth, and eyes, his other hand wrapped around her middle, hauling her off the bench.

Panic welled inside her, but it only lasted a moment before everything went black.

∾

Zane jogged from the fire station toward his car. He was late. He'd warned Abby he would be, but he hated leaving her waiting. He tugged his cell from his pocket and quickly typed in a text to let her know he was fifteen minutes out.

He jumped in his car and pulled onto the main road. The traffic was heavy, but he made it to The Crystal Palace in record time. Abby hadn't returned his text, but he hadn't said anything that required a response. Still, when he pulled up in front of the casino, he expected her to walk out the front door.

She did not.

He leaned to one side to extricate his phone from his pocket and found no new messages. He pulled around to the side street and parked before he sent her another quick text to let her know where he was and that he was coming inside.

No response.

He picked up his pace and headed for the front doors. However, his steps faltered when he spotted a man leaning against the edge of the building, smoking a cigarette and smirking at Zane. The man nodded, and Zane thought little of it until the guy spoke. "You lose something?" His thick Russian accent sent a chill down Zane's spine, and he stopped walking.

Zane stared at the guy, his heart beating wildly while the man took his time, inhaling again long and hard on his cigarette. Finally, he dropped it to his feet and crushed it with the toe of his shoe. "Cute little lady about this tall?" He held out a hand flat in the air. "Thick sexy hair, deep blue eyes a man could get lost in?"

Zane didn't move. *Fuck.*

The guy chuckled. "Yeah. You lost her all right. If you want to see her alive again, you'll come with me without making a scene."

Zane swallowed hard. *Fuck fuck fuck.* He glanced toward the front of the building, as though Abby would materialize, coming out the doors, a smile on her face, an apology about getting caught up in a conversation with coworkers.

That didn't happen.

The Russian guy was large, not as big as Zane, but fit. Zane doubted he could take the man in a fight. The guy would be trained to kill, not maim. And besides, if Zane started throwing punches, there was a good chance Abby's body would show up bludgeoned to death in an alley tomorrow morning.

Zane was fucked. Abby was more fucked.

The guy held out his hand. "Give me your phone."

Zane realized he still held it in his palm. Reluctantly, he handed it over. This scene went from bad to worse as the asshole pocketed his lifeline.

When the guy turned to walk toward the street, Zane followed, keeping his gaze pinned to the short spiky blond hair and broad shoulders in front of him.

He couldn't breathe. What did this asshole want with him? Or Abby for that matter?

The man led him to a black Cadillac with tinted windows. He opened the door to the back seat and motioned for Zane to get in.

Zane ducked and peered inside first. There was no one in the car except a driver, and that man was facing forward, paying him no attention.

With another silent *fuck,* he got in the back seat.

Spike shut the door with a finality that made Zane flinch. Normally he wasn't the sort of man who would fluster easily, but he'd also never been picked up by the Russian mob and shoved into a car against his will to be taken to an unknown location, either. Spike got in the front. He didn't bother to introduce himself, nor did he or the driver say another word to Zane. They exchanged a few words in Russian to each other, but that was it.

～

Abby blinked awake and moaned. She was uncomfortable and couldn't wrap her mind around why. Her hair lay across her face, and she started to reach for the lock to brush them away—only to come up short.

Instantly she was completely awake, her eyes wide open. The room was pitch dark. Her hands were secured behind her back. The arm she'd been lying on was asleep and tingling. Her head hurt. She tried to sit upright and relieve the pressure on her pinned arm.

Her ankles were also tied together.

Fear seeped into every corner of her body. She shivered, realizing she was also cold.

Her memory came slamming in. She'd been waiting outside the casino for Zane to pick her up. Stupid idea. Obviously. Someone had covered her face. That was the last thing she remembered.

She started to hyperventilate and tucked her chin down to her knees.

Where was she? Who kidnapped her? And what did they want?

After the events of the last week, anything was possible. If Anton Yenin had tried to kill her, there was every chance he had taken her now to finish the job.

Tears filled her eyes as she realized how much trouble she was in.

She screamed. Terror filled her more with every passing moment.

She heard not a single sound coming from anywhere.

"*Help.*" Her voice didn't sound loud enough to her ears. No one would hear her.

She scooted across the darkness, hoping to run into something. Finally, she hit a wall and wiggled up the side until she was standing. Her arms ached, and her wrists rubbed against whatever was tied around them. She twisted her fingers to attempt to figure out what the binding was.

Rope.

"Shit." Thick rope. Not something she could easily untie.

She hopped gingerly across the floor, keeping her hands to the wall as she moved. Her eyes didn't adjust to the darkness, which meant the room was very secure.

That made her feel even worse. What if no one ever came for her? Maybe the people who took her would leave her there for dead. It wouldn't take long.

She licked her lips. She was thirsty. Her throat hurt, burning as if she'd taken a drink of scotch without warning.

Finally, she felt a change in the wall, a metal surface. The door. She grabbed the handle and tried to turn it. Nothing. It was locked.

In a complete panic, she screamed again, as loud as she could. Not one sound followed her pleas for help.

Eventually she scooted back away from the door and slid down the wall to sit on her butt.

She dipped her head between her legs again and rested her forehead on her knees.

Think, Abby.

∼

Zane watched out the window as they headed south out of Vegas. They drove to an industrial site, too far away for Zane's taste, considering he was nervous as hell and couldn't stop pondering all the possible places Abby could be and how scared she must be. The area was covered with smoke stacks and metal buildings.

Zane gripped his knees as they drove, noting every detail. Obviously his chaperones had no interest in concealing their location. That fact didn't make Zane feel better. It only made him more suspicious of their intentions. The Russian mafia wouldn't reveal their hideouts unless they intended to kill whoever they lured in.

Eventually, they stopped next to a warehouse that was surely condemned or abandoned at some point. Zane recognized the place immediately and breathed a sigh of relief. It was a known location for the underground to use for fights. That meant half the city knew of its location. It was no secret.

Spike got out of the car first and opened the back door. "Come."

Zane climbed out of the car, scanning the area. Dozens of cars littered the street.

Spike started walking.

Zane followed, assuming that was the man's intended response.

Spike headed for a tall metal sliding door on the side of the aluminum building and tugged it open so it slid to the right. He stuck out a hand and Zane stepped inside as his guide slid the door shut behind him.

The warehouse was a wide open space filled with cigar smoke, filth, shouting, and the smell of blood and sweat. About a hundred people were inside, lounging around the cage in the center of the room where two men fought hard. Zane winced. This was not his kind of fighting. These guys followed no rules. He had a bad taste in his mouth. And there was a good chance the two guys in the ring were only sparring. None of the spectators seemed particularly interested in the outcome. They were just watching for the entertainment value.

Spike continued up a set of rickety stairs and to the left until he reached a room off to the side. He opened the door and ushered Zane to enter. This time he didn't follow. He shut the door behind Zane.

Zane squinted his eyes, still trying to recover from the sunlight. The room had more smoke in it than the main area of the warehouse, if that were possible.

It was an office of sorts. An enormous desk loomed on the far wall, and sitting behind it was Anton Yenin. "Ah, Zane Randolf. How nice of you to join me." He didn't stand from behind the desk, but he held out a hand to the chairs on the opposite side. "Please, sit."

"I'd rather not." Zane spread his feet wider and crossed his arms. "Where's Abby?"

"Now now, young man. It's rude to remain standing. Please, take a seat, and all will be explained."

Zane narrowed his gaze. He didn't like one aspect of this situation. Finally, he pulled a chair out and sat in it. "Talk, Yenin. Where is she?"

"Cute little brunette with blue eyes?"

"That's the one."

"She's safe."

"I want to see her for myself."

Yenin took a long puff off his cigar. "And you shall. All in good time."

"What do you want, Yenin?"

"Me? Oh, you misunderstand. I'm not the one who wants something."

Zane waited. Yenin was playing with him. There was no sense engaging the man any more than necessary.

"It's what my patrons want that matters."

"And what would that be?"

"A fighter."

Zane flinched. *Fuck.* "What makes you think I'll fight for you?"

"Oh, you'll fight for me all right. And you'll need to give it the best shot of your life if you ever want Abby to see the light of day again."

Fucking fuck. This goddamn asshole had Zane by the balls.

"You'll fight on my docket tonight. If you win, Abby

walks. If you lose, Abby's mine. She'd a cute thing. And it seems I've just lost my previous sex interest. I happen to have an opening." Yenin leaned forward, putting his elbows on the desk. "Ah, but you know all about that, don't you?"

"Why do you care if I win or lose?" Zane knew Yenin was in need of fresh meat. Wouldn't it be more of a crowd pleaser if Zane got his ass kicked?

"Because I want you to feel the gravity of what's at stake here. If you throw the fight or give up at any point, I'll have my cock buried so far in your woman's pussy by the end of the night, she'll never even remember your name."

Zane blew out a breath. He was fucked. Well and truly fucked. He was a good fighter. One of the best in the amateur circuits, but he was not trained to fight dirty, and he had no experience in a fight to the death. Zane leaned back in his chair. "You know good and well my chances of survival are slim."

"I do. That's why I needed your woman to add pressure to the arrangement."

God dammit. This had nothing to do with Abby. Yenin wanted Zane. "You've been following me."

Anton grinned. "Of course. I had my men follow Lauren right to Abby's door. Stupid bitch. I hit the lottery when they reported back who all came and went from that house." He winked.

Fuck. "When is this fight supposed to take place?"

Yenin glanced at his watch. "In about an hour. The first fight is at eight. You're second." Yenin stood and walked to a second door behind him. He yelled through the frame, "Erik, get my boy here suited up." He turned back to Zane, who had not moved from his chair.

"I want to see Abby first."

"You will, my boy. Later. Right now, I need you to follow Erik to the locker rooms and get some shorts."

175

Zane took a deep breath and stood. The last thing he wanted to do tonight was fight some asshole in a cage with no rules. Well, that was the second to last thing he wanted to do. The last thing he wanted was to let Abby fall prey to Anton Yenin. The thought of that man even touching her hand made him want to vomit.

~

Rider's cell phone rang as he shut down his computer to leave the precinct. He lifted it from the desk, his brow furrowed at the unknown number as he answered. "Henderson speaking."

"Rider. It's Mikhail." Rider could barely hear the man. It sounded like he was whispering in a noisy location.

"Who?"

"Mikhail. Mikhail Dudko. Listen to me. I don't have much time. Anton has Zane's woman."

Rider held the phone closer to his ear and sat back in his chair. "What? Where's Zane?"

"They have him too. They're at the old warehouse. You know the place. Huge fight night. You need to get your ass here fast and bring a shit-ton of backup. I gotta go." The line went dead.

Rider held the phone for several seconds longer, willing Dudko to say more.

"Fuck." He jumped from his seat and ran from his office.

~

Zane followed Erik without a word. The guy never spoke to him. He simply handed him a pair of shorts in the attached locker room and waited while Zane changed out of his clothes. When he was finished, he glared at Erik.

Erik paid no attention. "You want gloves?"

"Yes."

Erik chuckled. "Pussy." But he handed Zane a pair of gloves.

Zane followed Erik out to the center of the warehouse, glancing in every direction for any sign of Abby. He didn't see her, but he did see several other guys he knew— Russian guys he'd occasionally sparred with.

No one spoke to him. They kept their gazes focused on anything but him. He had no idea if every one of his Russian fighting friends was involved in this or not. And he couldn't help but wonder if the visit from Dmitry yesterday had anything to do with tonight's developments. There was little chance there was no connection.

Anton now sat on a high stool against the side of the cage. The first two fighters entered the ring while Erik led Zane over to Yenin.

"Where's Abby, Yenin. I'm not getting in that ring until I've seen her." He planted his feet, his hands on his hips, and stared hard at Yenin.

Yenin did nothing but smirk. "You'll do whatever the fuck I tell you to do. But as it happens, Abby will be here shortly. I don't want her to miss your fight."

Zane felt marginal relief at that notion.

The first fight began and Zane turned to watch. He recognized both men—Ivan Belinsky and Leo Gulin. They circled around the center, assessing each other for several moments after the bell rang.

Suddenly Yenin shouted, "Get a move on, boys. We don't have all night, and no one's paying to watch you two fucking dance."

Zane flinched as Leo threw the first punch. Ivan ducked, holding up one arm to block the attack. Something was off. Zane knew better. These guys were excellent fighters. They didn't miss, and they didn't need to block. He narrowed his gaze and watched as the dance continued.

Perhaps it was all part of their show. Staged.

Ivan swung around and planted a leg kick high on Leo's chest. Also a ruse. Ivan could easily kick a man in the head, especially before he was even winded.

Yenin stuck two fingers in his mouth and whistled loud. "My grandma can fight better than that. Get a fucking move on."

The crowd was also disappointed. Boos could be heard around the room.

Zane twisted his neck to see the crowd had doubled since he'd first arrived. Still not the level of patrons he would expect at an event like this, but certainly more than earlier.

What was Yenin's game?

And then he heard the betting. He narrowed his gaze on two men in the front as they shouted out their bets to a bookie walking by. Unbelievably fucking enormous bets. Not in the hundreds or even the thousands. This was a high-roller-only event.

The bookie made his rounds, taking bets from so many people at once, Zane didn't know how he could keep track.

Ivan and Leo upped the stakes, fighting hard. Five minutes went by, and then six. Nothing stopped the fight. There was no bell.

Zane scanned the ring. Unlike a sanctioned fight, the referee seemed to be more of a figurehead. He didn't stop the fight for any reason. If these guys didn't take a break soon, they would be exhausted.

Ivan got Leo in a chokehold and took him to the

ground. Leo bucked his hips and propelled himself back to standing before Ivan could get a good hold on him again.

They circled, their faces harder than when they'd started. Zane leaned closer. He couldn't believe what he thought he saw, so he wanted to be sure. And there it was again. Leo glanced at Yenin. He turned back to Ivan as though he had just caught the subtle instructions of his coach.

What the fuck?

Underground fighters did not take directions from anyone during a match. And Zane found it hard to believe either Ivan or Leo would ever take directions from Anton Yenin.

Sweat flew everywhere as the men fought. Zane tried to catch every subtle nuance, hoping to figure out what these guys were up to. He didn't catch anything as blatant as the glance at Yenin again.

Finally, Leo swung out his leg and took Ivan to the ground. They grappled for several tense moments until Ivan was pinned. Leo pummeled him hard. Just before it seemed Ivan was about to be knocked out, he tapped the floor to end the fight.

The crowd roared, some in protest, others in jubilee.

Yenin reached out and grabbed Zane's arm to get his attention. "You're up next."

Zane frowned at him. "I will see Abby first."

"You will. But get your ass in the cage. She'll be here."

Zane rounded to the other side of the cage where the gate was located. He climbed the steps and waited for Leo and Ivan to depart. Both men stared at him hard as they passed. They may have had a message in their glares, but either it was not a message Zane could read, or they had fucked with him for the last several years. Either way, it didn't change things.

~

Abby jerked her face up when the door swung open. She had resigned herself to the fact that she might die inside that room alone and scared.

She was almost relieved to find out that would not be the case.

The light from outside the room blinded her, and she squinted up to watch the enormous shadow of a man step in front of her.

He grabbed her biceps and yanked her to standing, roughly jerking her arms so hard she squealed at the pull of muscles.

"Shut up, bitch. Stop whimpering."

The burly man gripped one arm tighter and pulled her into the hall.

"Please. What do you want? I think you have the wrong person," she pleaded.

The man chuckled. "Yeah. I don't think so." He pressed her against the wall face first in the hall. "Hold still so I don't cut you."

She panicked as he twisted her hands higher. She felt the pull on her arms as he parted her hands with a flick of his wrist.

A second later he held the blade he'd used in front of her face, inches from her nose. "Stop moving."

Her eyes widened, and she held her breath.

His face was fierce, his brows furrowed. "Unless you want to hobble into the arena with your feet connected, you'll stand still and shut the fuck up."

Arena?

Where the hell was she? A fight? This guy was going to take her to a public place?

She nodded subtly and bit her lower lip hard enough to hurt.

The man kneeled in front of her and cut through the rope between her legs with the same speed.

She winced. That knife had to be sharp to so easily release her restraints. She didn't want it touching her skin.

He stood in front of her again, his breath hitting her face as he spoke. The scent of cigarette smoke filled her nose, forcing her to fight against the need to cringe away from his mouth. "You want that knife to cut through the soft skin of your face, bitch?" He cupped her chin roughly, his thumb dragging across her lower lip and up over her cheek.

"No." The one word was barely audible. She held her breath, praying it was the right answer.

"Then I suggest you follow me nicely and keep your mouth closed. Anton won't hesitate to kill you if you give him any trouble. You're the most expendable pawn in this game. You hear?"

Game? What game?

She nodded again.

Before she could gather another thought, the enormous brute grabbed her by one wrist and turned around to stomp down the hall, dragging her along behind him.

She had to jog to keep up, difficult in her low heels. Her legs hurt from the recently removed rope that cut into her ankles. She struggled to get her limbs to obey her commands.

~

Zane glanced around as he stepped into the ring. The referee dragged a wide mop around the center, doing a crude job of soaking up at least some of the sweat and blood. Zane had eyes for only two people, Abby and whoever the fuck his opponent would be.

Finally, he saw her. She walked into the room from behind Yenin, her arm in the firm grip of some Russian asshole Zane didn't know. She tried to wiggle free. He was hurting her. Her face was tight. She winced. But the asshole held her tighter and leaned in to share some stern words that made her mouth drop open and her eyes widen.

If Zane got both himself and Abby out of this alive, there was a good chance he would spend the rest of his life hunting these bastards to their early graves.

"You've seen her, Randolf. Now get to work."

Abby lifted her face and finally met Zane's gaze. He tried to communicate everything he felt with her, but there was no way for her to comprehend. Tears stained her cheeks, her mascara having run down to her neck. Her eyes were swollen and puffy from crying. She wore her black skirt and white tuxedo shirt from work. Her black hose were ripped in several places.

In addition, her hair was in wild disarray. He wondered how the hell they had taken her and what she had suffered since she'd been kidnapped.

She held his gaze, her eyes wide with concern and a sparkle of hope.

Zane just prayed he didn't let her down.

"Randolf," Yenin shouted. "Get to the fucking fighting now, or I'll stick my tongue down her throat right in front of you."

Zane jerked and turned around. What he found behind him took his breath away.

Dmitry Volikov.

Fuck fuck fuck.

Dmitry did not meet his gaze. He bounced around on his feet, popping his neck back and forth and stretching his arms in every direction as though nothing were out of the ordinary.

Zane didn't move a muscle to loosen up. He'd fought Dmitry before, at least sparring. But this had a dual taste of deception and betrayal. Was it possible that Dmitry was just as scammed here as Zane? Would the man betray him? Dmitry had insisted he did not work for Yenin. So, he either lied or he was in just as much deep shit.

Zane knew the Russian fighters had to work the underground. There was no way for them to avoid it. They needed the money. And somehow they were under Yenin's thumb. But this scene was beyond reason. Zane didn't know what to make of it.

A bell sounded, making Zane jerk to attention. He knew from watching the previous fight that was the only bell he would get. He glanced over his shoulder, risking a swing from Dmitry to pinpoint Abby. The asshole holding her arm had manhandled her onto a stool next to Yenin. He now stood back a pace in a stance that said if anyone even thought to fuck with him, they were dead.

Abby sat on her hands, her gaze on Zane, her lips trembling.

Zane gave her a nod and turned back around to find Dmitry bouncing toward him. Their gazes met, Zane's imploring, Dmitry's giving him nothing. If this guy fucked him over…

Yenin shouted again, and Dmitry threw a punch that nailed Zane in the cheek.

Zane stepped back and took a deep breath. He had to pull himself together and get serious. Anything other than a win wasn't an option. And although Zane may have outweighed Dmitry by a few pounds, he lacked the experience Dmitry had in the underground cage. He had no choice but to rely on strength and skill. Perhaps he would get lucky and outsmart Dmitry. There was about a one in a hundred chance, but it was his only option.

Zane spun around and kicked Dmitry high, hitting his shoulder.

Dmitry leaned at the last second, deflecting the majority of the kick. He swung a right hook, but Zane ducked and came back with two quick jabs to Dmitry's nose.

Dmitry stepped back two paces, shaking his head to clear his vision. And then he was back on his game. He swung again, narrowly missing Zane.

Yenin shouted from the side. "Come on, you pussies. Give my fans a show."

Zane tried to catch Dmitry's gaze to ascertain what the fuck was in his mind, but he never got the chance.

When they spun around, Zane caught a glimpse of Yenin with his arm around Abby, hauling her against his side. She pressed her palms to his chest, but he was way too strong for her. Zane saw nothing but red, which was exactly what Yenin intended.

Dmitry landed a hard kick to Zane's side, taking him to a knee. Dmitry wrapped his arm immediately around Zane's neck in a chokehold and leaned in close, trying to maneuver him to the ground. His teeth were gritted, but Zane heard his voice next to his ear all the same. "Fight, dammit."

Zane still didn't know whose side Dmitry was on, but he heard the words and bucked Dmitry off him. Zane jumped to his feet and bounced back a step to catch his breath. He'd never fought this long without a one-minute break. He had no idea how much time had passed, but he figured they were closing in on ten minutes.

The volume of the crowd increased, making Zane cringe. They were shouting bets. He wondered who they'd put their money on. Hell, he would put all his money on Dmitry. The man had more experience. However, the man didn't have quite the incentive Zane had. Dmitry didn't have a woman currently in the clutches of a deranged Russian mobster.

That was all Zane needed to catch a second wind. He came after Dmitry with a war cry, head-butting the man in the gut.

Dmitry flattened against the fence and fought to get out of his position while Zane punched him in the stomach.

Zane swung out his right leg, taking Dmitry down by knocking him off his feet. They grappled for position on the ground for long moments. Zane's left eye was swollen from an earlier punch. His vision was hampered. Somehow he managed to get the upper hand and landed on top of Dmitry's chest, squeezing his neck with both knees, hoping to make Dmitry pass out. He'd never choked anyone long enough to send them into blackness, but he'd also never fought under these circumstances.

Just before Dmitry's eyes rolled back in his head, all hell broke lose.

≈

Detective Jacobson hustled to the side of the building and flattened himself to the wall. He spoke succinctly into his mic. "Everyone in place? Unit one?"

"Good to go at the rear entrance."

"Unit two?"

"Copy. In position on the west side."

"Unit three?"

"Ditto. East side covered."

Jacobson motioned to the SWAT team that comprised his unit and gave his three men the signal to approach the front entrance on three. He said a silent prayer that none of his men got killed in this insanity. His objective was to create such total chaos that Zane and Abby could be rescued. His men had spotted both of them—Zane in the cage fighting Dmitry, Abby sitting on a stool next to Anton Yenin next to the fence.

"Show time in three," he announced.

~

A shot rang out.

Zane jerked his gaze upward to find the crowd screaming and turning in every direction.

Abby.

Zane swiveled to find her. The stool she'd been on was unoccupied. Yenin was also gone.

Another shot rang out. The screams around him increased.

Zane climbed off Dmitry's chest, heaving for breath, and he kneeled beside the Russian. He glanced down to find Dmitry clutching his throat and gasping for air, but not unconscious. Good. Zane needed to get the fuck out of this ring and find Abby. He didn't want to have to worry that he'd left a man behind for dead.

"Go," Dmitry whispered, his voice raspy. "Don't fucking let them take her to another location."

Zane jumped onto his feet. He ran toward the gate and flung it open. The referee stood next to it inside the cage, his eyes wide with fear. He paid no attention to Zane, which was fitting since he'd paid him no mind during the fight, either.

Zane scrambled down the stairs, but people blocked him in every direction. There were far more patrons now than had been in attendance for the first fight.

~

Abby struggled against Anton's grasp as he nearly dragged her away from the cage. He held her bicep tight and kept his head low, showing no interest in her well-being but keeping her by his side.

The room filled with chaos, smoke making it difficult to see. Her legs shook. Fear crawled up her spine as she twisted to look for Zane. She glimpsed him as he exited the cage, and then he was out of sight.

She needed to free herself from Yenin. That was her first priority. Letting the man take her somewhere else would mean death.

She jerked harder, surprised when her arm slipped free of his clutches. He turned toward her, but she jumped backward. His arm snaked out, but someone pushed between them, blocking Anton's attempt to secure her once more.

Abby pushed farther back into the room. She liked her chances better if she got away from Anton, even though there was gunfire inside the building. At least that foe was unknown.

Suddenly, another man wrapped his arm around her middle and lifted her off the ground. She screamed. It did no good. The entire metal building was filled with screaming. Her sounds blended in with the others. No one would notice or care that she was now in the clutches of someone else and being hauled against her will.

Weak and groggy from whatever she'd been drugged with, she hardly had the strength to fight back any longer. She grabbed the man's dark arm and tried to pry herself loose. He didn't budge. Like a bulldozer, he pushed people out of the way with clear purpose in mind.

In a moment she realized they were heading straight

for a back exit. She didn't know whether to be elated or more scared. Few people were heading toward that same door. Most had made their way toward the front of the building.

The man turned sideways as he pushed through the exit, carefully hugging Abby to his side to keep from ramming her into the frame.

"Please," she begged. "Put me down." She dug her nails into his forearm.

He didn't flinch. He also didn't say a word. As though she weighed nothing and was of no hindrance to him at all, he ran across the back lot. She couldn't imagine his intentions.

Suddenly a car swerved in front of them and came to a screeching halt.

Her new captor yanked the back door open, stuffed Abby inside, and climbed in behind her.

The car took off as she straightened herself and met his gaze. "Who are you?"

"Name's Leo. I'm a friend. Hang tight. I'm gonna get you out of here."

∼

Zane shoved people out of his way. Many of them grumbled and cussed at him as he met with their resistance. Few were as strong as him, though. He managed to make his way to the side of the room where both he and then Abby had emerged originally.

The crowd pushed and shoved for the main sliding door to the warehouse.

A third shot sounded.

Zane ducked, covering his head, and then he lifted his gaze, trying to figure out where the shots were coming from. The warehouse was too large and the echo intense. The shooter could be anywhere. He scanned wider and found nothing but a sea of men. Few women were in attendance. Abby was no longer among them.

Someone grabbed his arm and yanked hard.

Zane twisted to find Ivan had a hold of him. "This way." He nodded in the opposite direction and took off.

Zane followed. He had no better alternative. "Where are we going? I have to find Abby." He had no idea if Ivan gave a fuck about Abby or even Zane, but at this point Zane had no better option, so he followed Ivan even though Ivan didn't respond. Ivan began to jog. Zane stayed on his heels.

On the other side of the room, Ivan jerked open a door and the outside air filled the space. They burst outside. Zane's vision was less hampered without the thick smoke, but the sun was dipping low in the sky, making it difficult to make out anything specific.

And the crowd was almost as loud and thick outside as they had been inside.

Ivan kept running. He turned once to grab Zane's arm again. "Hurry."

Zane ran after him, feeling the burn in his lungs. He had nothing on his feet, and he wore only the borrowed shorts and gloves. He wished like hell he could remove the gloves to at least give himself the use of his hands, but there was no way he could pause to take care of the task.

A car peeled up to them, too close. It stopped inches from Zane's legs, and Ivan pulled the back door open. "Get in."

Zane hesitated. Could he trust Ivan? This evening was full of surprises. He had no way of knowing if anyone was who he thought they were at that point.

Ivan grabbed the hood of the car and swung inside. He

reached back out and wrapped his palm around Zane's wrist above the glove. "Get the fuck in the car, Zane. We need to get out of here."

Zane scrambled in behind Ivan, and the car peeled away, the door slamming shut as the driver hit the gas. "Where're we going?" Zane shouted. His ears were ringing and he could hardly hear himself over the pressure in his head. "I can't leave. I need to find Abby." He twisted toward Ivan. "I don't know what the fuck is going on, but you have to let me out. I need to go back." The driver made a sharp turn, slamming Zane into Ivan's side.

Ivan twisted to look out the back window. *"Duck!"* he screamed as he palmed the top of Zane's head and pulled him down.

The rear window shattered as a shot flew into the car.

Zane's breath caught in his lungs. He wasn't going to live through this, and there was no way Abby would survive. He nearly choked on this knowledge.

The driver careened to the right and then the left several times. A quick glance out the windshield told Zane the driver was trying to avoid hitting anyone. People were running in every direction. Many of them had a head start, having escaped the warehouse long before Zane.

Zane slouched down in the seat in case another bullet passed through.

Ivan reached under the seat and pulled out a .38. "You know how to use this?" he asked, handing it to Zane.

Zane nodded as the gun landed in his lap, and he worked his gloves free with his teeth. It was the first real indication he had that Ivan was on his side.

Ivan reached under the seat again and extracted another gun.

The car lurched to a stop, slamming both Zane and Ivan forward. The front door opened and Dmitry jumped in, shocking Zane. He slammed his hand on the dash. "Go. Fucking drive, man. Before we all get killed."

The driver shot off again. This time he swung wide to the right, and Zane had the chance to brace himself before landing on Ivan's lap.

"You have another one of those?" Dmitry asked, his neck twisted to the back to face Ivan.

"No." Ivan turned around and braced himself to shoot into the night through the back of the car. There was nothing left of the glass. It was in pieces all over the seat.

"What the fuck is going on?" Zane asked.

No one responded. They were all busy. The driver had eyes only for the road ahead. Ivan peered intently into the dusk, watching for whatever the fuck he thought he might need to shoot at. And Dmitry was on the phone.

He was on the *goddamn phone* for fuck's sake. He spoke in Russian, his voice carrying over the engine. Zane had no idea what he said, but suddenly he ended the call and turned to the back seat. He met Zane's gaze. "She's safe."

Zane exhaled on those words of hope. He had no way of knowing if Dmitry was telling the truth, but he had nothing else to trust, so he chose to catch his breath and wait.

Two minutes later, the car suddenly turned a sharp right, pulling off the main road onto another gravel drive. The ride was bumpy at the speed the driver kept up.

Zane was unprepared when they came to a sudden stop, the driver slamming on the breaks and squealing in a half circle until they were finally at rest.

Ivan reached across Zane and opened the door. He shoved it hard. "Go." He pointed to another car parked several yards away. "Hurry," he shouted. "We don't have all fucking night."

Zane jumped out. This was ludicrous. He didn't know

who to trust. He was completely at the mercy of these underground fighters, whom he'd always considered more of the good-guy class than the mob scene. He hoped his gut was right because he was now careening toward another vehicle at a full run with no certainty he wouldn't be left standing between the two of them left to die.

The back door opened and someone reached out to grab his hand again. Zane nearly fell into the car as it sped away almost before he was fully inside.

A whimper he knew well drew his attention at the same time Abby leaped across the seat and landed on him. She planted both hands on his face and held it, scanning as though ensuring he was actually there and alive.

Zane wasn't so sure himself at that point.

This car was bigger, a limo. The man who'd pulled him inside sat across from them.

The driver hit the gas even harder than the first crazy driver, but this time no one shot at them and the car moved in a more direct path to wherever.

Abby gripped his face harder, crying so loud, Zane couldn't hear anything the other man said.

Zane set his hands on her back and pulled her close to his chest, taking his first real breath in forever. She was right there, on his lap, alive. He closed his eyes for a second and then opened them to find Leo across from him.

CHAPTER 16

Abby was a mess. She'd never been so scared in her life. She wasn't at all sure she wouldn't still suffer from a stroke. And they weren't out of danger yet. The car was moving fast, weaving back and forth with the speed.

She squeezed Zane too hard. It had to hurt. And she didn't care.

"Baby." He soothed her back, but she wasn't consolable. Far from it. "It's okay. I'm right here."

She lifted her face and stared at him again, making sure her eyes hadn't deceived her. She didn't care that she straddled his lap and her skirt rose up her hips. She only cared about touching him everywhere, ensuring herself he was alive and unharmed.

"Are you hurt?" he asked. He pulled her away from him a few inches and scanned down her front.

"No." She shook her head. "*You* are." She touched his cheek below his swollen eye, wincing. He needed a doctor.

"I'm fine." He smoothed his hands up her back until he threaded them into her hair and pull the long waves away from her face. His thumbs hit her cheeks, wiping away the tears. They didn't stop flowing. She knew she was hysterical. She couldn't stop it. She kept staring at him, glancing up and down, wondering if her eyes were deceiving her.

"Baby, you're okay." He didn't sound convincing.

She knew they were anything but okay. All she cared about was that she had a grip on Zane.

A phone rang. The man behind her who said his name was Leo answered. "Yes... Yes... Two minutes..." That was it.

Abby held her breath again. Two minutes until what?

Zane grabbed her face tighter. "Abby, look at me."

She met his gaze, finding it difficult to concentrate on any one particular spot.

"Abby, you're okay," he repeated, though she knew otherwise. "Breathe, baby."

She inhaled deeply and then let it out.

The car came to a sudden halt. Zane grabbed her back firmly so she wouldn't fall off his lap.

She twisted toward the door as it was yanked open from outside. The man who leaned in made the breath whoosh from her lungs.

"About time you guys got here." Rider grinned and reached for Abby, helping her off Zane's lap and out of the limo.

She didn't release her grip on Zane's arm, and he followed her out of the car. He dipped his head back inside to say something to Leo, and then the car sped away.

Abby lifted her gaze to find them once again on an abandoned road. It was dark, but this time she was with people she knew she could trust. Rider eased her toward a police cruiser.

Zane wrapped his arm around her and helped her into the backseat before sliding in next to her. She started to shake and then giant sobs that wouldn't stop took over her frame.

Zane belted her into the car and then pulled her head against his chest. It almost seemed absurd to take that small step to protect themselves after what they'd been through. Zane tipped her head back. "Baby, I'm here," he repeated. "You're safe now."

The cruiser sped away, not nearly as erratically as the previous car she'd been in.

Rider sat in the front passenger seat, twisting around to face them. Another officer drove.

Abby did her best to stop sobbing. She knew there were a thousand things that needed to be said.

"How did you find us?" Zane began.

"Mikhail called me," Rider said. "What the fuck happened?"

Abby could feel her chest pounding hard as she held on to Zane's bare chest and listened to what he knew. She tried to focus. Zane explained how he'd come to pick her up from work and found some Russian guy threatening him instead. Next he moved on to everything she'd witnessed in the warehouse.

Zane lifted her hair off her shoulders and furrowed his brow as he stared at her. "Rest. You can tell us your end when we get to the station."

When they finally pulled up to the police station, Abby was relatively calm. At least she managed to walk inside of her own accord, and she had on clothes. Zane wore nothing but boxing shorts and he was a complete mess. He paid no attention to his own plight though, clearly only caring about her as he held her hand and angled her to follow Rider.

A hush fell over everyone as they walked through the station, several officers lifting their gazes to stare.

Rider led them to a locker room. No one was inside.

Zane lifted Abby onto the counter at a row of sinks and quickly pulled off a row of paper towels from the dispenser to soak with warm water. He wiped her cheeks while she stared at him.

It took her a minute to process what was happening. Finally she grabbed the wad of wet towels from his hand. "Zane, I'm fine. It's just makeup." She glanced in the mirror and winced. She did look pretty bad, but at least she wasn't injured. She turned back to face Zane.

He stopped moving, his shoulders slumping and his chest heaving while he came down from an adrenaline high right in front of her. He held her gaze and took the last strides to plaster himself against the counter between her legs, tugging her head against his slick chest.

She didn't give a fuck about sweat or blood. All she cared about was listening to his heart beating under her ear.

Rider cleared his throat behind them. "I'll give you two a minute. I set some clothes behind you."

Abby heard him leave the room, the door shutting with a snick. She would have resumed crying if there had been tears left to fall.

Finally, Zane lifted his face. "I was so fucking petrified."

"I know." She held his cheeks in her palms.

"If anything had happened to you…"

"It didn't."

"Did that jackass hurt you?"

"No. Not like you're thinking." She reached up his face to touch his eye. "You need to have this looked at."

"I've had worse. It'll be fine. I just need a shower. Most of the blood will wash away. It's not all mine." He grinned.

Abby glanced past him toward the row of open showers across the room. "Go. I'm fine."

Zane followed her gaze. "I'm not leaving you to shower right now."

"Of course you're not. I'm gonna stand right next to you. But you need to wash away all that blood so I can stop freaking out."

Zane stepped back and Abby hopped down from the counter. She took his hand and pulled him along. When she got to the edge of the tiled row of showers, she leaned against the wall. "Go to it." She pointed inside.

Zane smirked. "You're gonna watch."

"Yep."

"That's a lot of pressure for a man."

"More than fighting your friend in a fake set up to win back your woman?"

"Well, put that way, no." He turned on the water and shrugged out of his shorts.

Abby watched as he stepped under the steaming spray. His tight ass made her swallow a lump in her throat. He was so fucking sexy. The muscles of his back rippled as he reached for the soap dispenser and squirted some in his palm. He looked immediately better from just rinsing.

Her heart rate slowed as she realized he was right. Most of the blood had not been his. When he turned around, she sucked in a breath. His front was so much more magnificent, all abs and pecs and cock. God, she was lucky. She leaned her head against the wall and watched the show. As long as she didn't stare too hard at his swollen eye, she could convince herself this never happened. Sort of.

When Zane shut off the water, she handed him a towel from the shelf against the wall. He rubbed it over his head and then wrapped it around his body. Immediately he moved back into her space, pinning her to the wall with his arms around her and his forehead against hers. "Better?"

197

"Immensely. You almost look human."

"So, sweaty bloody guys aren't your thing?"

"Not so much." She smiled, wanting to kiss him, but afraid to hurt his obviously cracked lip.

He closed the last few inches himself and took her mouth. His kiss was gentle and sweet, reminding her they were both okay. They lived, and they would survive. Now, she just wanted to make their statements to the police and get the hell back to his house. She felt gross herself, but she didn't want to shower here at the precinct.

Zane barely stopped touching her while they made their way over to the bench by the sinks. He managed to shrug into the sweats and T-shirt Rider left him while still strumming a thumb up her arm or across her face. When he sat to put on the pair of tennis shoes, he tugged her down next to him.

Before they left the room, Zane pulled her close again. "I'm never going to be able to let you out of my sight again. You realize that, right?"

"I feel the same about you, but I'm thinking it will be tough to do our jobs if we stay pinned together."

"Maybe they need an EMT at the casino, one who guards the blackjack tables."

She giggled. "Maybe."

When they finally stepped back into the main section of the police station, Abby was shocked to see her boss and Lauren both in a conference room across the hall.

Rider stood outside. He opened the door and nodded for Zane and Abby to go in.

Lauren jumped up and crossed toward Abby, throwing her arms around Abby's neck. "Oh God. Abby. I'm so sorry."

Abby hugged her back and then met her gaze. "Not your fault."

"Somehow I got you into this mess. I should have listened to you from the start and broke things off with Anton. Now look what happened." Lauren's face looked much better than it had yesterday. She was still a mess and would have a black eye to rival Zane's, but at least the swelling had gone down and she could see.

Rider spoke up from his side of the room. "I'm not convinced both of you aren't pawns in a much larger scheme."

Abby's boss came around the table next. "And I can't believe all this keeps happening in my casino. Abby, are you okay?"

She nodded. "I'm not a very reliable employee, though. I was only there a month before I needed a week off for a car accident, and then at the end of my first day back I manage to get kidnapped." She tried to smile.

"Yeah, well, in both cases your danger was caused by patrons to my establishment. If we don't put an end to this, I'll never be able to hire waitresses and dealers."

The door to the conference room opened again, and the officer in charge of the investigation, Jacobson, stepped in. He shook Zane's hand and then reached for Abby's, nodding at the other occupants. "Everybody. Please sit. Let's sort this out. I need to hear from Abby, and then we'll go over a few things." He turned toward Abby again. "You want to make your statement in my office? You don't have to do this in front of everyone."

She shook her head. "No. I'm fine. Here is fine." She sat in a chair Zane pulled out for her, perched on the edge, wishing she could just go home.

"Okay. Give me an account of what happened from your eyes first." Jacobson pulled out a notepad and a pen and set a recording device on the table.

"Unfortunately, I have very little to tell. I was waiting

outside The Crystal Palace for Zane to pick me up." She lifted her gaze when Zane squeezed her hand. "I know, stupid, but I thought it was safe. Anyway, some guy grabbed me by the face and smothered me with something that knocked me out fast. I never saw him. When I woke up, I was alone in a dark room, my wrists tied behind my back and my ankles tied together. I screamed, but no one heard me. Or no one cared.

"Eventually, the door opened and some Russian guy with spiky blond hair cut me free and yanked me to my feet. He cut me free and dragged me into the arena where I saw Zane in the cage about to fight." Renewed tears fell as she told the tale.

Zane wrapped an arm around her shoulders and pulled her against his chest until she was half on the chair that was butted against his.

Jacobson spoke again. "Abby, we'll need a doctor to do a blood test to find out what they gave you. It could prove to be vital evidence later."

She nodded.

The door to the room opened, making Abby twist in her seat to see who was there. She was jittery, and with good reason.

The man who leaned in wasn't someone she'd met before. He appeared to be about fifty, and he glanced around before meeting Jacobson's gaze. "I need a word." He backed out of the room.

Jacobson stood and followed, apologizing over his shoulder. "Be right back." He shut the door behind him, but Abby could see him speaking with the older man outside the long window between the conference room and the hall.

No one said a word.

Jacobson reentered a few minutes later. "Sorry about

that. That was Chief Edwards, by the way." He looked at Abby and then Zane. "They picked up Anton."

Zane gripped Abby tighter. "Jesus. Thank God." He turned toward Rider. "How the hell did all this go down? I was so caught up in the mayhem, I didn't even know what happened. There were shots fired, and then everyone started running."

Rider leaned forward onto his elbows. "I got a call from Mikhail Dudko."

"Who's that?" Abby interrupted.

"Another Russian fighter. One of the good guys. I think," Rider explained. "Anyway, he happened to see one of Anton's minions carrying a woman into a secure room. She was unconscious."

"Yeah. She was me," Abby added, as though this weren't obvious.

Rider nodded. "He didn't know who you were at the time. But a few minutes later he passed by Anton's office and heard the man telling Zane he had to fight and win to get his woman back."

Zane squeezed Abby's shoulder. "And he called you?"

Rider nodded again. "Like I said, he's one of the presumed good guys. I'm not sure why these guys fight for Yenin, but he has some sort of hold over them. Other than that illegal activity, it seems there are a group of fighters who live relatively clean lives. I don't think they do Yenin's dirty work. They stay low, fight, and send every dime they can afford back to Russia."

"How do you know all this?" Zane asked.

Jacobson chimed in next. "We've been following these guys for over a year. We know when every Russian in this city eats and when they take a shit." He winced and glanced at Abby. "Sorry."

Rider continued. "Anyway, Mikhail called me. He knew

something horrible was about to go down, and neither him nor any of the other guys he trains with are interested in participating in anything that sinister."

"Why did he call you?" Abby asked.

"Probably because he had my number." Rider shrugged and glanced at Zane. "I'm sure he has yours too, but you were busy."

"Quite." Zane rolled his eyes. He turned toward Abby. "Like I've told you, we train with these guys sometimes. They often come to the gym and work with us. Even though they fight in unsanctioned venues, they need people to train with that will give them a challenge. We have each other's numbers."

Abby bit her lip. This was beyond complicated.

Rider cleared his throat. "So, I called Jacobson, and then I jumped in the car with an officer who was on duty and headed toward the warehouse myself. I knew the SWAT team would move in and take over. I wanted to be close by in case…" His voice trailed off. The "in case" was obvious. Zane was his friend. If there had been anything he could do, Abby was sure he would have done it. In fact he had.

Zane reached for a bottle of water from the center of the table and twisted the cap off with one hand. He took a long drink and then handed it to Abby. "So I fought Dmitry. Before that, Leo fought Ivan. I watched them. They were the ones to help get me out of there and meet up with Abby and then Rider."

Abby twisted in his arms. "The man who must be Leo grabbed me the first second I was separated from Anton. He lifted me in his arms and ran from the building. I don't know why I trusted him, but eventually I stopped fighting. I was out of options, and I didn't want to get shot. After he shoved me into the limo and we took off, he explained that he was going to make sure I met up with you." She gripped

Zane's forearm, her heart pounding once again. The adrenaline wouldn't stop.

"I was in a similar situation relying on Ivan. He drove to an arranged spot, and that's when I was reunited with Abby in Leo's car." Zane stared at Jacobson.

"Where was Yenin? How did you get separated from him?" Jacobson asked Abby.

"I have no idea. After the first gun shot rang out, he jumped from his stool and fled. He tried to tug me along, but I broke free."

"Who fired the first shots?" Zane asked.

"Our guys," Jacobson answered. "They were shot into the air to create a diversion. We knew Abby was inside that warehouse, and then we saw you in the cage," he said to Zane. "When people scrambled, it made it much easier to take down Yenin."

"Wasn't he armed?" Zane asked.

"He wasn't personally armed. Frankly, I think he's a pussy. His entourage of men were armed, but they were stationed at the doors, not next to him. He was easy to spot because he perched himself front and center on a stool with an unwilling woman at his side." Jacobson stood. "I'm sorry. I need to wrap this up and go deal with Yenin. The streets of Vegas will be a little bit safer tonight." He turned toward Abby. "I'll check in with you tomorrow to see if there's any other detail you remember." And with that, Jacobson was gone.

A quiet woman with kind eyes came in as soon as Jacobson left. She set several items on the table and turned toward Abby. "You're Abby Burns, right?"

"Yeah." Abby rolled up her sleeve, realizing this woman was taking her blood sample.

"This'll just take a second." Abby turned toward Zane

and sighed, and moments later the woman was done. She left hastily.

Rider turned toward Zane and Abby. "Why don't I take you two home? I'm sure you could use some sleep." He stood. "We can pick up with anything new tomorrow."

Abby's boss stood also. "I'll check in with you in a few days, Abby. Stay home. Recuperate. Don't worry about your job. It isn't going anywhere."

"Thank you, sir. I appreciate that."

Her boss left first.

Zane helped Abby to her feet. She looked at Lauren. "Are you sure you're okay?"

"I'm fine."

Rider nodded. "I'll take her back to my house for the night. I think she'll be safe now. The reality is, although I'm sure Anton was originally out for revenge against Lauren, in the end this was about money. He saw an opportunity to make a buck off Zane and he took it."

"I heard some of the bets people were making. They were outrageous," Zane added.

Abby's brain felt like it actually hurt. Too much information to process. She doubted she'd be able to fall asleep for a week. But that wasn't going to keep her from trying. She needed a shower and a bed in that order. She lifted her gaze to Zane. "Can we go home?"

"Yeah, baby." He held her firmly against his side.

Rider stepped toward the door. "Let's get you guys home. I'll send some guys to get your car from the casino."

CHAPTER 17

Abby couldn't stop shaking. She rode in the back of the squad car with Zane. Rider drove. Even though it was Vegas and the air was still warm late at night, she couldn't stop the chill she felt.

Zane helped her into the house and immediately led her to the bathroom. He flipped on the hot water to fill the tub and then turned toward her. "Let's take a bath. The warmth might help you stop shaking."

The idea sounded heavenly. She wanted to wash off the filth of being in the presence of Yenin.

Zane worked the buttons free down her tuxedo shirt and eased it over her shoulders. "Are you injured anywhere?" He lifted her wrists and checked both sides. They were pink from being tied together, but the skin wasn't broken.

"I don't think so."

Zane lowered the zipper on her skirt next, and it fell to the floor.

Forcing her brain to cooperate, Abby kicked off her shoes and stripped off her ruined hose. While Zane removed his own clothes, she managed to divest herself of her panties and bra too.

Zane took her hand and helped her into the tub, climbing in behind her. He settled on one end and tugged her down between his legs so her back rested against his front.

Immediately the hot water soothed. She took several deep breaths and closed her eyes as some of the tension leaked out of her.

Zane pressed her head against his shoulder and kissed her temple from the side. "Relax, baby. Your entire body is stiff."

"You fought for me," she whispered as the events of the evening crashed in from all sides.

"What?"

"You fought for me. You would have beaten Dmitry in order to win me." She twisted her neck and sat up straighter to meet his gaze. "Oh my God, you *fought* for me." She nearly shrieked that time.

Zane gave a wry smile. "Of course I did."

This was serious. Zane could have been injured or even killed trying to save her.

He brushed her hair away from her face and furrowed his brow. "What's the matter?"

"What if the police hadn't arrived? What if you had lost? What if your friend had killed you?"

"Well, first of all, it wasn't quite that dramatic because like you said, Dmitry is my friend. He wouldn't have let me lose."

Abby gasped. "He would have let you win?"

"I believe so. It sure seemed that way. We had to put on a good show, but in the end he wouldn't have let anything happen to you."

"In the end he saved my ass, and yours."

"Yes, he did."

She leaned back against him. "I'm never going to be able to sleep. I don't even think I'll ever be able to turn out the lights."

Zane reached for the soap and started washing her. "You will. Eventually. It's understandable. Don't beat yourself up over this. You were kidnapped and held hostage. People don't rebound from that in an hour."

She closed her eyes and let him wash her. It felt good to be pampered. And unbelievably her body came alive under his touch. She didn't think she would be capable of anything sexual after what she'd been through. But she was wrong.

When they were both clean, Zane didn't move to get out. In fact, he added to the hot water and eased her back against him again. He stroked his fingers up and down her belly forever, gradually reaching higher and lower with each pass until he came close to her clit and grazed the undersides of her breasts.

Her breathing increased. She finally felt warm. Hot in fact.

"Abby?" Zane whispered.

"Yeah?"

"Sub for me."

"What do you mean?"

"Let me dominate you. Trust me to make your body hum."

"Isn't that what you always do?" How was this different?

"Mmm. I want to up the stakes a bit. It will help you release the tension." He kissed her neck, and she tipped her head the other way to give him more space.

"Okay." Her nipples stood at attention, and her pussy flooded under the water. His words alone, the promises he made, drove her arousal sky high. She clenched her legs together between his.

Zane nibbled a path up her neck to her ear. "I'm gonna push you. I want you to trust me. You won't regret it."

"Okay." The word came out on a weak breath.

Zane smoothed his hands down her thighs until he reached her knees. He lifted her legs and draped them over his own, spreading her wide.

Abby moaned, already so horny it hurt.

Zane set his palms on her inner thighs and stroked the sensitive skin without touching her center. He continued to kiss her ear until she shivered. He lifted his knees, forcing her legs wider. "So sexy, baby. I love when you're open for me like this."

She let her head roll farther to the side as his breath hit her ear. Her arms were pinned at her sides under his.

When his fingers finally grazed her lower lips, she lifted her hips.

Zane grasped her thighs again and held her down. "Uh uh. Let me, baby." He resumed his light touches to her outer sex.

She needed more. She willed him to stroke deeper, her hands fisted at her sides.

Instead Zane abandoned her pussy altogether and smoothed his hands up her body until he cupped her breasts, his thumbs flicking over her nipples. "Love how your breasts swell under my touch." He nibbled around her ear again.

She didn't respond, though if she had, it might have been to scream from frustration. She could feel his cock pressing into her lower back. Why didn't he get the show on the road and press into her?

He set his lips on her ear again. "Let's go to the bedroom, baby. The water's gonna get cold again."

Abby nodded.

Zane wiggled out from under her and stood, hauling her limp body up with his. He lifted her from the tub and stood her on the mat. "You steady?" he asked before releasing her.

"Barely."

Zane stepped out behind her and grabbed two fluffy towels, handing her one while he dried with the other.

When she finished, she started to wrap the towel around her middle. It felt awesome to be clean. Just knowing Anton touched her skin anywhere made her sick to her stomach.

Zane grabbed the towel before she finished and set it on the counter. "You won't need that."

He set his on top of hers and lured her toward the bedroom by the hand. When he reached the bed, he sat on the edge and pulled her between his legs, facing him. He cupped her face with both hands, forcing her to meet his gaze. "Trust me?" he asked for the third time.

She nodded. "Of course."

"I want to spank you."

She flinched, but held his gaze. He didn't allow otherwise.

"It can be an amazing way to release stress. I know you've never tried it, but until you have, you can't realize the adrenaline rush. After what you've been through tonight, you'll relax much better after submitting to me."

She chewed on the inside of her cheek. It seemed ludicrous. How could she possibly release stress by letting someone spank her? She was a grown woman.

"Remember the woman you saw at the club on the cross?"

She nodded. That woman had indeed been enjoying

herself. She seemed to have slipped into a trance. "She was like hypnotized or something."

Zane smiled. "It's called subspace. People often describe it as feeling like they disconnected from their body, or like they have a natural high. It can be incredibly pleasant."

"I don't know, Zane. That's a huge step."

"I know it is, baby." He pulled her face closer. "And I think you can handle it. If it gets to be too much, use a safe word. *Red*. But I'm a good judge of where you're at. I would never push you further than I thought you could handle."

She shivered, once again, feeling a chill that wasn't from the room.

Zane pulled her the last few inches and kissed her gently on the lips.

She relaxed against him, grabbing his forearms as he deepened the kiss to something much headier. His tongue delved between her lips, and she melted into his taste. Gradually she relaxed enough to slump against his front. Her nipples grazed his chest, making her moan.

Zane broke off the kiss. "Will you let me spank you, baby?"

She hesitated. "You'll stop if I don't like it?"

"Absolutely."

She stared at him.

"What's the worst that can happen?"

"I disappoint you," she muttered. That was her main concern. What if she hated it and it was something Zane really needed in their relationship? She was afraid to find out. She really liked him. She more than liked him. She was in love with him. No way would she say it out loud yet, but she knew it deep inside. It scared the hell out of her to take this next step. So much more important than sleeping with him.

"Oh, baby. Never." He narrowed his gaze and lifted her

chin with his thumb. "Never. Do you realize how much you mean to me? I know we've only known each other a few weeks, but it seems like longer. I can't remember what it was like not to be with you. I don't even want to know. I would never be disappointed in you. If you don't like it, we won't do it again. Your call entirely. I don't want you to think spanking you is a deal breaker. Not even close. I'm getting my cues from you. I think you'll enjoy it. I think tonight is the perfect opportunity for you to give it a try. Your entire body is revved and anxious. Let me take that stress away."

His words rang in her head. *Do you realize how much you mean to me? I don't want you to think spanking you is a deal breaker. Not even close...* She found herself nodding consent. Worst case, she called *red* and Zane stopped. She knew he would.

"I need you to say it out loud, baby." His intense gaze still bore into her.

"Please spank me." That sounded so awkward.

Zane smiled. "Safe word?"

"Red."

"Good girl. Use it. Nothing we ever do or don't do will change the way I feel about you. If you never submitted to me again, I'd still be by your side. Ecstatic like I won the lottery. Use the safe word."

"Okay." She swallowed. He meant every word. And those words meant the world to her.

Zane gently nudged her back a step and pulled his legs closer while he guided her to one side and then pressed her lower back so she leaned over his lap. "Lie across my thighs, baby."

His lap? He was going to spank her over his knees? This hadn't occurred to her. The idea was so foreign, she'd only been able to visualize the woman on the cross at the club.

Instantly wetness filled her pussy. She took a deep breath, unable to understand why she would be aroused by the notion. She was losing her mind.

Zane helped her lie across him so her upper body rested at a slight angle on the bed at his side. Her toes still reached the ground. When he had her where he wanted her, he set one hand on her lower back and squeezed her butt cheeks with the other. "No pain from the puncture?"

She shook her head, biting her lower lip. Her pussy flooded with need as he stroked her skin.

His hand massaged up and down her ass and thighs for so long, she almost grew too relaxed under his touch. "I'm gonna start easy and build up."

She didn't respond. Her hair almost concealed her face as it fell across her cheek.

The first swat was easy enough. Still she flinched. Her thighs stiffened. The second spank landed on her other cheek, and then Zane rubbed her ass again. She felt the slight burn. It wasn't so bad.

His hand roamed up and down her thighs. And then he swatted her again, harder this time.

Abby jerked under his spread fingers on her lower back. The sting raced up her spine and down her legs. It wasn't unpleasant, though. In fact, she felt warmer. Even her face felt heated.

Zane struck her again, and then squeezed her cheek. "You okay, Abby?"

"Mmm hmm." She wasn't really sure what she was. She teetered on the edge of someplace unrecognizable. Her mind warred between finding his actions humiliating and arousing. She gritted her teeth as the wetness at her entrance increased.

His next two strikes landed at the juncture of her thighs and her ass cheeks.

There was no mistaking the direct effect on her clit. Her pussy throbbed with need. Her eyes opened wide at the shock. How was she aroused?

Zane squeezed her cheeks again, one at a time, rougher than before. His touch soothed. "Baby, the pink marks are so sexy. You're doing so good. Can you take more?"

She nodded against the mattress.

"Words, baby. Tell me where you are."

"I'm okay," she whispered.

"Good girl." His hand landed again, harder this time. And again.

She lost count. Was that eight? How many times would he spank her? She felt the burn as each strike landed on an earlier one. The next spank landed low and center.

Abby moaned. She couldn't prevent it from happening. Holy mother of God she was aroused. Her pussy throbbed with need.

Zane's hand remained in that spot, rubbing, reaching lower. He changed his direction and reached between her legs. "Are you wet, baby?" His middle fingers slipped between her folds and stroked through her wetness. "Oh, baby. Do you know how hot that is?"

She didn't respond to either question. They were rhetorical, anyway.

Zane thrust two fingers inside her and scissored them with no warning. She almost came. Her spine stiffened. She turned her face so her forehead rested on the bed, and her hair fell around her face.

Oh God.

His hand disappeared just as quickly, and he slapped both cheeks at the juncture to her thighs in quick succession.

Abby let out a yelp. She grabbed the blankets with both hands at the sides of her face and fisted the material.

She was going to come. Hard. While Zane spanked her. *Shit.*

"That's it, baby. Let it go." He spanked both thighs next and then thrust his fingers into her again with no warning.

Abby screamed into the mattress, muffling her sound as much as possible when she heard her voice. Her pussy gripped his fingers as her orgasm raced through her system. There was no way to stop it.

Zane fucked her fast with his hand. Before the waves of release were over, he removed his fingers and lifted her off his lap, turning her at an angle. "Crawl into the center of the bed, baby. Get up on all fours."

Her body still pulsed. She barely had the motor skills to do as he said. The bed sprang up when he stood, and then she heard the faint sound of a condom wrapper. Two seconds later, Zane crawled up behind her, nudged her knees open wide, and gripped her hips. His cock plunged into her so fast, she rocked forward. She lowered her forehead to the bed once again, unable to hold it up. Her arms shook so badly they seemed to not have enough blood flow to properly follow directions.

He thrust fast, his grip holding her steady. She could hear him moaning.

She held rigid when she realized a second orgasm was looming on the heels of the first that had never fully ended.

"So tight," he gritted out. "Your pussy has a grip on me. I'm not gonna last." His words were muttered. Clipped. Every time his cock was fully seated, she felt the sting of his body flattening against her enflamed ass.

Zane released one hip and reached around her belly to stroke her clit. That was enough to blur her vision. *"Zane,"* she yelled, her voice stopped by the bed.

"Come for me, baby." His thumb landed on her clit and

pressed while his cock thrust one final time deep inside her.

As she went over the edge, she felt him go stiff. Her pussy gripped his cock tight as he pulsed his orgasm deep inside her.

Her ears rang as she crested the top and slowly floated back to earth. The first thing she noticed was her entire body shook as though she were once again cold. Her limbs probably were cold, from lack of blood flow.

Zane leaned over her body and nudged her to fall to her side as he took her down with him.

She lay spooned by him, his cock still inside her. And she'd never been more consumed by a man. She fought to catch her breath while Zane brushed her thick hair from her face.

His lips landed on her temple, and then he dropped his head to the side behind hers. "So sexy." His hand danced up and down her arm, rubbing gently. Finally he threaded his fingers with hers from the back of her hand and tucked both their hands around her under her chest. "Hottest thing I've ever experienced. You sure you've never been spanked before?" he teased.

She was stunned herself. Too stunned to speak in fact. Almost embarrassed. It seemed as though she had separated from her body and was just now coming back into it.

Finally Zane gave her a squeeze and let himself slide out of her. "Be right back. Don't move." He crawled from the bed and padded to the attached bath.

She listened to the sound of the water running for a few minutes, and then he shut it off and came back.

He rolled her onto her back gently and pressed her knees open wide.

She winced at the sting of the bedding beneath her ass.

Her gaze landed on his head as he cleaned her up. He was so tender. Emotion overwhelmed her as she watched the way he cared for her. Her knees were like noodles. She couldn't lift them to bring them back together.

When he finished, he set the cloth aside and helped her turn onto her belly. The next thing she knew he was massaging her ass again, this time with a cool substance that he spread against her heated skin. It felt wonderful, and she sighed several times.

She let him manipulate her body.

Zane helped her flip over onto her back again and pushed her thighs wide. He climbed over her between her legs and reached across to flip off the bedside lamp. He hovered his torso over her body and kissed her lips. "You didn't use that safe word."

"You didn't mention I would get aroused."

He shrugged, a coy grin spreading on his face. "I thought it might happen, but not everyone needs the sexual part. Some people are content with the release from the spanking alone."

"I wasn't expecting that."

"I know. It's not possible to understand until you do it." He kissed her lips again. "So fucking beautiful, baby. I'm humbled."

"I'm a little embarrassed."

"Don't be." He set his forehead on hers. "It's perfectly normal. And do you feel more relaxed now?"

"Yeah, but two orgasms would do that."

He set his lips on hers again and spoke against her mouth. "Come on. Admit it. That was way better than two vanilla orgasms."

"Scale of one to ten?"

"Yeah?"

"Fifty."

LUST

He grinned again and then kissed her senseless. When he broke the kiss minutes later, he climbed over her leg and lay down on his back. He hauled her over so she had her front against his side, half sprawled over the top of him. "Think you can sleep now?"

"Mmm hmm." Not a doubt anymore.

He squeezed her tighter and then reached down to pull the covers over them. His hand drifted down to her ass and lightly stroked the skin. "You okay, baby?"

"Mmm hmm," she repeated. *Better than.*

Zane kissed the top of her head. "That was a subspace."

She smiled against his chest. If that was a subspace, she could live with it. It felt like everything he'd described and more. Entering into a serious relationship with Zane was not going to be a hardship. She started to drift asleep, and then she was reminded of something. "You fought for me..."

Zane's breath hitched. He paused only a fraction, and then he responded. "Would do it every day for the rest of my life if it meant sleeping like this with you forever."

Her throat clogged at those words. She decided not to speak for fear she would start crying. She'd cried enough lately. Right now she needed to ignore the emotions he was dragging to the surface and let her body rest.

She drifted for only a few minutes before sleep dragged her under.

CHAPTER 18

A ringing noise yanked Abby from a deep sleep. She opened her eyes a slit. The room was dim, and she was still tightly snuggled in Zane's embrace.

His grip loosened a moment later, and he twisted away from her.

She heard his hand slap against the bedside table and then the distinct sound of his cell phone dragging across the top as he located it. "Rider?" He sat up.

Abby rolled onto her back to look up at him in the early morning light. Why would Rider be calling so early?

"What?" Zane shouted this word. He jumped from the bed and ran his free hand through his hair.

Abby pulled herself upright on the bed, holding the sheet up to her chest. Something was terribly wrong. Fear crept up her spine. She'd felt that fear yesterday several times. This morning it was back in full force.

"When? Fuck… No… Goddammit…" He turned to face her.

She pursed her lips, unwilling to ask the hard questions.

Zane turned around and grabbed his jeans off the floor. He tugged them on while holding the phone between his ear and his shoulder. He pointed at Abby's bag in the corner and mouthed, "Get dressed." And then his attention was back on Rider. "Yes… We'll be there in ten minutes… No… Fucking…well, just fuck."

Abby was wide awake mentally and racing across the room to grab clothes so fast her legs almost buckled.

Zane set the phone on the bed. He crossed the room while tugging a T-shirt over his head. When he reached Abby's side, he grabbed her shoulders. She was still naked. Her mind hadn't quite figured out what to put on yet. He didn't mince words. He looked her in the eye. "Lauren's missing."

"No. Oh God."

"I'm so sorry, baby. Let's get rolling. Emily is distraught. Rider is fucking pissed."

"I'm sure." She leaned down to grab panties and a bra. As fast as she could manage, she put on jeans and a T-shirt and tugged on her tennis shoes. Her hair was a wreck, but she could pull it up into a bun in the car.

She raced from the room, following Zane's near jog.

She'd never in her life gone from completely unconscious to driving down the road in so few minutes. But today was a first. Every day was a first lately. And frankly, she was growing tired of all the action.

Zane drove as fast as he dared, and they made it to Rider's house in record time. Two squad cars sat out front, lights blaring. The sun was still creeping over the horizon.

Abby ran toward the house before Zane. The front door was open and she didn't pause. She scanned the room.

Emily sat on the couch in a tight ball, her eyes

bloodshot, her nose running, a tissue clutched in her hand. "Abby."

Abby went to her side and hugged her. "What happened?"

Rider greeted Zane, and then men both sat on the coffee table.

Rider explained. "Something woke me up. I thought I heard a noise. Sounded like a crash. For a moment I assumed I'd been dreaming, especially since Emily hadn't moved. But my heart was pounding, so I climbed out of bed and headed down the hall to check on Lauren. When I opened her door, she was gone. The window was broken and the curtain was hanging toward the outside, blowing in the wind."

While he explained this, four police officers padded around the house on a mission. Now, one of them came closer. "I think we're done here, Rider. I'm so sorry, man. There isn't much to go on. Jacobson is on his way to the station. He'll drag Yenin's sorry ass out of bed ASAP and question him. I doubt we'll be able to get much out of that asshole, though. We're probably going to be on our own."

Rider stood. "I understand. I'll be in soon. Let me get Emily calmed down, and I'll meet you at the station."

A second officer came from the hall holding a plastic bag with a phone in it. "Is this Lauren's?"

Abby responded at the same time as Emily, "Yes."

The officer shook his head. "I'm gonna take it in. I'm betting it's bugged."

"Fuck," Rider said. "How the hell did we miss that?"

Zane stood also. "We had no way of knowing anyone was still interested in grabbing Lauren. Hell, we still don't know who took her. Obviously not Yenin."

"Who then?" Rider asked. He paced.

The cops let themselves out.

Abby held Emily against her. She could feel the tears welling up in her eyes, but she kept them at bay to focus on Emily's state of shock.

Zane responded, "Probably one of his men. But why?"

"Easy. I should have thought of it too," Rider said, hands on his head.

"What?" Abby asked.

"Anton does not let people walk away from him. Ever. He's not that kind of man."

"He told Lauren to leave. He told her to," Abby insisted.

"Yeah, he was just fucking with her. Leaving him was never an option," Rider said.

Abby was confused. "But he's in jail. Why would he be concerned about some woman who left him from jail?"

"His reach is far. I'm sure he ordered his men to pick her up," Rider answered.

"What will they do with her?" Emily asked this.

Rider glanced her way, but didn't respond. He stomped across the room and grabbed his boots from next to the door. As he put the first one on, he lifted his gaze. "We're all going to the station. Em, get some clothes, honey."

Abby released Emily and noticed she was only wearing a tank top under the blanket she was wrapped in.

"Why?" Emily asked.

"Baby, I need to go in, and there's no way in hell I'm leaving you alone anywhere. Those fuckers know where we live. If they would kidnap Abby and then Lauren, they won't hesitate to take you also. They have a point to make, and they intend to make it, even if their leader is behind bars."

Abby helped Emily get to her feet. Nerves were the rule rather than the exception once again. "He's right."

Zane reached for Abby as Emily padded away.

"God." Abby set her hand on her chest. The number of ways she could feel violated kept rising.

Emily reappeared, looking about like Abby felt, same level of dress, same crazy hair. "Ready." She turned toward Rider. "What are we going to do about the window?"

"We'll worry about it later. I don't think anyone is interested in robbing us today. They got what they came for."

They stepped outside and Zane put his arm around Abby. "We'll follow you to the station."

Rider nodded, his own arm wrapped as tightly around Emily. "Meet you there."

~

Zane was exhausted. Even though he had slept like the dead next to Abby for five hours, it hadn't been enough. And the stress alone was wearing on him. The five seconds of elated safety he'd felt after finding Abby alive and well dissipated quickly as it sank in that Anton was not done. The man liked revenge, and he could exact it from prison just as well as outside. He had connections that ran far and wide and deep. He also had money.

By the time everyone had coffee and was seated in a conference room at the station, Jacobson came in holding up Lauren's phone. "Yep. It had GPS tracking. It also had an open mic." He glanced at Abby. "That must be how he knew about your conversation with Lauren when you encouraged her to leave him. He was listening in on every word."

Zane grabbed Abby's hand and squeezed. He knew instantly where her mind went.

"So this is all my fault. If I hadn't butted in and tried to talk Lauren into leaving that asshole, none of this would have happened." Abby's voice shook.

Rider spoke next. "Abby, that's ridiculous, and you know it. If you hadn't interfered, where would that leave Lauren? You think she should have sat back and spent her life under Yenin's thumb?"

"No." Abby's shoulders slumped. "True. But now she's right back where she started."

"Maybe, but honey, you can't know for sure what would have happened. We have no choice but to work with what we know and find her." Rider took a sip of his coffee. "And we will. Yenin can only do so much from behind bars. Jacobson's team knows a great deal about the way this group operates. They've been tracking their movements for years."

Zane had an idea. "Let me see if I can get ahold of any of the guys. Maybe Dmitry or one of the other fighters has some intel."

Jacobson nodded. "Good idea. They trust you. But how well do you trust them?"

Zane thought about that for a moment. During the events of last evening, he'd had his doubts, but in the end the men he knew all pulled through for him. He knew now more than ever that his Russian friends, although they did fight in the underground, were good guys. He would put his life in their hands any day. And he said so. "With my life."

Zane sat forward. "Look, it's well-known that Dmitry, Leo, Ivan—hell, even Mikhail, Nikolav, and Sergei—are not clean fighters on the up-and-up. But I'm betting the reality is they need the money badly. If Anton brought them over to the United States and got them all green cards, he also holds them by the balls. They fight in his venues, but I don't believe any of them are truly dirty.

"When push came to shove yesterday, Dmitry would have died before he let Abby suffer. I saw it in his eyes. He may not have had the opportunity to say many words, but he told me without speaking to put up an impressive fight for the audience and then take his ass down. Those were the terms. I had to win to get Abby back."

"What were Dmitry's terms?" Rider asked.

Zane shook his head. "I tried not to think about it at the time." He knew whatever Anton had threatened Dmitry with, it had to be bad. Anton's men weren't allowed to lose for any reason. That was why Dmitry fought as hard as he did. If Yenin had suspected for a second that Dmitry threw the fight, he probably would have had him shot in the forehead before he left the cage. In the end, the fight never ended. Thank God.

Rider's phone buzzed in his pocket. He leaned to one side to pull it out. "Speak of the devil. Dmitry sent a text."

"What does it say?" Abby asked.

"'I have my sights on Lauren. Tell the cops I need a few hours. If the police move in, I'll lose her.'"

"Fuck," Jacobson exclaimed.

Rider cleared his throat. "This is probably a good thing."

Jacobson leaned on the table. "Dmitry is a known underground fighter for the Russian mob. Why should I trust him?"

Zane stood and leaned in Jacobson's direction. "Did you not hear a word I said? If the man says he needs a few hours, we need to give him that. His life is at stake too. If you think he doesn't know that, you're crazy."

Jacobson exhaled slowly and righted himself to run a

hand through his hair. "You're right." He turned and left the room. Or stomped rather.

Rider looked at Zane. "He's okay. Don't worry about Jacobson. He's just stressed. He won't fuck this up."

"Hell," Zane said, "I don't even know how he could. It's not as though we know where Lauren's being held in order to bust in and fuck anything up."

"True. But I'm betting Jacobson's men know a lot of spots to start looking. He needs to call them back and hang tight just in case. If they happened to hit the right hideout before Dmitry's ready, she could be killed." Rider put his hands on his head and leaned back. "Jesus." He tipped his head toward the ceiling.

Emily leaned into his side. Her face was swollen from crying. Her heart was too soft for this sort of thing. "Dmitry will get her out. We have to trust that."

Zane sure hoped she was right.

Rider tapped into his phone. "I'll let Dmitry know we're giving him some time."

Jacobson came back into the room thirty minutes later looking calmer. He held a giant paper bag up and then set it on the table. "I thought you might be hungry."

"Thanks, man," Rider said. "You okay?"

"Yep. Sorry about earlier. I'm running on very little sleep, and I'm pissed that this slippery bastard has the better of us even from behind bars."

"Totally understandable." Rider stood and pulled breakfast biscuits out of the bag. He passed them around the table.

Zane stared down at the one in front of him, wondering how the hell he was going to swallow a single bite. He had barely managed to stomach the coffee in his plastic cup so far.

Abby must have thought the same thing because she didn't even glace at her sandwich. She sat huddled in the chair with her feet on the seat and her knees pulled up to her chest. Her arms were wrapped around her legs. "Why does Anton have his sights on me? I'm not the one who left him."

Jacobson pulled out a chair and sat. "Initially, when he had his men run you off the road, I suspect he was pissed at your interference, and he intended to either eliminate you or teach you a lesson."

"But why kidnap me and then not either kill me or worse?"

Zane flinched. He knew exactly what the "or worse" entailed. "That's on me. I'm sure Yenin saw an opportunity when he realized you were connected to me and reached for the dollar signs."

"Fighting?" she asked.

Zane nodded. "He's been hounding me to fight for him for months. I've turned him down every time. He knew if he raised the stakes, I would have no choice. He tried and failed to blackmail Conner into fighting for him a few months ago also. I'm surprised he was willing to take such a risk again so soon. But all he saw was money. And then he put me up against a man he also knew was a comrade in the sport. I'm sure the bets placed around that room were enormous."

"Yeah, I heard some of them." She gave Zane a slight grin. "I never knew I was dating such a celebrity."

Zane leaned down and kissed her forehead. "Hardly. But underground fighting is definitely where the money is."

"So, you think his men will come after me again?"

"Doubtful. Unlikely that Yenin cares much about you personally," Jacobson said. "He saw an opportunity, and he took it. He doesn't even know how it might have panned out in the end. I'm not surprised about him coming after Lauren from behind bars, but the vendetta he had against her is personal. She dissed him. He doesn't take no for an answer. Lauren's life will never be hers again. She will need to be relocated and given a new identity."

Zane set a hand on Abby's shoulder when she flinched. "Once someone is involved with the Russian mob, they don't escape, baby. That's just how it is."

"I'm giving Dmitry one more hour to contact us, and then I'm going to mobilize my men." Jacobson said all this while staring at Zane.

Zane nodded. He hoped to hell Dmitry had Lauren safe and sound somewhere before the hour was up. He also wondered if he'd ever see either one of them again. Dmitry was a good guy. Zane knew that. But he wasn't so squeaky clean and wonderful that he would put his life on the line for a random woman. If Dmitry intended to rescue Lauren, were his motives altruistic? Or did he intend to have Lauren for himself?

Zane was sharp enough to realize that. He almost smiled at the notion of rock-hard, serious Dmitry Volikov falling for a woman.

Zane sat in his chair again and opened the sandwich. He nodded at Abby. "Eat, baby. Could be a while."

But it wasn't as long as expected. Half an hour later, Rider's phone vibrated on the table top. He stared at it for a split second and then snatched it up.

"'She's safe. I'm going to ground with her,'" Rider read.

"What?" Zane asked when Rider finished reading. "Is he crazy?"

Rider smiled. "Nope. He's perfectly sane."

Zane hesitated. "You think—"

Rider chuckled. "Come on, man. You know Dmitry. Have you ever seen him with a woman?"

"Not more than once."

"Ever seen him stick his neck out for one?" Rider asked.

Zane smiled now too. "Not once."

"What the hell are you guys talking about?" Abby asked. "What does Dmitry mean by 'going to ground'? Is he gonna bring her here?"

"No." Jacobson shook his head. "He's taking her safety into his own hands." He exhaled slowly. "As much as I hate to admit it, he's probably doing the right thing. The department is stretched thin. Keeping her safe is a huge undertaking. If Dmitry can do it, let him." He turned to Rider. "Think you can get him to put Lauren on the phone so we'll know she's okay?"

"I'll give it a shot." Rider started typing.

Zane stared at Rider's phone, hoping Dmitry would understand what they were really asking—for proof that Lauren was okay so Jacobson would call off his men. They didn't want to outright insult Dmitry, but the phone call would give the cops something to breathe easier about.

The phone buzzed again. Rider read, *"Of course. And then I'm ditching this phone. I'll contact you or Zane in a few weeks when things calm down."*

Rider waited another minute, and the phone rang.

He handed it to Abby and let her answer. "Lauren? Thank God. Are you okay? No one hurt you?" Abby looked at Zane. "Yes, Zane knows him. I think you're in good hands. But please be careful and stay alive. That's what matters. If something doesn't feel right, you can always get to a police station and get help… Okay, sweetie. Be safe. Talk to you later." She ended the call and handed Zane the phone. "I think she sounds appropriately scared out of her mind and safer."

"That's what matters," Jacobson said. "Now, if you all don't mind, I could use a short nap." He stood and faced

Rider. "I'll be in touch if I hear anything you should know." He turned to Abby next. "Stay with Zane or Rider. Don't go back home yet. It's just a precaution, but I wouldn't take any chances."

Abby nodded and reached for Zane's hand to squeeze it. "Thank you," she directed at Jacobson.

EPILOGUE

Two months later...

"Baby, are you ready?"

Abby spun around to check the back of her hair in the mirror, ignoring Zane's voice traveling from the living room. She set the hand mirror down finally and met her gaze over the vanity. *You look fine.*

When she stepped into the living room, Zane was standing by the front door jiggling his keys. He lifted his face to meet her, a smile spreading across his lips as his gaze roamed up her body and back down. He gave a low whistle.

Abby flushed. She loved that he found her so attractive, but she still felt embarrassed when he so plainly admired her body.

"Sexiest dress ever, baby." His voice was low and rough. "Aren't those things supposed to be ugly and ill fitting?"

She giggled. "Usually. But Sabrina has good taste." She turned around. "Is the back okay?"

He ambled toward her as she tipped her head over her shoulder to look back at him. "I'll have to beat men off you all evening." He wrapped his arms around her from behind and pulled her into his front, his mouth landing on her neck to gently nibble her skin. His hand trailed down the bare skin of her back. "Lord, this is sexy."

"It's not too low?"

His hand dipped inside the opening above her butt and stroked her cheeks. "For what?" he whispered.

She shivered at his touch and leaned her head against his chest. "Stop that," she muttered. "We'll never get there on time if you keep that up."

"What? This?" He reached farther and danced his fingers down her crack. "Hmm."

Abby groaned and reached over her head to grab his head as he nudged her hair aside and nibbled her neck. "Zane…"

Suddenly his hand was gone and he gripped her hips, his breathing erratic against her bare skin. "We have to go. But I can't wait to dance with you."

She spun in his embrace to face him, tipping her head back to see his eyes. The look of lust that met her made her pussy clench. Her nipples already stood at attention. She closed her eyes, fighting to recover enough to exit the house. "You've turned me into a nymph."

He chuckled as his hands wandered around to her back once more and spread across her bare skin. "And this is a bad thing?" His lips landed on hers, briefly. "I don't want to mess up your lip gloss, but if we don't leave this instant, I'm going to mess up far more than that."

Her eyes popped open. "I'm not standing at the front of the church with just-fucked hair." She pressed on his chest. "Let's go."

He released her, but his shoulders slumped.

Abby grabbed her purse and stepped toward the door on wobbly legs that wanted to collapse. The thong she wore was drenched. And her chest had expanded until her nipples rubbed against the satin of the front of the dress provocatively. It would be a miracle if no one noticed the tips. The dress didn't permit a bra.

Zane opened the door for her and took her arm to help her to the truck. When they reached the passenger side, he lifted her into the seat and shut the door.

Abby squirmed. She squirmed nearly every time she was with Zane, and that was a lot lately. She'd all but moved in with him.

Her mind wandered to other things as Zane drove. "Do you think she's okay?"

"Who?" Zane twisted around to look at her, his brow furrowed, a smirk playing at the corners of his mouth.

"Lauren. It's been weeks. Dmitry said he would be in touch."

"He will. When it's safe. Yenin has only been arraigned so far. It will take months for him to go to trial. And now that his father is on the scene, I don't see the local Russian mafia falling apart any time soon. Lauren is safer with Dmitry wherever they are."

"I guess so." She lifted her gaze farther. "Where did Yenin's father come from?"

"New York. He's a big member of the mob on that side of the country. He gave his son free reign to take on this territory. Now that Anton has presumably fucked things up, Grigory has decided to step in and run the Vegas contingency himself."

"That can't be good."

"Not really. We'll have to wait and see." He set a hand on her thigh and squeezed.

Every time he did that she fell under his spell. He knew exactly what he was doing. Distracting her.

She set her head against the seat and took a deep breath. "This still feels a bit awkward."

"What?"

"Me being a bridesmaid in Sabrina's wedding. I just met her two months ago."

He glanced at her smiling. "That may be true, but it's perfect. Every member of The Fight Club and their significant other is in the wedding party. Besides, you and Sabrina are like peas in a pod. I can tell she will be a lifetime friend. You're closer to her already than any of the other women."

Abby smiled. "True."

"What were the chances that two of us would meet a woman secretly working on the next great American novel?" He winked at her.

"I do love her, and she's a godsend when it comes to helping me understand the publishing world. Without her, I never would have had the balls to finish my book. Besides, she's also volunteered to whip it into shape for me before I submit it anywhere."

Zane's hand traveled up her thigh, pushing the silky black material of her dress higher.

Abby set her hand on his to halt his progress before she lost her mind.

When Zane wanted to distract her, he was an expert. "Let me touch you, baby. You're uptight."

She was uptight all right. Every time she thought about Lauren, she stiffened. She'd only known her a month, but it worried her that her friend had now been off hiding with some Russian guy for twice that long. What if she was being held against her will? She squeezed his hand tighter. "Being in this truck is no safer for me than the living room.

You'll mess me up and I'll look like I've been rolling around in the hay at the front of the church."

He chuckled. "I promise no hay. And I promise not to mess up a hair on your head. Now, remove your hand, baby."

She glared at him, but the tone of his voice had slipped into Dom mode.

His face was on the road, but his hand gripped her thigh harder. "In fact, take off your panties." He released her.

Abby wasn't sure about this plan. It could only lead to messy hair and skewed makeup.

Zane stopped at a light and turned to face her. "Now, baby. Take them off and spread your legs."

More wetness flooded her pussy as she squirmed against the seat, her hands fisted in uncertainty. *In the car?* How was he going to drive and touch her at the same time?

"Unless, you want me to spank your sweet ass over my lap inside this truck in the church parking lot, I suggest you do as I've asked twice now."

Abby flinched. She bit her lower lip as she lifted her butt off the leather seat and wiggled her thong over her hips and down her legs.

"I'll take that." He reached out his hand.

She set the scrap of lace on his palm and watched as he pocketed her thong. When his hand came out of his suit pocket, he held something else. He'd traded her panties for what?

She couldn't see, but she didn't have to wait long.

In a second, he flipped his hand over and revealed the contents.

She gulped. She was already hot and bothered from his play on the way out of the house. His dominance in the car was making it seem warmer than it was. And now this.

"What is it?" She knew it was some sort of vibrator. And she was smart enough to realize it was going inside her, but if she could buy a bit of time with small talk, perhaps they would run out of minutes. No way could she endure something like that right now.

"It's an egg. Put it in you. Don't hesitate."

So much for stalling… Abby reached with shaky fingers and picked up the oval from his hand. How bad could it be? She flipped it around, looking at it.

"Enough examination. Press it in your pussy as deep as possible."

With a deep breath, she spread her legs and reached between them to do as he asked.

Oh. It was more filling than she expected. Her pussy gripped at it as she slipped it deeper. After a second, she had control of herself. As long as she didn't move…*shit*. It started to vibrate. Abby twisted her face to find Zane smirking, not glancing her way. He lifted up a small black box, which she realized was a remote control.

"No."

He gave her a sharp glance. "What was that?"

"Zane. I can't." She lifted her ass off the seat as the vibrations grew stronger. A moan already slipped out. "You can't…" She panted as it got even stronger.

"I can. And you will. Sit down, baby. Hands at your sides."

She let her ass fall back against the leather, but that made the egg press in deeper.

"Look at me, baby." His voice was hoarse. She affected him.

She turned her face toward him, her hands in tight fists, her teeth gritted together.

He couldn't watch her because he was driving, but she didn't dare take her eyes off him.

The vibrations increased and decreased seemingly at will. She wasn't sure if it was a setting or if Zane was continually pressing buttons on the remote. Finally, he pulled into the parking lot and chose a spot at the end of a row of cars, not directly under a street light. He shut off the engine and turned toward her.

It seemed she could hear the egg throbbing inside her. Was it loud? Or just in her mind? "We need to go inside," she whispered, trying not to move too much or breathe.

"We will." He didn't touch her, but the vibrations shot higher again. "After you come. Eyes on me, baby."

Oh God. It was unimaginable that he wanted her to come in the front seat of his truck in a church parking lot...and without touching her. It was also inevitable. She was so close.

She panted through the waves of intense pleasure driving her higher by the second. "Zane..."

"Baby, you're so gorgeous when you come." He reached for a lock of her hair and lightly bounced it on his finger, casual as can be. "Come for me."

She inhaled deeply and held that breath, all her energy focused on her pussy and how close she was. She kept her gaze locked on Zane's face, but she no longer really saw anything.

"Come, baby. Let it go."

That was it. She tipped over the precipice, gripping the console with one hand and the arm rest on the door with the other, gasping as her pussy gripped the egg and pulsed around it over and over. The vibrations gradually decreased as she came down.

"So beautiful," he muttered. He leaned over the console, pushed her dress up above her waist and reached inside her with two fingers to ease the egg out of her pussy.

The contact made her groan with renewed need.

Zane chuckled. "You're wet, baby." He lifted the egg to his mouth and popped it inside.

Astounded, her eyes went wide, and her mouth fell open while she watched him suck the egg and then pop it out and put it back in his pocket. "Mmm." He licked his lips as he handed her a few tissues. "You can clean up a bit with these." And then he offered her panties. "You want these back?"

She snatched them from his hand, feeling every bit of the heat that crept up her face. How was she going to face their friends after having an orgasm in the church parking lot?

He closed the gap between them, gripped her chin, and leaned the last few inches to kiss her gently. "I love you, Abby."

Her breath caught in her throat. Tears welled up in her eyes. *No. Shit.* She didn't want to cry and ruin her makeup after managing to keep herself presentable through an orgasm.

He smiled. "I think I fell in love with you before I ever saw your face."

Yep. That was it. A tear slipped down her cheek uninvited.

"I saw that sexy ass and legs sticking out from under your porch, and I knew the woman attached to them was mine."

And there went another tear.

Zane released her, yanked open his door, and jumped down from the cab. Seconds later he opened her door and lifted her to the ground. He set his forehead against hers and wiped the two lines of tears. "Sorry. Didn't mean to mess up your makeup." He took her hand and gave a tug to head for the church.

Abby stayed where she was, pulling back on him.

"What, baby?"

"You can't just lay that on a girl and then walk away like nothing happened."

His smile lit up his face. "Guess I can."

She shook her head and inhaled slowly. "I love you too."

Now he froze. His eyes widened. "I didn't mean for you to have to reciprocate just because I said it."

She shook her head harder. "Of course not. I've known for a while. I was just too scared to say anything."

"Why?" He cocked his face to one side.

She shrugged. "I wasn't sure how you felt."

He surrounded her with his hands at both sides of her face, leaning against the side of the truck. "Well, you don't have to wonder anymore. I love you, baby. You're stuck with me. In fact, I want you to stop going back and forth pretending to maintain your own house. Move in with me."

And the shocks kept coming. "Now?"

He smirked. "Tomorrow is okay too."

"But I have a lease. And there are the roses. I can't let Mrs. Lamphry's roses die."

He laughed, tipping his head back and filling the evening with his gorgeous voice. "We'll check on her roses as often as we need and make sure they're fed. But I want you in my bed every night, your clothes in my closet. All of them. Not half of them. Not a suitcase that we trip over."

She chewed on her bottom lip and stared at him. He was serious. "Okay."

His eyebrows shot up. "Oh, thank God." He took both her hands in his and kissed her knuckles. "I was afraid you might put up more of a fight."

"Most of my stuff is at your place already." She shrugged. "Might as well."

He laughed again. "Oh, so it's a matter of convenience, huh?"

She swatted at his arm and then got serious. "Zane Randolf, I've never been so happy in my life. I'd be delighted to move in with you, and my heart is beating out of my chest that you're in love with me."

"Good." He kissed her again. "Now, my love, let's get inside and get this wedding over with before the bride and groom wonder where they hell we are. The sooner we get this out of the way, the sooner I can have you back at the house naked on your knees at my bidding." He took her hand, entwining their fingers together, and led her toward the church just as someone opened the front door and glanced around. It was Conner. Of course. He waved at them, his shoulders visibly relaxing even from a distance.

Abby's knees threatened to buckle. So much information in such a short time, and all that following a mind-blowing orgasm in the car. But her world was perfect. Every part of it. She held Zane's arm tightly as they made their way to the front door.

The sooner they got inside, the sooner the rest of her life would start.

AUTHOR'S NOTE

I hope you've enjoyed *Lust*, the last book in The Fight Club series. Please enjoy the following excerpt from *Force*, the first book in The Underground series.

FORCE

THE UNDERGROUND, BOOK ONE

"Volikov, what the fuck are you doing in there? This isn't a tea party. It's a fucking fight."

Dmitry glanced from the corner of his good eye without moving his head to glare at his best friend, who stood outside the cage with his fingers threaded through the holes of the fence. "Fuck you." His other eye was swollen almost shut. And even if it hadn't been, he would have squeezed it shut to avoid the sting of sweat and blood running from his forehead. He winced when his cornerman dabbed at the cut above his brow. The older man had a serious expression on his wrinkled face, a lock of white hair hanging across his brow. He ignored Dmitry's flinch and continued mopping his forehead.

Mikhail smirked. "You look like a total pussy tonight. Get your head in the game. Find some hot chick in the audience to focus on and pretend you're fighting for her honor or something. I don't give a fuck what it takes, but make it happen. We need this prize money. The fucking rent is due."

Dmitry didn't need the reminder. He was well aware of

his financial situation. He was in over his head, a head that grew more clouded every day he tiptoed around the sexy woman currently living in their apartment.

Clearly he'd been short a few circuits when he stepped up to the plate and took Lauren Schneider under his protection. A stupid move on his part. And now he was stuck watching her fucking hot ass and fantastic tits sway in front of him every time he came home—which he tried to ensure wasn't often.

Mikhail released the fence and slapped a hand onto the pole at the corner. The actual fence put up for the fight in this venue was a rare treat. There was even an MMA floor inside the ring. Often Dmitry fought on bare dirt with a circle drawn on the floor in one of these basements in downtown Chicago. Most of the locations were "renovated" speakeasies from the thirties. The ceilings were low. The floors were crude. The lighting was bad.

The money was good.

Mikhail leaned in a few inches before stepping back. "Get this over with. You want to stay here all night getting your face smashed in? Or would you rather head for Lorde's and enjoy a few beers?"

Now, that wasn't a bad idea. *Think about how good beer tastes after a victory instead of concentrating on thick, glossy, brown hair swaying down the back of a narrow-waisted model's body.*

The trouble was, Lauren was exactly that—smoking hot. Smoldering. Just like a cover model—long, wavy hair that begged him to run his hands through it. Deep green eyes that sucked him in every time he made eye contact. Hourglass figure. A bombshell. And he wasn't the only one who knew it. Everyone who laid eyes on her did a double take—or often a triple take. The only thing that kept him from self-combusting over the last six months was not letting her leave the apartment. If he had to take her out in public and share her with other people on the street, he feared he would have to kick some pervert's ass and bring the Underground aboveground. Just the thought made his blood pump faster.

Perfect. Because he needed the adrenaline rush. Round two needed to look a whole lot better than round one, or he and Mikhail were going to have to find more nefarious means of paying the rent. And he shivered to consider their options.

He blinked as he sucked in oxygen through his nose— or tried to anyway. One side was completely clogged, and the other was hardly better.

The bell rang.

He was on his feet once again, bouncing into the center of the cage, his arms held in his usual protective stance in front of his face. He stretched his neck both ways while he danced around his opponent.

Jackson Delgado. The son of a bitch was tough. Dmitry had to give him kudos for his tenacity. The kid was relatively new by unsanctioned boxing standards, but he made up for his lack of knowledge in stamina.

For the first time in years, Dmitry felt old. At thirty-one, his body was growing tired of the constant barrage of beatings. He'd been fighting more than half his life. Mostly to survive. And that included now. How he'd managed to stay so fit and able for so many years was a mystery. Must have been in the Russian blood, though, since he and all five of his friends were still on top of their game.

Delgado threw a punch, which Dmitry deflected easily. Delgado was darker skinned than Dmitry. And his short-cropped hair was black. Even his eyes were the darkest brown Dmitry had ever seen. Hell, the only clothing the man wore was his loose shorts, and they were black also.

The crazy tat he had running down his right arm covered almost every inch of skin—whatever it was. Some sort of snake or reptile.

Deprivation fueled Dmitry. And for the next ten minutes he intended to funnel that need and focus. Delgado might be young, and there was no doubt he was spry, but the man had never known the kind of hardship Dmitry endured on more than a few occasions. He had a look about him that said he fought for the sport, for the excitement, for the rush of participating in the illicit. The lack of lines across his forehead and the way he had walked into the ring with a smile on his face, his head held high, told a fraction of his story.

The man had not known true hunger or deprivation.

Dmitry intended to use that to his advantage. It was time to get control of this fight.

Stretching his brow, he forced his swollen eye to open enough to aid in his depth perception. On a deep breath, inhaling stale cigars and spilled vodka, he gauged his opponent's moment of weakness and lifted his right leg to kick the man high across the chest.

The crowd roared, drawing Dmitry's attention. He'd been oblivious to the dull sound of bets being placed and people cheering around him until that moment. Hundreds of people packed into a small space. That scream of excitement fueled him enough to follow up with a sharp series of jabs that had Delgado staggering backward into the fence.

When Jackson threw his arms higher in front of his face, Dmitry lowered his shoulders and tossed an uppercut that hit his opponent square in the jaw. Blood spattered around both men. Stupid fool wasn't wearing a mouth guard.

Dmitry went for the legs next, kneeing Delgado in the side of his thigh.

Delgado buckled and went down on his knees. He wrapped his arms around Dmitry's torso and held on tight, trying to get a moment's peace to regroup.

Dmitry had no intention of letting Jackson get a break, however. He pummeled him around the head and shoulders as he dragged his body away from the fence.

Finally, Dmitry bent at his own knees, his intent to force Delgado to fall backward. Landing on top of him wasn't an issue. Dmitry had the element of surprise on his side. He went down over Delgado, landing on his chest and immediately pinning the man on his back with a forearm across his throat.

Jackson struggled.

Dmitry pressed harder. Any more and the kid's air supply would be cut off. Dmitry would never let it go that far, but it would sure help if Jackson would tap out instead of forcing Dmitry to switch to other tactics. Dmitry wanted to win, but he wasn't the kind of guy who enjoyed injuring his opponent in any permanent manner.

Some said that made him weak. Dmitry knew it made him stronger. He'd never killed a man, and he didn't intend to start tonight. "Fucking tap out, Delgado," he muttered through his mouth guard.

The noise around them increased as the spectators shouted above each other, perhaps cheering on whoever was their favorite.

Dmitry heard nothing concrete. It was all white noise to him. It was always the same—hundreds of people gathered in a circle that squeezed tight against the ring—tensions escalating as the match wore on.

Jackson squirmed beneath him, his eyes growing larger as he fought for oxygen. He wrapped his hands around

Dmitry's forearm and tugged, his legs bucking behind Dmitry's torso.

"It's over, asshole. Give it up."

Finally, Delgado blew out the last of his oxygen and closed his eyelids, his hand snaking out to slap the floor.

The referee jumped back, taking Dmitry with him by the arm and lifting it into the air. "And the winner is Dmitry 'The Cossack' Volikov."

Dmitry's thoughts were clouded, so he didn't hear another word the ref shouted to the crowd over the dense ringing sensation that made the entire room seem to be underwater—not just from his lack of sense of hearing, but his blurry vision too.

He didn't need to hear the referee, however. He knew the routine. He'd been in this situation so many times in the last fifteen years, it all blended together.

Dmitry glanced down to watch Delgado roll onto all fours and drag himself off the sweaty ground. He staggered from the cage with the aid of his cornerman and disappeared into the crowd.

By the time Dmitry was finished waving to the screaming audience, he was exhausted. He had to work hard not to let it show as he walked down the four steps that led to the edge of the raised fenced area and made his way across the room toward the exit.

Mikhail took his arm. "Thank fuck. You had me worried."

Dmitry smirked as he ran a hand over his shaved head. "Why? When was the last time I lost?"

"You want a list?"

"No." Dmitry sobered. He'd lost a match last month. And the only thing that kept them afloat had been Mikhail's winnings that week.

Dmitry had to admit several realities. He was so

fucking tired from not getting enough sleep. He was growing too old to keep up this pace. And all of this was his own damn fault.

There was no reason he and Mikhail needed to keep Lauren and Mikhail's younger sister living in the particular apartment they had rented. It was bigger than they needed, and it cost more than they could afford. But they did it anyway. And neither of them was willing to verbalize the stupidity.

Dmitry knew Mikhail kept up the farce for the same reason Dmitry did. After years of finagling, Mikhail had finally managed to get his sister into the US. The woman had lived an impoverished life, and the last thing Mikhail wanted to do was perpetuate that way of living.

Dmitry knew his friend would rather sell his soul than allow his sister one more day of shit. She deserved better. They all did. Even if they had to fake it to make it.

It was hardly different for Lauren. She was in a fucked-up situation no one could have prevented. For years she'd lived hand-to-mouth working her ass off as a waitress in a Vegas casino while trying to put herself through college. All of that had been shattered when she found herself in the hands of the local Russian mafia tycoon. That bastard, Anton Yenin, fucked with both her mind and her body. And he had no intention of ever stopping. Even from his jail cell, he managed to have Lauren kidnapped in order to prove his power.

Dmitry shivered as he recalled the way his heart pounded that fateful day. He'd seen Lauren around the estate and warehouse several times in Vegas when he'd been there to train or hang out with the guys. He'd known by the look on her face she was too innocent for the likes of Yenin, but once someone got under the thumb of the Russian mafia, they never got out.

Never.

Unless they had a knight on the inside willing to give up everything to sneak them out of that existence and drag them to a better world—if living in sequestered hiding could be considered "better."

The woman was smoking hot. He'd had a hard-on for her from the first time he laid eyes on her. Taking her from under the control of Yenin's men had been risky, but he hated the way she'd been punched around by Yenin and his cronies. He didn't like blood on a woman. Especially not her own blood. Any man who would put it there was a snake. Including Yenin.

Dmitry may have Yenin to thank for bringing him into the country, getting him a green card, and putting him to work, but Dmitry drew the line at watching a beautiful woman get punched in the face.

And Lauren wasn't just any woman. She was intelligent, hard-working, sexy, and brave. She wasn't the usual type of whore Yenin brought home. She tugged at Dmitry's heartstrings.

Dmitry yanked off his gloves and then his shorts. He angled for the makeshift shower in the corner of the tiny locker room and tipped his head back to rinse off the grime of the fight.

He glanced several times at Mikhail, who leaned against the brick wall of the underground establishment and counted the pile of money someone had handed him on Dmitry's behalf.

"We good?" Dmitry asked.

"Yep. For another week at least." Mikhail pursed his lips as he stuffed the wad of cash in his front pocket.

Dmitry blew out a breath and leaned his forehead against the cold tile in front of him. The shower was no more than a spigot coming out of the wall where years ago someone had rigged up this disgusting excuse for a shower. Nearly every pale yellow tile was cracked. The caulking had long since eroded away, leaving most of the tiles askew. It smelled like old sweat—one hundred years of old sweat.

With a shiver, Dmitry righted himself and turned off the water. "Let's get out of here. It's late."

"We stopping by Lorde's for that beer?"

Dmitry shook his head. "I need sleep more than alcohol. Tomorrow's another long day in paradise."

Mikhail followed Dmitry to his bag and sat on a crooked bench while Dmitry tugged on his jeans and T-shirt.

He didn't say another word. He didn't have to. All he could do was pray and hope for a better tomorrow.

ALSO BY BECCA JAMESON

Hot SEAL, Red Wine

Hot SEAL, Australian Nights

Hot SEAL, Cold Feet

Dark Falls:

Dark Nightmares

Club Zodiac:

Training Sasha

Obeying Rowen

Collaring Brooke

Mastering Rayne

Trusting Aaron

Claiming London

Sharing Charlotte

Taming Rex

Tempting Elizabeth

Club Zodiac Box Set One

Club Zodiac Box Set Two

The Art of Kink:

Pose

Paint

Sculpt

Arcadian Bears:

Grizzly Mountain

Grizzly Beginning

Grizzly Secret

Grizzly Promise

Grizzly Survival

Grizzly Perfection

Arcadian Bears Box Set One

Arcadian Bears Box Set Two

Sleeper SEALs:

Saving Zola

Spring Training:

Catching Zia

Catching Lily

Catching Ava

Spring Training Box Set

The Underground series:

Force

Clinch

Guard

Submit

Thrust

Torque

The Underground Box Set One

The Underground Box Set Two

Saving Sofia (Special Forces: Operations Alpha)

Wolf Masters series:

Kara's Wolves

Lindsey's Wolves

Jessica's Wolves

Alyssa's Wolves

Tessa's Wolf

Rebecca's Wolves

Melinda's Wolves

Laurie's Wolves

Amanda's Wolves

Sharon's Wolves

Wolf Masters Box Set One

Wolf Masters Box Set Two

Claiming Her series:

The Rules

The Game

The Prize

Emergence series:

Bound to be Taken

Bound to be Tamed

Bound to be Tested

Bound to be Tempted

Emergence Box Set

The Fight Club series:

Come

Perv

Need

Hers

Want

Lust

The Fight Club Box Set One

The Fight Club Box Set Two

Wolf Gatherings series:

Tarnished

Dominated

Completed

Redeemed

Abandoned

Betrayed

Wolf Gatherings Box Set One

Wolf Gathering Box Set Two

Durham Wolves series:

Rescue in the Smokies

Fire in the Smokies

Freedom in the Smokies

Stand Alone Books:

Blind with Love

Guarding the Truth

Out of the Smoke

Abducting His Mate

Three's a Cruise

Wolf Trinity

Frostbitten

A Princess for Cale/A Princess for Cain

ABOUT THE AUTHOR

Becca Jameson is a USA Today best-selling author of over 90 books. She is most well-known for her Wolf Masters series and her Fight Club series. She currently lives in Houston, Texas, with her husband and her Goldendoodle. Two grown kids pop in every once in a while too! She is loving this journey and has dabbled in a variety of genres, including paranormal, sports romance, military, and BDSM.

A total night owl, Becca writes late at night, sequestering herself in her office with a glass of red wine and a bar of dark chocolate, her fingers flying across the keyboard as her characters weave their own stories.

During the day--which never starts before ten in the morning!--she can be found jogging, running errands, or reading in her favorite hammock chair!

…where Alphas dominate…

Becca's Newsletter Sign-up:
http://beccajameson.com/newsletter-sign-up

Join my Facebook fan group, Becca's Bibliomaniacs, for the most up-to-date information, random excerpts while I work, giveaways, and fun release parties!

Facebook Fan Group:
https://www.facebook.com/groups/BeccasBibliomaniacs/

Contact Becca:
www.beccajameson.com
beccajameson4@aol.com

facebook.com/becca.jameson.18
twitter.com/beccajameson
instagram.com/becca.jameson
bookbub.com/authors/becca-jameson
goodreads.com/beccajameson
amazon.com/author/beccajameson

Printed in Great Britain
by Amazon